Free
(Against My)
Will
A Novel

By Michael Lauer

Copyright © 2019 Michael Lauer

Printed in the United States of America

Free (Against My) Will/ Lauer —1st Edition

ISBN: 978-1-7338764-2-1

1. Fiction 2. Relationships 3. Lauer   4. Love/Loss
5. Title

Although based on real events this is a work of fiction. Events have been changed and altered, characters have been invented. Any resemblance to actual events or locations, or persons, living or dead, unless specified, is entirely coincidental.

No part of this book may be reproduced or transmitted in any form by any means, electronic or mechanical, including photocopying, recording, or by any information storage and retrieval system without permission in writing by the author.

NFB Publishing
<<<>>>
No Frills Buffalo/Amelia Press
119 Dorchester Road
Buffalo, New York 14213

For more information visit
nfbpublishing.com

DEDICATION

While I was readying this book for publication, I came across a video of Lynyrd Skynyrd performing their anthem "Free Bird" to a throng of thousands at Oakland Coliseum in the summer of 1977. Recorded just months before their tragic plane crash, this video captures everything that makes this song one of the most requested rock songs of all time.

The song itself is of a young man telling his lover why he cannot stay with her any longer. He tries to break it to her gently, telling her that it is not her fault. He just can't be tied down because there is just too much that he has to do. He is a free bird, and he cannot change.

It's me, not you.

In the live version, the two verses are separated by an emotional piano solo by Billy Powell. Throughout the song, the simple chord changes supporting the ballad are augmented by the mournful slide guitar of Gary Rossington. Ronnie Van Zant sings sweetly, tenderly, trying to let the young lady down as easily as he can. You can hear the truth in his voice: he really *can't* change. If only he could, you think.

As the second chorus wraps up, the guitars start speeding up. Then Mr. Van Zant delivers the line that unleashes what comes next: "Won't you fly-y, oh, free bird."

On the studio album, what follows is a classic guitar solo that every guitarist dreams of nailing. That every rock fan has heard a thousand times. That never, ever gets old or boring or any less spectacular.

God created music. He may not endorse the message that this song conveys, but there is no doubt that the talent behind the creation of this guitar solo could only come from Him.

I have a live version of "Free Bird" on my iPod mix from *One More from the Road*. I frequently skip the song and go immediately to the guitar solo. There are times when I stop what I am doing to listen to the solo, whether it's yard work or writing or driving (I don't stop driving, I just stop paying attention—but maybe I shouldn't admit that publicly).

Something interesting happens in the video, however. As Van Zant sings that last line—"won't you fly-y, free bird"—the audience goes wild. Okay, that doesn't surprise me in and of itself. But as the video pans the crowd, it hits me why they go wild; why that solo is one of the best-known guitar solos ever recorded.

There is release.

Resolution.

Freedom.

For over six minutes, the band has been building the tension. The ballad, the lyrics, the piano solo, the slide guitar. The pace of the song increases. Every piece of the song deliberately builds on every other piece, until, finally, we are given permission to let it all out: "Won't you fly-y free bird?"

When those first few notes of Allen Collins's guitar hit you, there is nothing you can do except to let it all go. And now you have five minutes or more to do so, as Allen Collins and Steve Gaines trade licks.

This book is my release. My resolution. My freedom.

§§§

This is a work of fiction based on significant events that occurred in my real life. Most of the minor events in this book never happened at all, while others are a composite of stories of myself and others that fit the overall theme of the book. It should be read with that in mind.

Because of this, the book may hit close to home for some even though I used numerous composite characters. For the real characters, I changed names to protect identities and privacy, and have gone out of my way to portray people in a positive light. However, this book does broach some dark subject matter, and even people behaving at their best in these situations do not always come out looking their greatest. For this, I ask for the forgiveness and redemption that, ultimately, is the theme of this book. Time and maturity heal a lot of wounds, and I, in no way, mean for this book to reopen any. It is because of the characters in this book that I became who I am, and for that reason, I thank each and every one of you.

This book takes place shortly after the events of my previous book, *The Complete History of Cheektowaga (As I Remember It)*. In that book, Rob Becker, a dear friend of mine from childhood, drowned during a family camping trip in Ontario. His passing left a significant hole in my heart that I did not know how to deal with at that point in my life, or for many years after. His death is the subject of Chapter 2 of this book. Rob visited me often in my dreams. He was and is my ghost. His dreams guided me for years, appearing regularly when I needed him. These dreams occur throughout this book as well.

This book deals with a drinking problem. My solution was my solution only and is not meant to be a scientific or a medical one, or a cure-all for someone who is struggling with this addiction. I realize from first-hand experience what a devastating disease this can be, and I do not want to minimize the seriousness of it. So while my solution in this book is simplistic, it is what it took to kick start me at that point in my life. It will not work for everyone. If you are struggling with an addiction, please seek out a medical professional, God, and a loved one, in whatever particular order works best for you. But please seek help.

I once again unashamedly dedicate this book to God the Father, Jesus Christ my Savior, and the Holy Spirit. I will warn you that there are Bible passages throughout! I have used the World English Bible, a not-for profit, Public Domain version of the Bible, as my source of quotes. If they pique your interest, please go to the source and find the Truth.

I wish to thank Dan Shields, Joe Feick, the late Tom Bellin, Dan Gochnour, Rick Dickerson, Lori Thee, Jeff Jimerson and all the rest of the Orchard Hill Church band that played the music that touched my heart that Easter Sunday in 2009. Through your immense talents, God was able to break through a heart hardened by years of agnosticism and self-righteousness. I offer a sincere thank you as well to Orchard Hill's Senior Pastor, Kurt Bjorklund, for delivering the message that day, and for numerous other messages throughout the years, that brought me, and ultimately my family, to God.

My love of music has once again bled into this book. In writing this book, I was inspired by certain songs. I have included those songs as "Suggested Listening" at the beginning of each chapter. Listen as you read to get to the same place that I was as I wrote this. I have once again created a Spotify playlist to make this possible.

https://open.spotify.com/playlist/1VN7iSMIl5HijhTYc44Rp7

I also include a few words to the real-life Jenny. I tried my best to walk the line between being accurate of my feelings and cognizant of yours. I think that the reader will see that what we went through was painful for both of us. I needed to write this to finally exorcize this portion of my life, in the same way that I needed to write *Cheektowaga* to face John. All my best in whatever the future holds for you. May there be happiness, grace, and love.

Thank you once again to Sarah Page for editing, and to Jeannie Schott for the excellent cover. Once again, you nailed it!

Finally, I dedicate this book to my amazing wife of more than 25 years. Many of the stories in this book took place before I met her, but they contain as much pain for her as they do for me. I am revisiting them to get rid of them. She is just revisiting them. So I dedicate this book to the strength, loyalty, trust, and support that she has given me throughout the amazing journey that has been our marriage. I love you, Meg, with all my heart, soul and life, and I wouldn't be here without you! Here's to at least 25 more years of joy, tears, and wonder (i.e., everything that a marriage should be)!

Introduction:
Of Faith and Swimming Naked

Suggested Listening
"Land of Beginning Again" – Neal Morse
"One" – U2

God created man in his own image. In God's image he created him;
male and female he created them.
Genesis 1: 27 (WEB)

I just need to make it through until morning, I say to myself. Joy comes in the morning.

It's funny I would say that. That comes from some Psalm in the Bible, I think. The situation I'm in right now couldn't be further from church. Not that god has been interested in me lately. Or ever.

Besides, I realize it is already morning as I attempt to open my eyes. And there is no joy. Just a pounding headache and a real need to get sick.

But I'm sure I said that because I said it every day. That's what the medication was for. To make it through until morning.

The medication, of course, was anything that would numb me. That would keep the thoughts at bay. The memories. The hurt, the betrayal, the loneliness.

Beer most nights, but I was okay with something harder if I needed it.

At first, I'd drive over there to see what she was doing. Even after trying to numb myself. I would find myself in front of her house at least once a week. Knowing what I'd see but needing to see it anyways. She lived too far away for me to go there now, but my thoughts still wandered there.

When I was out of town, the nights never ended. It seemed that the alarm never rang, the sun never rose. But when the alarm did actually ring and the sun did finally rise, my head always hurt as the previous night's medication left its mark. And there was no joy.

Just like today.

Of course, some nights it isn't alcohol. This particular night, it is a woman. A woman and alcohol.

I finally open my eyes to see someone lying next to me. She is topless and very much not Jenny.

My head is throbbing too much at this point to try to figure out just who she is. Or where I am. I have a pretty good idea of why my head hurts, though. It definitely has something to do with the number of empty Genesee Beer cans scattered about the room and on the nightstand.

I reach for my glasses when I can no longer ignore the necessity to find somewhere to be sick. The topless woman is sound asleep, passed out, and will still be there when I am done. She didn't hear me or move the two times I got up to puke in the middle of the night.

I stumble out of bed, realizing that I am naked. Again, she will never see me in my current condition. Luckily, I make it to the bathroom just in time.

Nothing sexier than a naked, fat, drunk guy puking his guts out in the morning. Unless it's a naked, drunk woman snoring and drooling in her boozy unconsciousness.

Once my prayers to the porcelain god(dess) are finished, I stay kneeling on the dirty, cold tile floor trying to put together where I am. Why would I be drinking Genny? I'm a Labatt guy. That's probably why I got sick. Then I remember the sheer quantity of empty Genny cans scattered around. No, I would have been sick with that many Labatts, too.

A voice comes groggily from the other side of the locked door. "Hey, babe, you okay?"

"Yeah, just give me a minute, please," I plead, trying to make sense of my situation.

At that point, I remember her name. Stacy. There, that helps. This was our first date. We had gone to dinner. Red Lobster, I think. Lots of beer. Then back to her place with a twelve pack of Genny. Then…

No, THAT never would have happened. I must have dreamed it. But she was lying there topless, and I was naked, so maybe it did happen. Shit, if it happened, I wish I could remember more of it. Or any of it for that matter.

The smell of bacon, of all things, starts wafting through the door. Rinsing my mouth out, I slowly and painfully emerge from the bathroom. In the kitchen, Stacy stands at the stove, frying up some bacon, wearing an oversized Pat Benatar t-shirt and nothing more.

"Good morning, you lightweight. It's bad when you can't even keep up with a girl."

If only that were the first time I woke up not knowing where I was. Or remembering what I was doing.

Or the last.

§§§

When you lose a childhood friend, especially one who is only 21 years old, it has an effect on you. You start to look at things a little differently. You ask questions. And maybe you lose a little bit of childhood yourself. You become an adult against your better judgement. Against your will.

Your previously precious, privileged, protected life is yours to live now. Yours to fuck up on your own terms. Mommy and Daddy aren't there anymore to bandage your boo boos. You need to stop the bleeding yourself.

First, though, you have to recognize that you are bleeding.

Rob Becker was gone. That was easy to see. His death left a huge hole that shouldn't have been there so soon.

What was not so easy to see were all the others who left me too. They didn't leave as dramatically. They left me the same way that I left them. They grew up. I was struggling to do the same.

I was raised Roman Catholic, going to church regularly at Our Lady Help of Christians in Cheektowaga, New York. I was a good Catholic. I went to confession, confirmation, and communion. I didn't eat meat on Fridays, I did not have sex before marriage (not because I didn't try, but I'm going to take credit for it anyway), and I didn't take God's name in vain (I had other go-to curses that worked even better). I could recite the whole mass by memory. I knew when to kneel and when to stand. I went to Catholic elementary school, Catholic high school, and a Jesuit college.

I went to Catholic elementary school because that's where Mom and Dad sent me. In the same way that I went to church every week because they told me to, I went to Our Lady Help of Christians School, better known as Chapel School, because they told me to. I went to Canisius College because Canisius had a good accounting program, because friends were going there, and—because it was local—I didn't have to come up with more money for room and board.

The decision to go to St. Mary's Catholic High School was mine as well. I could tell you that I made the choice to go there because of their superior academics. I could tell you that I went there because some of my best friends were going there. I could tell you that I was nervous about going to a big public school, or that I wouldn't fit in, or that I was afraid I would get beat up. Even though all of those things are true, none of them were the reason.

I went to St. Mary's because it did not have a pool, and I did not want to swim naked at Maryvale.

I don't know if this was a Buffalo-only thing, but public high schools in the 70s required the boys to take swimming classes in gym if they had a pool, and, for some reason known only to them, they had to swim *au naturel*. *Sans* bathing suit. Butt-ass naked.

The girls did not have this requirement. Girls also swam in gym class but were provided swimsuits (or brought theirs from home, I don't know). But the boys were afforded no such covering. Theirs was to show it all, wild and free.

Gym class started with the boys emerging from the locker room wrapped in towels. They were then told to line up along the side of the pool for attendance, where they dropped trou (or more accurately, towel). The gym teacher, generally a middle-aged guy, then went down the line to make sure everyone was accounted for. The boys were then allowed in the pool. After class, the boys were required to shower (again, obviously, naked) before dressing and returning to class.

Rumor has it that some schools (I don't know if Maryvale was one of them) had windows from the main hall into the pool. Often, girls would "happen" to wander by the windows during swim class, especially during the line-up.

One guy I used to work with had a very embarrassing incident occur during one of his classes. For some reason, he was running late the morning of his gym class, and showed up in the locker room after everyone else had already reported for attendance. Scared that he would get in trouble for his tardiness, he simply ditched his clothes, grabbed a towel, and ran out to the pool.

Unfortunately, it was Parents' Day, and the pool area was filled with the parents of his classmates, as well as his teacher and his classmates. It was at that point that he remembered that the boys were allowed to wear bathing suits on Parents' Day, so he was the only person in the auditorium in his birthday suit.

Luckily, this tradition no longer exists, in Buffalo or, hopefully, anywhere else. In the era of increased attention on issues like child pornography and sexual abuse of minors, it is amazing to me that this situation not only occurred, but was required.

So, while I can now express my faith and the reasons for it, one of my most prolonged exposures to God was the result of not wanting to expose myself.

The underlying message of Catholicism was lost on me. My time in church growing up was either as a meeting place for Rob, Mike Wolf, Brian Marino, Chuck Dempsey, Rick Werner and me to discuss that Saturday night's itinerary, or as a weekend requirement to check off my to-do list on my way to Heaven. Heaven, of course, being a concept that one just accepted.

Scholarly knowledge of my faith was minimal. My biggest attempt of actively learning about it was a sixth-grade debate that I had with Father Paul during one of his class visits.

Father Paul was the pastor of Our Lady Help of Christians and would frequently come next door to the school to teach. His lesson this day was on free will. He did a wonderful job explaining it, but it obviously didn't sink in with the sixth-grade version of me.

"How can we have free will if God knows what we are going to do?" I inquired.

"He knows what you will do, but you still have to choose to do it," was Father Paul's explanation.

"Then I didn't really choose it, did I? I was just doing what I was made to do."

"You could have chosen to do something else."

"But God knew that I wouldn't," I argued.

"But it was you choosing your actions, not God," Father Paul countered.

"Regardless of what I choose, God knows. That does not seem like free will. It seems like God's will."

Frustrated with arguing with a sixth grader, Father Paul ended the discussion with a curt "Well, it's free will. Okay?" Then he was on to another, less controversial, subject.

We were not encouraged to read the Bible. That might have explained some things, or it might not have. The Bible is an amazing book, but you need to work at it to understand it. There is a reason that there are so many different Bible studies, why preachers can do a weekly sermon, and, most importantly, why there are so many interpretations by different religions. There is a central and consistent message, but it only reveals itself to you over time. Sixth grade wasn't the time for me.

I was able to fulfill all of my religion requirements in my curriculum at Canisius with classes that had nothing to do with the Bible. Classes like philosophy and logic were considered religious enough to count, as did god-free interpretive classes like Evil in Fairy Tales.

By the time of Rob's death, I still went to church every week with Jenny. With Jenny's encouragement, I finally tried to learn what this whole "God thing" was all about. I volunteered at our parish, I occasionally read Scripture at mass, I became involved in the community. But I did not know anything about the main topic on which I spoke. That would take another 20 years or more.

And then, of course, Jenny left…

Chapter 1:
The Courtship

Suggested Listening:
"End of the Innocence" – Don Henley
"Beginnings" – Chicago

Therefore, a man will leave his father and his mother, and will join with his wife, and they will be one flesh.
Genesis 2:24 (WEB)

I met Jennifer Keller at a friend's house when my band was practicing in the White's basement. She wanted to meet the guitarist (as do all fans), but she got stuck with the bassist. Somehow, that seems to be a metaphor for most of the people in my life.

See, the bassist "anchors the bottom." A good bassist is behind the music, just out of sight. You would know something was missing if it were gone, but you might not be able to put your finger on what it was. The bassist will support the music, be the foundation for the rest of the band. Occasionally, he can drive the action, but it is rare that the bassist is out front. The bassist is more like the administrative staff rather than the superstar salesperson. Necessary, but not the one making the bonuses.

Think of some of the songs with great bass lines: "Billy Jean" by Michael Jackson, "Caribbean Queen" by Billy Ocean, anything by Motown artists. If you took away the bass line in any of those songs, you would not have the song. But, can you name the bassist on those songs? I know I can't (of course, I could Google it, but I'm busy writing this).

There have been some great bassists, many of whom I could ramble on about for hours. Geddy Lee of Rush, Billy Sheehan of Talas, Flea of the Red Hot Chili Peppers. But these are the exception rather than the rule. Most bassists are more generic: Chuck Panozzo of Styx, Dougie Thomson of Supertramp, Cliff Williams of AC/DC, Danny Klein of the J. Geils Band, and Matt Christopher of Baron Blood and Matthias.

In retrospect, bass was the perfect instrument for me. I was generic.

Mike Wolf and I had been jamming a few times with some of his Kaisertown friends. Even though I was a trained guitarist (I had taken almost a dozen lessons), Mike thought I was better playing single notes rather than chords. He was right, so I became the bassist one afternoon when I went to U-Crest Music Center on George Urban Boulevard and plunked down $100 for my new tool, a Big Stud. (Okay, that sounds inappropriate somehow. The Big Stud was the brand name of the bass. Carry on.)

So our new band, Baron Blood (so named for maximum shock value), was set to practice one Friday night. Beforehand, Mike was informed by the lead vocalist that a certain young lady would be among the audience (of two) that evening, and that she was interested in meeting him.

Baron Blood had a brief and tragic history in the Buffalo music scene. Its brevity (three months, tops) was caused by its tragedy (we sucked). I could write an entire book about the inner workings of the band, the personalities involved, the impact of the music, and stories from the fan base. But if I did that, it would still only be a two-page book.

Imagine a band consisting of a lead vocalist, guitarist, bassist, and drummer. The guitarist is a natural: able to listen to a song one or two times and be able to play it. A guitarist with a unique style of soloing that combined speed with feel. A guitarist with passion and an ear for songs that kicked ass. An ear for songs that, maybe no one had heard yet, but were on the edge of breaking through (AC/DC, Ozzy, and Def Leppard are just a few of the examples). A towering figure with long flowing hair, ripped jeans, and snakeskin boots.

Then put that guitarist with three guys who all wore thick glasses. A bassist who weighed 250 pounds. Three guys whose combined wardrobes cost close to $30 at Sears or Twin Fair. Oh yeah, and three guys who know nothing about their respective instruments.

Now, frankly, the last part of that story that sounds a little bit like the origins of the band U2. When U2 was formed, the guys just chose what instruments that they wanted to play, and they played them to international fame and glory. Suffice it to say that our band did not coalesce in that manner. Instead, we simply chose what instruments were available and made noise with them.

There are many words in the English language for noise. Some of those words evoke pleasant feelings. Some of those words include "tuneful" or "harmonious" or "melodic." I wouldn't use any of those words to describe Baron Blood. Instead, I would use words like "cacophony," "dissonance," "din," and "racket." Any of these words would accurately describe what our guests were in store for that evening.

Of course, I am exaggerating. We were much worse than that.

But we still showed up that night and diligently went through our set list of Ozzy tunes and two originals in front of our two guests. And Mike and Jenny went off to talk after we packed up the gear. And they decided that they were not right for each other, but that I might make a good substitute.

So it was that I started dating Jenny.

My family was very happy with my new relationship. They met Jenny and found her to be a very respectful young lady. But more importantly, they noticed her effect on my attitude. I no longer moped around. I would rush to answer the phone in case it was her. Not because I had to, but because I wanted to. After a long and unsuccessful relationship with a girl who demanded my presence at the phone each night to take her call, I looked forward to Jenny's call rather than dreading it.

My sister Sara found an immediate way to ingratiate herself to my new girlfriend. She invited us to her house one Friday night. Because Sara's brother-in-law sold arcade games and bar equipment, she had a full bar in the basement with pinball machines and a jukebox. Knowing that Jenny was more than two years younger than me, Sara started the jukebox when we went to her basement. Benny Mardones' voice greeted us: *She's just sixteen years old, leave her alone they say.* When I saw that Jenny was not offended by this and that she had, in fact, thought it funny, I knew that I had found someone special.

Looking back, this may have been the greatest time in my life. I looked forward to something almost every night. A few nights a week, I had to work at Perkins Restaurant, but even that was usually fun. I was a cook there, so even when I was working, I felt like I was creating something. A few nights a week, I would get together with Jenny. I still had school, and that meant homework. But I knew that I was working toward something longer term, so I could make myself work hard at it.

In fact, "homework" wasn't all that bad. Most times, "homework" was a euphemism for making out somewhere. Jenny and I would frequently park my dad's Ford Fairmont in the ring road of South Park behind the Botanical Gardens to do homework. After ten minutes or so of looking at our work, we would then spend an hour or more in each other's arms. If it wasn't at South Park, we also enjoyed "studying" at the pit behind the Becker's house, Jenny's front hallway, the band's practice room, or anywhere else that we could sneak away for a half-hour or more.

I want to make clear that nothing immoral happened during our "homework" sessions. Jenny and I planned that one day we would be married, and that we would have our time together then. Not that I didn't try to convince her that now would be a good time to practice! But we stayed away from crossing that line. There are few enough lines that I didn't cross that I am going to give myself credit where I can.

And then there was band practice.

Baron Blood broke up when Mike lost patience with us. What was, for the rest of us, a fun night of making noise and drinking became a serious undertaking for Mike, who was looking to make a living playing guitar. God knows he was good enough for this to be a possibility. When it became painfully obvious that his friends were not going cut it, he went looking for a band that he could succeed with.

It didn't take him long. Through his contacts at the Canisius College radio station, Mike knew a ton of people in bands or looking for bands. He soon befriended a senior, also named Matt, an accomplished drummer looking for a band. One of the DJs at the station, Jim, was a natural for a lead singer: a sharp dresser, good looking, an innate ability to talk to people, and a deep knowledge of music. He could even sing! Pat Hartmann and I rounded out the new band. Not for our talents, per se, but because Mike needed a bassist and a second guitarist regardless of their skill level. And we fit the bill.

Naming ourselves Matthias after a character in the movie *The Marathon Man*, we started practicing. Not getting together to drink, but actually practicing! (We drank too, but only after practice.)

Our drummer had been renting some space in an old apartment building in North Buffalo used by numerous bands as practice space. Although we never saw them there, Matt said that Talas rented a room in this building for their practices. That didn't matter to me. We had our own room!

This felt like independence. We could go there any time we wanted, so Jenny and I would occasionally go there just to make out. The rest of the guys (okay, I did too) brought porn mags up there, and there was always at least some beer, even if it was warm. To me, it felt like my first apartment, and my bandmates were my roommates.

When Matthias practiced—at least once a week—was when life stood still. We would work out new songs, listen to other songs that we wanted to learn, and practice the ones we already knew. We weren't great yet, but we were all there to get better. We challenged ourselves with the songs that we chose. Mike was becoming a better guitarist by the day, and we were looking for ways to incorporate the lyrics that I was writing. Music was the focus, and I was a part of it.

And we got noticeably better. Our practices were no longer frustrating because someone forgot their part. Everyone showed up having practiced on their own whatever new song we were learning, so we were able to play a rough draft of the song our first time out. By the end of the night, we were able to run through a 40-minute set, front to back, with no interruptions, and very few mistakes.

My bass playing was never going to be compared to Geddy Lee or Billy Sheehan or Flea, but I could "anchor the bottom." The rest of the guys could count on me to be there when the solo came up. They did not worry that I would throw a wrong note in the mix because I forgot a part. Not to say that I was perfect; I struggled keeping the pace in the bridge of "Run to the Hills" by Iron Maiden because my fingers got tired. Practice helped with this, but using a pick instead of my fingers worked better. That felt like failure to me, though, because Steve Harris was able to play it with his fingers.

I wrote the lyrics to numerous songs during this time. Mike always wanted to do original songs, and I was able to provide the words to the numerous riffs that he could (seemingly) spontaneously create. Very few of the lyrics remain today, as they were frequently left with someone during practice or lost over time. Jim probably had some of them because he would try to memorize them. Unfortunately, some also disappeared because I read them while I was drunk years later, was embarrassed at my youthful optimism, and threw them away.

I found one of them recently and I reluctantly include it below. Keep in mind it was the first "real" song I tried to write. For your perusal, I present:

<u>WHY DID I EVER?</u>
On the first day I said I love you
On the first day you were untrue
You used me for your own ends
On the first day you asked out my friends
How the Hell could I be so wrong?
Two years was way too long
How the Hell could I have loved you
After all the things you do?

CHORUS: Why did I - ever put up with you?
Why did I – ever love you?

All the things you said were just lies
Can't imagine all the worthless ties
The nights alone when we just fought
Won't be long before you get caught

CHORUS
You really screwed up our nights alone
Arguing all day on the phone
You made me be with you all the time

Although when I was it was a crime
Trying to choose between you and me
You're the loser 'cause I chose me
You're the loser, I'm no longer a pawn
I'm the winner 'cause you're gone

Add in a pretty solid bass line and a typical eight-bar Mike Wolf kick-ass guitar solo, and this song was one of our stronger offerings.

We were able to score a few live gigs with this band. Our largest gig, playing in front of nearly 20 people at the West Seneca Community Center, was certainly the highlight. We had access to a professional sound system, and we put in almost nightly practice for weeks to prepare. We sounded pretty good and the show went off without a hitch, but the next band, who were regulars on the Buffalo bar circuit, made us look and sound like the amateurs that we were.

That show drove Mike to be even better. He saw the disparity in the bands, and drove Matthias even harder. This was when we went our separate ways. Pat and I were trying to juggle work, school, and relationships, and could not commit more time to the band. Matt graduated and went out to California looking for work as an actor or a musician. He ended up as a stuntman, and has been in numerous movies (although I can never pick him out). Jim landed an internship at a company out of town. Mike found a bassist that sounded like Billy Sheehan, and they formed Sacred, their first of many bands together, all of whom played professionally in Buffalo.

Senior year of college for me should have included going to job fairs and networking, just like the counselors and professors at Canisius said I should have been doing. But, instead, it was spent dating Jenny, working at Perkins, and playing bass for Matthias. So when I graduated, I had no job prospects. Even though I was engaged to Jenny, I was still a cook at

Perkins when I graduated. My entry into adult life was simply to go full time, and eventually into management.

Jenny and I were married in October, in a small ceremony at the Old Chapel at Our Lady Help of Christians, officiated by her cousin, Father Jack. The reception was in the back room of a VFW post. We wanted nothing more. Our friends and family were there to witness our union and to wish us well. Mike Wolf was my best man, and Rob Becker was a groomsman. Pat Hartmann couldn't make it because he was away at boot camp for the Army Reserves. My other groomsman, therefore, was a long-time friend of Jenny's from South Buffalo that I had known for only a few months.

By this time, I had landed a job in management with Wendy's (a real career!), while Jenny juggled two or three jobs to make ends meet financially. One of these jobs, which she landed while I still worked there, was as a waitress at Perkins. Given our respective jobs in retail service industries, our shifts were erratic, inconsistent, and low paying. Not the greatest way to start a life together.

We moved into an apartment in South Buffalo on Ashton Street, not far from her parents. This flat became our sanctuary, our nest, as we nurtured a new family of two. Our first six months of marriage were defined by constant money shortages, way too much drinking, and never seeing each other as we juggled numerous part time jobs.

Our cars were whatever beaters we could find for a few hundred bucks and keep running for a few months. One of our cars was a '64 Ford Falcon with a passenger side door that wouldn't open because it had been in an accident. We couldn't get it started one night when we were out drinking, so we just abandoned it in a parking lot. I hope that the City of Buffalo has stopped charging me penalties on the unpaid towing charges after all this time!

Three months after we were married, we woke up to what I came to call "Black Friday." Lying in bed at 9:55 one Friday morning, we were listening to the radio, trying to gather the motivation to face the day, which almost certainly involved one or both of us trudging somewhere to make up to $7.50 per hour with no benefits. The song "American Woman" by The Guess Who came on 97 Rock. Not the greatest way to start the day, but it would get me out of bed.

When the song was over, the station ID came on to mark the top of the hour. But rather than hearing the familiar spot for WGRQ, there was a spot for WRLT, Lite FM. Huh? Then came the shock of a lifetime as the next song played was Barry Manilow's "Copacabana!"

Without warning, 97 Rock was no more! Everything I learned about music, the music that meant so much to me, was learned at the altar of 97 Rock.

This was a time when radio ruled. There was no internet to hear whatever genre of music you liked non-stop. No satellite radio playing 24 hours of Elvis or Bruce or Tom Petty or Pearl Jam. No Pandora or Spotify choosing some new music for you based on whether you gave a thumbs-up or a thumbs-down to the last song played.

My radio friends were gone. No more Bearman and Norton, no more Carl Russo, no more Cindy Chan. Even though 97 Rock had recently embraced the corporate rock sounds of Journey and Styx and REO Speedwagon, they did not embrace the lite, airy sounds of this…this abomination that appeared out of nowhere.

Because 97 Rock did not magically reappear after a week or so, everyone I knew was trying to make sense of our new musical world. A few of us went over to WPHD, with Taylor and Moore "perkin', perkin', perkin', even though we're working" and visiting the Land of Fa (a recurring bit that allowed them to use the phrase "Fa King" without getting in trouble with the FCC). Some threw in the towel and went pop over at Kiss 98.5. But many of us hardcore music-holics became honorary Canadians for our music, just like our beer.

The wonderful thing about Buffalo is that we were, in many respects, distant suburbs of Toronto. Less than 100 miles away along the shores of Lake Ontario, Toronto represented big city life. They were the clean version of New York City. They had plays (*Phantom of the Opera* played there for years), museums (the Hockey Hall of Fame), and concerts that Buffalo never got.

They also had an excellent radio station, CHUM-FM at 104.5 on your FM dial. I would listen to them occasionally in my 97 Rock days for variety, so I immediately tried to transfer my music loyalties there. Unfortunately, the distance made reception hit or miss. Mostly miss. I could listen to them in the apartment most days, but listening to them in the car meant frequent fuzz as the signal was lost due to houses, bridges, and other cars getting in the way of the signal.

Mike and Pat soon found a compromise: CHTZ (that's CHT Zed for all you Canadians reading along) 97.7FM broadcasting from St. Catherines, Ontario, about 20 miles from Niagara Falls. Reception was not usually an issue, and they played some good rock music. Their DJs were not as polished as those on CHUM or 97 Rock, but they provided the music fix that I was jonesin' for.

The blessing to both CHUM-FM and CHTZ was that they were bound by "Canadian Content" laws governing their output.

Canadian Content laws required all Canadian stations to provide a prescribed number of minutes each hour to purely Canadian content, be it news or music. For rock stations like CHUM-FM or CHTZ, it meant that they had to play songs by Canadian artists, or songs that were recorded in Canada. A few 97 Rock bands qualified because they were recorded in Canada. For example, Aerosmith albums produced by Bruce Fairbairn qualified under this law because they were recorded in Canada.

The more exciting part of this law was that I was exposed to truly Canadian bands that most people in other parts of the US have never heard of: Max Webster (not a person, but a group led by Kim Mitchell), Triumph, Coney Hatch, and Gowan are just a few examples. Kim Mitchell went on to have a prolific solo career, scoring minor US hits like "Go for Soda" and "Lager and Ale." Triumph took the power trio format of Rush and combined it with a stage show to match KISS (complete with pyrotechnics and the Triumph logo in 20-foot lights). Larry Gowan used much of Peter Gabriel's back-up band (including Tony Levin on bass), and later replaced Dennis DeYoung in Styx. His "Criminal Mind" is a frequent addition to Styx live shows.

I could list more songs that I love that folks in other parts of the US have never had the pleasure of listening to: "I'm an Adult Now" by The Pursuit of Happiness, "Hands On" by Lee Aaron, "Battlescar" by Max Webster (featuring all three members of Rush). Other acts that have made it big in the US, like Bryan Adams, Barenaked Ladies, and the Tragically Hip, all got their start on the radio largely because of the Canadian Content laws.

Another Canadian phenomenon appeared at about this time: the comedy team of Bob and Doug McKenzie. These were actually characters played by SCTV veterans Dave Thomas and Rick Moranis. Much like SNL's "Wayne's World" (whose Mike Myers was also Canadian), Bob and Doug "broadcast" a low budget cable show called "Great White North" from their basement. Dressed in parkas and toques (Canadian for ski cap), they discussed "two-fours" (cases of beer), back bacon, donut shoppes (because that's how you spell it in Canada), and all else Canadian.

Bob and Doug are now mostly forgotten cult figures in Canada, although they occasionally appear in beer commercials or one-off appearances on certain shows. Rick Moranis became a recognizable actor in the US, with his most famous roles being Louis Tully (the "Keymaster" in the original *Ghostbusters*) and for the *Honey I Shrunk the Kids* series of movies. Dave Thomas likewise continued in movies and television, doing frequent voice acting work in animated series.

Canada itself featured prominently in the lives of many Buffalonians, especially before 9/11 made crossing the border more difficult. Growing up, Canada was sort of like another state, truly our "neighbor to the north." There is so much to love about Canada: the language, the sports, and, of course, the beer.

Canada has its own language, eh? It sounds a lot like American English, but there are noticeable differences that a Buffalonian could point oot. For example, Canadians pronounce the word "schedule" with a "sh" rather than a "sk", and the word "again" with a long "a" rather than a short "e" (so "a-gay-n" as opposed to the American "a-gen"). Or that there is no letter "Z" in spoken Canadian, only the letter "Zed." One of Canada's favorite bands in the 80s was Zed Zed Top.

When you read a newspaper in Canada, don't think that the words "colour" or "honour" are misspelled. Or that the temperature in July is incorrectly reported as "a high of 30", or that the speed limit is 100. With the metric system, they are just saying that the temperature will be about 86 Fahrenheit, and that the speed limit would be about 62 mph.

And that thing about Canadians always saying "eh?" at the end of their sentences? There's nothing to that, eh? Sometimes, they replace the "eh?" with "right?" So don't stereotype Canadians and their language, right? They're no different than Americans, eh?

Everyone knows that Canada's national sport is hockey. As hard as it is for Americans in the heartland to believe, hockey is much bigger than football in a Canadian's life. But the other Canadian sport is one that most Americans do not know: curling. For my US brethren, think of shuffleboard played on ice, and you get a pretty good idea of what curling is. It finally made it as an Olympic sport in 2014.

And beer. Yes, beer! The words "Canadian beer" to a Buffalonian were like the word "water" in the desert. (Not that I've ever been in a desert, but I think the comparison is apt.) We knew that a bottle of Tuborg Gold, or Molson Export, or Grizzly, or Moosehead, or Carlsburg would be better than anything that Wilson Farms sold. Better yet, each of these had the alcoholic equivalent of two beers.

Trips up to Canada were frequent. Crossing the border simply meant answering a few questions at customs and declaring that you were American and that you were not bringing anything across the border. Unless, of course, you were bringing back a case of beer. Each adult in the car was allowed to bring back a case of beer, so once you declared that, you were on your way home. The border patrol never bothered you—unless you were a bunch of kids heading to a concert.

One summer, Kingswood, an outdoor amphitheater outside of Toronto, was putting on a show by Roger Waters (ex-Pink Floyd) that was not coming to Buffalo. Being huge Floyd fans, Mike, our friend Ken, and I hopped in my 1978 Chevy Monza with no seatbelts, an iffy muffler, and a significant inventory of rust to see Mr. Waters.

The guard at the border was polite. "Destination?"

"We're going to a concert in Toronto," I replied as the guard surveyed the scene. Mike was wearing his best concert gear, and his hair was fine form. Ken was in the back seat with his Pink Floyd t-shirt. I was a cross between business casual and punk, wearing ripped jeans and a polo shirt.

"How long in Canada?" the guard continued, making note of the car and its license plate.

"We'll be back tonight," was my answer.

"Anything to declare?" he asked, gesturing to one of his colleagues down the line.

"Nothing," I responded.

The guard was joined by another. The two talked quietly out of earshot, pointing to the car a number of times. After a minute or so, the guard came back and solemnly informed us to pull the car over to a designated spot, and to follow the officer into the building. Once we got out of the car, a team of uniformed agents began going through every inch of the car, while we were politely, but sternly, taken into the offices and told to sit quietly. We were informed that the car was being searched for drugs.

It dawned on us then that three scruffy young adults crossing the border in a beater car heading to a concert by an artist associated with a stoner band might give authorities something to suspect us of.

But, because we were planning on getting our beer at the concert (it was going to be Canadian beer, after all), and because none of us did any sort of illegal substances, the car checked out clean after 15 minutes or so, and we were sent on our way. (The concert was awesome, by the way.)

My favorite trip to Canada, though, was our honeymoon trip to Niagara Falls. Staying at a cheap, touristy hotel on Lundy Lane, Jenny and I spent two nights in newly-wedded bliss, unfazed by the Canadian bands, language, sports or beer. In fact, I'd be hard pressed to tell you anything that happened outside of that room, if we left it at all.

It was after that trip that the rest of this story occurs.

Chapter 2:
That Day

Suggested Listening
"Gone Away" – The Offspring
"The Gap is Too Wide" – Mostly Autumn

We know that all things work together for good for those who love God, for those who are called according to his purpose.
Romans 8: 28 (WEB)

In May, Jenny and I moved to a three-bedroom apartment on the East Side of Buffalo near the Cheektowaga line. Owned by the sister of my brother-in-law (there is probably a more correct way to refer to that relationship, maybe sister-in-law once removed or something), it was the first time Jenny had ever lived outside of South Buffalo. But even with two and three jobs apiece, we could no longer afford the rent on our Ashton Street apartment.

Part of this was the result of having Jenny's brother move in with us the previous January. When her brother moved in, he brought along his girlfriend and their three-month-old daughter. All of them had been kicked out of their houses and needed somewhere to go. So it was a family of five that moved into the two bedroom apartment on Roebling.

Truth be told, the newlywed bliss of the first few months was starting to wane even before Vince and his family arrived on the scene. Our lack of time together, combined with being tired from multiple shifts at low paying jobs, meant that we didn't have a lot of time to talk about us. To tell the other that they were loved. Instead of a purr of delight and lovemaking, there was often a grunt of annoyance as we crawled into bed with an already-sleeping partner. Or there might have been an earful about finances when one partner went to take $10 out of the bank to fill up the gas tank in one of our beater cars, or to buy a meal on our shift at work, only to find no money left in the account.

Throughout it all though, Jenny and I generally managed to keep each other smiling. We knew that we had each other, which made everything else bearable. Even with her brother and family being in the middle of it, things settled into something resembling a routine. Maybe it wasn't a perfect life, but it was our life.

Once we moved to the east side apartment, I began submitting resumes to get an accounting job. I knew that starting a career (instead of just having a job) meant that my salary would increase. At that point, maybe we could have a nicer apartment, reliable transportation, and normal working hours, and maybe Jenny and I could see each other every night. Or at least on weekends.

In the meantime, we decided that we could at least ask our respective employers for the same days off each week. Starting that summer, most weeks we were able to have Monday nights off together. We would generally celebrate with dinner at Perkins or a fast food joint, followed by a night curled up on the couch with a bottle of Canei wine. We tried to make time for each other in the bedroom as well, assuming that her brother's family was out of the house or already asleep.

In this apartment, we were visited more frequently by Rob Becker and Mike Wolf. They would stop by with beer, and we would sit and listen to albums and talk. Mike was in his senior year at Canisius, and Rob was working many nights at a local restaurant. Sitting in the apartment, frequently in the absence of Jenny, was a much cheaper alternative than going to a bar. Plus, we could control the music we heard.

The weather that summer was perfect (for Buffalo, that is). Trips to the lakefront or the Riverwalk were frequent. Our apartment had a front porch, where many nights were spent with a six pack of Labatts or a bottle of Canei (when Jenny was home). In July, Rob invited me to go to Sherkston Beach, Ontario with him for the day, but I had to work. Jenny went with Rob instead.

Jenny's brother and his family were around less and less as the weather improved as well. They were as frustrated living with us as we were with them. They began looking for a cheap apartment for themselves in South Buffalo now that both of them could work. Grandparents, who at first were angry with them for the unwanted pregnancy, quickly began to see the joy that the baby could bring and were soon taking turns caring for her while her parents got their lives together.

As summer was winding down, Rob Becker stopped over one Friday night with a case of Grizzly Beer that he had brought back from Ontario. Rob was grateful for Jenny's company that day at Sherkston, telling me that he just needed to get away, and the Grizzly was to thank me for giving up my wife one beautiful summer day to clear his mind. He and Jenny had talked quite a bit, but I had never really asked Jenny for any of the details.

As he was leaving that night, Rob reminded me that he was leaving for his family's annual camping trip up in Canada the following day. Each year, the entire Becker family, along with their significant others, drove into Ontario to a secluded campsite on the shores of Lake Ontario to spend a week camping, fishing, and swimming.

Rob was not a swimmer, so he did not fish either. He would frequently go out into the water up to his knees with family members and splash around, though. Most years, he spent his time back at the campsite reading or simply enjoying the weather. The campground also had a lodge where you could play video games or board games. Now that he was older, he brought along beer for himself, as well. The previous year, he and his soon-to-be brother-in-law Don had spent a number of days just sitting lakeside with some beverages and talking.

Rob was looking forward to this trip. He told me that night up on our front porch that he was burnt out. His job at Salvatore's was high pressure, because the patrons were paying top dollar for good food and didn't like to be left waiting. He worked full-time, but also was required to work significant overtime when a dinner party went longer than expected, or when he was called in a sixth (or seventh) day because a coworker didn't show or walked out.

He was also feeling down because his luck with the ladies was non-existent. While there were numerous waitresses at Salvatore's that he was interested in, he was convinced that none would go out with him. Of course, he never asked any of them to go out.

On his way out, Rob offered to pick up another case of Grizzly for me on their way home from the family trip. Having put a good-sized dent in the current case, I took him up on his offer.

Grizzly Beer was a favorite among our crowd. While it could be found in the States, it was not as prevalent as other brands. And even then, like other Canadian beers, it just wasn't the same. So Grizzly from Canada, even more so than Labatt, was what we brought back. Unfortunately, Grizzly Beer, like more and more parts of my early years, is now nothing but a memory.

Sort of like Rob Becker.

Chapter 2:
That Day

Suggested Listening
"Gone Away" – The Offspring
"The Gap is Too Wide" – Mostly Autumn

We know that all things work together for good for those who love God, for those who are called according to his purpose.
Romans 8: 28 (WEB)

In May, Jenny and I moved to a three-bedroom apartment on the East Side of Buffalo near the Cheektowaga line. Owned by the sister of my brother-in-law (there is probably a more correct way to refer to that relationship, maybe sister-in-law once removed or something), it was the first time Jenny had ever lived outside of South Buffalo. But even with two and three jobs apiece, we could no longer afford the rent on our Ashton Street apartment.

Part of this was the result of having Jenny's brother move in with us the previous January. When her brother moved in, he brought along his girlfriend and their three-month-old daughter. All of them had been kicked out of their houses and needed somewhere to go. So it was a family of five that moved into the two bedroom apartment on Roebling.

Truth be told, the newlywed bliss of the first few months was starting to wane even before Vince and his family arrived on the scene. Our lack of time together, combined with being tired from multiple shifts at low paying jobs, meant that we didn't have a lot of time to talk about us. To tell the other that they were loved. Instead of a purr of delight and love-making, there was often a grunt of annoyance as we crawled into bed with an already-sleeping partner. Or there might have been an earful about finances when one partner went to take $10 out of the bank to fill up the gas tank in one of our beater cars, or to buy a meal on our shift at work, only to find no money left in the account.

Throughout it all though, Jenny and I generally managed to keep each other smiling. We knew that we had each other, which made everything else bearable. Even with her brother and family being in the middle of it, things settled into something resembling a routine. Maybe it wasn't a perfect life, but it was our life.

Once we moved to the east side apartment, I began submitting resumes to get an accounting job. I knew that starting a career (instead of just having a job) meant that my salary would increase. At that point, maybe we could have a nicer apartment, reliable transportation, and normal working hours, and maybe Jenny and I could see each other every night. Or at least on weekends.

In the meantime, we decided that we could at least ask our respective employers for the same days off each week. Starting that summer, most weeks we were able to have Monday nights off together. We would generally celebrate with dinner at Perkins or a fast food joint, followed by a night curled up on the couch with a bottle of Canei wine. We tried to make time for each other in the bedroom as well, assuming that her brother's family was out of the house or already asleep.

In this apartment, we were visited more frequently by Rob Becker and Mike Wolf. They would stop by with beer, and we would sit and listen

That Monday night, Jenny and I had the day off together as we did every week. This particular day we spent together grocery shopping and hanging out at a record store. I remember hoping to find a copy of an imported live Marillion album, *Real to Reel,* but the store did not have it. After dinner at the apartment, Jenny and I sat down to relax in front of the tube.

The phone rang about 8:15. It was Jenny that answered it.

"Oh, hey Mike," I absent-mindedly heard her say. I did not pay attention past then, although I did wonder why she didn't call me to the phone right away. Maybe Mike was propositioning her. He would frequently make lewd suggestions to Jenny, like he did to any other woman that he was comfortable with. Knowing this, Jenny would play along and challenge him to come up with his most outrageous suggestions.

Instead, a moment or two later, I heard a subdued, "Matt?" Looking up, I noticed that Jenny was not smiling. Far from it. Getting up from my chair, she covered the receiver and said, "It's Mike. I think he's crying."

She had to be mistaken, I thought as I took the phone. Either she's mistaken or it's not Mike. Mike was never serious about anything. It was one of his charms. He could take the most solemn situation and make it bearable with a quick joke or comment.

I was quick to find out that he was, in fact, crying. In a broken voice, Mike told me, "Rob Becker is dead."

Just like that, everything in my life changed. My cozy, little, safe world was shattered. I experienced a total loss. My childhood ended. I tasted adulthood. Real life in the form of death.

Yes, I had lost loved ones before. All of my grandparents had passed. Aunts and uncles were gone. But these were adults. Old people. Not kids.

I always saw myself as a kid. Which meant my friends were kids. And kids don't die. It just doesn't happen like that!

All of this struck me at once, while Mike was still talking. I wasn't listening anymore. In the midst of my best friend's tragedy, I couldn't stop thinking of what this meant to me. How was I going to make sense of this?

Mike was trying his best to give me what few details he knew, telling me in a broken voice that Rob had drowned. That he had been in the water when an undertow had pulled him under. How Don had not been able to rescue him.

"Matt?" I heard from the other end. "Are you okay, dude?"

I guess I had been quiet for a while, trying to make sense out of what I was hearing. Looking back, I know I never asked Mike how he was holding up. The crying should have been an indication.

Eventually, the phone call ended. I don't know how long I was on that call or who hung up first. I just remember crying in Jenny's arms, and her holding me saying, "I'm so sorry, baby."

When I wasn't able to answer even the simplest question of what Mike had told me ("When did it happen?"), Jenny called Mike back. What I know about Rob's death was what Jenny found out from Mike that night.

By the time Jenny hung up from Mike the second time, I had already cracked open a beer, and was considering going to the store for more. I knew I was going to need them.

"Mike is really upset," Jenny informed me as she came into the kitchen and opened up her own beer. Sitting down, she continued, "I've never heard him cry before, but he could barely talk. Matt, you need to call him. He needs some support. Invite him over here. Have him spend the night here. But do something!"

I silently killed off the rest of my beer. Whatever Jenny had just said did not register with me as I considered what this meant to me. My friend, who would still talk me through issues at the bridge next to his house, was gone. Who would listen to me bemoan the fact that I wasn't getting laid enough, or grumble that I needed a raise, or complaining about my crappy car, all the while handing me fresh Michelob Darks? If he could go, he who was younger than me, that meant that I could go, too.

This was not possible. There was still so much we still had to do, so many places we had to go, so many dreams we had to make real. My life couldn't be just working at some thankless job for the next 40 or 50 years. What about becoming a rock star, or being a hockey player, or a writer? Did this mean that those were just dreams, that real life didn't always work out the way you wanted it to?

My future dreams, anchored in the memories of my past, were stolen by the reality of the present.

And with it, I had a choice to make. I had to grow up. My only other alternative, the one that I had clung to right up until the phone rang, was to keep looking ahead and telling myself, *"someday…"*

"I was in a band once…"

"I remember the time that I…"

"Check out the new Marillion album..."

"Let's go get some beer..."

But still Jenny sat there, expecting a response, expecting me to join her in real life.

But isn't that what most of our problems were all about up until this point? Real life? The finances and the arguments over sex and the multiple jobs and her brother's kid crying in the next room and the job search and every other fucking thing that dragged us down; all the things that kept me away from everything that I ever wanted and deserved and was entitled to in this miserable existence that Rob was no longer a part of? All because this God that I believe in, who is supposed to be here for me, decided that He would just rip him out of my life with no warning?

Real life. Jenny sat there, waiting in it. I wanted to stay here, wherever I was. Real life couldn't get me, not if I had another beer. But there was no more beer. Jenny had grabbed the last one and was still sitting there waiting patiently for me to say something, anything, that would give her some insight as to how I was feeling.

How was I feeling? Could I still feel? I was hurt. I guess that's a feeling, but one that comes with a chilling numbness, evidently.

"Matt?"

She still wanted to engage, to know that I was alright. The answer to that, though, was a judgement that I was not qualified to make. Not tonight, maybe not ever. I was. Wasn't that enough? Maybe it was too much.

I noticed that the television was still on, spewing white noise into the landscape of my thoughts. Blue light flashed in the background as Jenny sat beside me stroking my back, tears staining her soft cheeks. I kissed them and tasted their salty warmth.

"But…" was all I could get out as my own tears started again. Jenny held me against her chest as the weight of my loss washed over me and cleared out the confusion. Finally regaining my composure, I joined the real world once again.

Silence was the best I could do to communicate my feelings. In the silence was my loss, my feeling of emptiness, and my inability to do a fucking thing about it. Somehow, Jenny knew, and did not want anything more from me. She handed me what remained of her beer.

Picking up the phone, she invited Mike to come over for the night. She also told him to stop at Wilson Farms along the way for a case of beer.

She then called her parents and told them to find Vince, and to let him know that he and his family would have to crash somewhere else that night because Mike Wolf would be staying the night.

After that she called both of our employers and left messages that we would not be making it into work the following day.

Finally, when Mike showed up with a case of Labatt, she made sure that we all had a beer in our hand for the rest of the night.

Rob's funeral was at Our Lady Help of Christians on my birthday. The pall bearers were Don, Mike Wolf, Brian Marino, Chuck Dempsey, Rick Werner, and me.

Happy 23rd birthday, Matt.

Chapter 3:
Welcome Home

Suggesting Listening:
"There was a Time" – Spock's Beard
"Torn" – Natalie Imbruglia

Let your spring be blessed.
Rejoice in the wife of your youth.
A loving doe and a graceful deer –
Let her breasts satisfy you at all times.
Be captivated always with her love.
Proverbs 5: 18-19 (WEB)

Shortly after Rob's death, we moved again to a crappy apartment in South Buffalo across the street from Jenny's parents, as our financial picture deteriorated. Our landlords were completely unhinged. They owned two giant, vicious dogs that were always outside. Our only entrance to the apartment was the front door, because the side door would have meant walking through the fence into the dogs' territory. The dogs were still able to bark and jump at us when we were walking in the front door, and I think it would have only have been a matter of time until one of them jumped the fence to get to us.

Any request to fix something in the apartment meant finding one of them outside, because you couldn't get to the door to their apartment without dealing with the dogs. If you did happen to find one of them, they would tell you to fuck off or to fix it yourself. But they had no problem coming to our apartment to ask us for the rent money on the first of each month, or occasionally a few days early. One time, on the 27th of the month, the wife came to our apartment to demand the rent. Of course, we didn't have it, which sent her into a frenzy. Noticing that we had a cat, she told us that if we didn't have the rent by the following morning, she would feed the cat to her dogs.

We left that apartment as soon as we could, and found one three streets south. That apartment was the top floor of a home owned by a handyman and his wife. An upgrade in both apartment and landlord!

This new apartment was much more spacious, having a large dining room and two big bedrooms. There was a front porch where we could sit outside on nice evenings. The fixtures worked, and the landlord was always asking us how things were working. The landlords were friendly, and truly wanted their property to be your home. And the rent was only $10 more than at the previous place.

Living in South Buffalo was a change for me. Pat Hartmann and Mike Wolf would not come out there just to visit, unless it was on the way to some club that they were already going to. I was working as a manager at a Wendy's, while Jenny was juggling a number of minimum wage jobs, and trying to go to college for a culinary arts degree.

At some point, I finally got a huge break in my professional career. To this day, I do not know how my resume got there, but I received a call from Marine Midland Bank. I had had numerous job interviews before, mostly with CPA firms that never called me back for a second interview, so I was well-prepared for this interview.

Which I bombed.

I had no idea about half of the things that the interviewer was talking about. Something about collateral, commercial loans, and… stuff. I remember that there was something about travel, and would I be interested. Although I had never been on a plane in my life, I evidently said that I was very interested. Anything to get a job, I suppose. When I told Jenny this little tidbit, she was not happy.

But I got a second interview anyway, this time with the manager of the department, and I studied up a little bit. Going to the library, I looked for books on lending, and tried to get a few ideas of what lay ahead. When the interview came, I must have sounded at least a little coherent because I was hired. Compared to Wendy's, my salary was immediately doubled!

Jenny liked this development, even though she still did not like the thought of me traveling.

My first day on the job was March 17, Saint Patrick's Day. With my German heritage, and living in Cheektowaga with people of primarily German and Polish descent, I was never introduced to the importance of Saint Patrick's Day. Jenny, on the other hand, lived in South Buffalo, which was primarily Irish, all her life. Her ancestry was mostly Irish. So this was a big day for her.

As it was for Buffalo overall. With only a few exceptions like Boston, Saint Patrick's Day in Buffalo is celebrated like no other city in America. A huge parade takes place downtown, usually in a snowstorm of some variety. That never bothers the residents who line the streets. In Buffalo, everyone is an Irish Catholic that day regardless of skin color or religion. The parade is then followed by a night at the bars. This part of the celebration is generally held the weekend before March 17; that allows for more celebrations on the actual Saint Patrick's Day!

My new coworkers had planned to go out after work that day anyway. My first day was just another reason to go out. I figured that we would go for a drink, and I would be home by six or six-thirty. I soon found out that this was a bunch of professionals, and I had a long way to go to keep up with them. Rolling out of the bar after 10, I was in no shape to drive, but I did anyway. Showing up massively hungover on the second day of your professional career is generally not something that I would advise, but that is admittedly what I did. The only thing that kept my career from ending before it began was that I was one of the least hungover people in my department (boss included).

The previous Saturday night, I had gone out with Jenny to celebrate Saint Patrick's Day as well. Pitchers of green beer were consumed in large quantities. Again, not unique to Buffalo, the concept of green beer for Saint Patrick's Day was new to me. Simply taking the cheapest piss-water and adding green food dye to it does not make the beer taste different (or better), but we Buffalonians drink gallons of the stuff the week of St. Patty's Day anyway. I discovered that the amount of dye used by the bars is important. Most bars add enough dye that the resulting beverage is a deep Kelly green, the color of Ireland. If they skimp on the dye, though, the beer looks more like the piss-water it was made from.

This night, we were out with a few friends of Jenny's at one of South Buffalo's infinite number of bars, taverns, pubs, clubs, watering holes, gin mills, and other assorted drinking establishments. Among the crowd was a guy that I had assumed (in my previous meetings with him) was gay. But this night, he brought along one of the hottest women I had ever met and announced her as his girlfriend. A petite blond with an oversized chest packed into a low-cut blouse who hung on his every word. He introduced her as a modeling student who was looking for a start in the movie business. If he were there, Mike Wolf would have had a field day with this!

At our table, everyone was partaking of the many pitchers of green beer that magically regenerated every 15 minutes or so—except for the blond model, who was drinking a fruity concoction ornamented with a paper umbrella. This being South Buffalo, I didn't even know that paper umbrellas were allowed. Maybe she brought her own.

I will readily admit to staring at her ample cleavage a good portion of the night. She caught me one time, and called me on it. Having apologized, I refilled my clear plastic cup with the dark green swill we were drinking and took a long drink in shame.

"That stuff looks awful," she commented. "What does that even taste like?"

Having just been caught lusting after someone else's date while my own wife sat only a few feet away should have humbled me a bit. But instead, I wanted to get back some of my dignity via my sharp wit. So I answered, "The green is a mint flavoring. It tastes a little bit like a candy cane. You know? Minty."

"Mint flavored beer?" She looked at the pitcher disapprovingly.

"It's actually kind of refreshing," I continued. "Unexpected. That's why so many people drink it on St. Patty's Day. It's something different."

"I thought it was just green food dye."

"No, it's like a peppermint flavoring. You want a sip?" I asked, pouring her a small glass.

Taking it hesitantly, she sniffed the cup. Most of the table had quieted their conversations and were watching us, knowing that I was messing with her. The guys, of course, were also taking this opportunity to ogle the goods without fear of being caught like I just was. Looking nervous, she slowly brought the glass to her mouth and took an exploratory sip.

Her face brightened. "Oh my God, that IS minty!"

Incredulous, I played along, knowing now that I was going to get told what a big jerk I was later on by my wife. "Yeah, I told you. It's different, isn't it?"

"I don't even like beer," she continued, "but this is great! It's not peppermint, though. What is it?" She took another drink. "That's spearmint! Wow, you really do learn something new every day."

So it was that she drank her new favorite, green spearmint beer, for the rest of the night.

Not long after I started at the bank, Jenny landed a steady, full-time job as a dispatcher for an appliance repair service. Not only did her salary greatly increase, but we now both worked nine-to-five, Monday through Friday type jobs. We had an opportunity to improve our finances, as well as strengthen our marriage, which was still shaky after the months with her brother and his family living with us.

Not that he was out of our lives completely. Vince now lived with his girlfriend and their daughter in an apartment in South Buffalo as well. We still were dragged in when they were fighting, either because of a phone call from Jenny's mother or from Vince's girlfriend. I remember one night where Vince was running through some neighborhoods eluding the police, who were looking for him because he threw a rock through his apartment window! His girlfriend called the police on him because she was afraid that he would hurt her or the baby.

But Jenny and I were in love, and that was all that mattered. Rob's death brought us closer together somehow. Neither of us had ever lost a friend before, so we chose to lean on each other for support. I started having disturbing dreams, and woke up in Jenny's arms crying at least once a week. Jenny sought refuge in the Catholic Church, encouraging me to do the same. She knew that Rob had gone home. I was not as sure.

The stresses remained, even as we looked to each other for comfort.

While the concept of traveling seemed exciting, I soon found out the truth. First, I never went anywhere exciting, but I went there almost weekly. While never the same place twice, it was always some small town

60 miles from a city with any sort of nightlife. Then, I had to work. I was an auditor, so I no one was ever happy to see me. I was given a tight budget, and most nights had to work until seven or eight to get the job done. Finally, there was the travel itself. Getting up at four in the morning on Monday to catch a flight, and not getting home until ten or eleven Friday night, was certainly not what I had had in mind.

A few nights a week, Jenny and her friends would hit one of South Buffalo's numerous bars. They would frequently go dancing. And because we were both making some decent money, it didn't matter that she dropped $30 or $40 a night.

The weekends were ours, though, and we took advantage of them. Every Saturday night (and Friday night, if I got home early enough), Jenny and I would hit the bars. Some nights would end up very well, with some passionate lovemaking and a strong sense of togetherness. Other nights did not go so well.

One night, we had both been drinking. Jenny was dancing with her friends, and she had been drinking way more than me. Damn, I thought, she looked good tonight. Maybe I'll get lucky!

But when we got home, the room started spinning on her, and she went into the bathroom to puke up the night's good times. The combination of her sickness and her drunkenness made her start to freak out. She began crying hysterically. Rather than being understanding, I did something that I regret to this day: I slapped her in the face to try to get her to pull herself together. I had never hit a woman before or since, but it seemed like a good idea at the time. The fact that I had also been drinking did nothing to dull the sickening shock of that incident for either of us.

Finding places to go drinking was easy. At that point, South Buffalo had an inordinate number of bars, mostly storefront pubs offering cheap beer, darts, pool, and friends. I don't know how true this "fact" is or was, but I know I heard it said that the South Park strip of South Buffalo had more bars per foot than any other place on earth. Of course, I've heard that claim in a number of cities during my travels.

That was just the neighborhood bars—the ones you could pop into anytime for a quick one or six. That did not take into account the clubs.

Buffalo had some legendary rock clubs during this time. One of the first rock clubs I ever went to was Harvey and Corky's Stage One on Main Street in Clarence. Owned by Harvey Weinstein whose subsequent claim to fame was the ownership of Miramax Studios (and subsequent sexual molestation scandal), this club hosted quite a number of big acts in its infancy. U2 played their first show in Buffalo at Stage One on the *Boy* tour. The Police played there during their *Outlandos D'Amour* tour.

I was familiar with Stage One because Talas was a regular there. Mike Wolf and I would go a few times a year to see them. I would stand on Billy Sheehan's side of the stage and watch him in awe, trying to pick up something, anything, that would help me with my bass playing. Hoping that physical proximity would somehow transfer talent to me via osmosis.

It never did. I am living proof of that.

Jenny and I never went to Stage One together (we lived more than 10 miles from it), but we did see Talas a number of times at the Salty Dog Skyroom on Abbott. This club was one of the largest in Buffalo. Boasting the longest bar in Buffalo, the Salty Dog occupied the entire top floor of an old shopping center. This club could hold over 1,000 patrons and still look empty. Generally featuring heavy metal bands, groups like Metallica, Motörhead, Poison, and L.A. Guns played here on their way to fame. It also hosted the likes of Melissa Etheridge and R.E.M. along the way. One of my great disappointments in life is that I never got to see Marillion play the Salty Dog on their first ever US tour; I had to work.

Jenny and I would go to the Salty Dog on weekends with friends to check out bands, but she would frequently go to one of the smaller clubs on South Park during the week when I was away. A favorite with her and her crowd was the Blarney Castle on South Park. On the infrequent weeks that I was not scheduled out of town, Jenny and I usually chose to stay home throughout the week. As such, Jenny's friends did not see me very often.

Regardless, my drinking was starting to get to me without my noticing it. When I was on the road, we were given a per diem, so it didn't matter what you spent it on; you could choose any food or drink you liked. We were given the same $34 per day whether we ate every meal at McDonalds or every meal at a steakhouse. This made the accounting for the bank easier, because they did not have to go through receipts and make judgement calls about whether a steak was an allowable expense over a burger (or whether to reimburse someone's alcohol consumption). So most of my new coworkers would order a few drinks with dinner each night (and sometimes with lunch).

On the few nights that I was out of town by myself, I found myself homesick and did not want to sit in a crowded restaurant watching happy families eat. Instead, I would get fast food take out, and a six pack of some sort of cheap beer. The six-pack was meant to last for most of the week, but as time went on, that happened less and less.

On one of our good Saturdays, Jenny and I were lying in bed after happily enjoying each other. "Sara is so full of shit," Jenny declared, apropos of nothing.

"About what?"

"That I would be happier single. If I were single, THAT would never have happened!"

I was perturbed. "You mean she said that you should be single?"

Jenny realized the can was opened and the worms were coming out.

"She didn't mean anything by it. You know how she is. She's just jealous because, even though she's dated most of South Buffalo, she's never found a guy that she is interested in. She thinks they're all out for one thing, so that's her opinion about marriage."

I wasn't ready to let this pass. "What exactly did she say?"

"Let it go," Jenny deflected. "We just had a great night, and you're worried about something my friend said."

"Yeah, I'm worried," I continued. "I think that she is putting thoughts in your head. You're married, babe. She's not. You have different responsibilities than her. You have a new family now."

"And that's what she warned me about."

"Warned?"

"Not warned. That's the wrong word. Anyway, she told me that she is worried that I got married too young. That I'm too young to be tied down when there is still so much living that we haven't done."

"What did you say? I hope that you told her that this was a choice that you made willingly. That you knew what you were getting into."

"No. Truthfully, I do worry. I'm still overwhelmed by all this," she confessed. "I'm an adult. I have responsibilities. I can't just drop everything I have to go out with friends or to explore the world. My money isn't my money. It's our money. What if it's not enough? What if I'm meant to do something else, and I'll never know it because I'm with you?

"And what about you? Half the time, I don't know where you are. Or what you're doing. Drinking? Strip clubs? Something worse that I don't want to think about?"

"Well, I hate to tell you this, my love, but it's too late to think about that now," I tried to reassure her. "I'm an adult now, too. I don't know what will happen either, or what the future holds. I just know that, whatever that future does hold, I want you to be a part of it.

"We took a vow in front of God and man, and our friends and family witnessed it and promised that they would support us in our life together. It doesn't sound like Sara is supporting us right now. As far as the rest of that stuff, I took a vow that I intend on honoring."

"What do you mean, Sara's not supporting me?" Jenny interrupted. "She's the only one that cares how I'm doing in all of this. I just said I'm scared, and you pretty much told me 'too bad.' At least she sees the issue for what it is. I got married too young!"

"What are you saying?" I asked, incredulous. "You want out? I know things were rough with Vince, and with the multiple jobs and all, but we're finally in a place where we can grow together. As a family."

"Really?" she wondered. "So when you are off in East Bunglefuck for a week, we're a family? You come home on the weekend to give me a quick one, and then you're off again. That's what I get out of this marriage?"

"I'm not always going to be on the road," I offered. "At some point, I'll have an opportunity for something different. We're starting to dig out from our financial mess. That will give us freedoms that we never had. Buying a house someday. Getting reliable cars. Maybe having kids."

"Kids? I'm not raising kids by myself while you take your weekly vacations."

That was enough for me. "Vacations? Listen, I work my ass off on the road to get back home as soon as I can! To provide for my family. I didn't plan on being on the road, but that is the hand we've been dealt at this point. Just because Sara thinks it sucks doesn't mean that you have to agree with her. If you truly think it sucks, then I will put out my resume again and try to find something that doesn't require travel. Will that ease your mind?"

"I hope so," was the best I could get out of her at that point.

Money is a great thing. I place great value in it for obvious reasons.

At the point in my life where this story takes place, I had never had any. Now I was making a good living, providing for my new family, and had an honest-to-goodness career path. Money allows you to get nice things, be prepared for future uncertainties, and keeps you from having to make bad decisions. It does not *prevent* you from making those bad decisions, though.

I am quick to point out to people that money is not everything. It needs to be pretty high on your priority list, but should never be at the top. When someone (your wife) tells you that she doesn't like the results of your (comparative) wealth, I recommend that you take that conversation seriously. I did not. I only heard the part about her getting married too young.

So Monday inevitably rolled around again, and I boarded another plane. Chicago? Been there. Boston? Yep. Minneapolis? Only in winter. Dallas? Only in summer. Most weeks were a blur. My sightseeing was the accounting department offices, the warehouse, and the fast food strip closest to the hotel.

My evening phone call home generally resulted in listening to the phone on the other end ring 10 times because no one was home. Nothing that another beer or three couldn't fix.

Atlanta was the last trip before a long Thanksgiving weekend the following week. My Friday night flight home touched down early for a change, so I rushed to claim my luggage and get to my car. I was tired, but I knew that I had at least the next ten days to be in town, and to try to make things a little better on the home front.

The letter was sitting in the middle of the table.

> *While you were gone, I packed up my stuff and took it to my mom's. I can't make myself love you, and I'm done trying. I filed for divorce, and you will be served papers*

next week. Give me a few days to get my head together, and we can meet for coffee and talk. Sorry it has to end like this.

The kicker was that she had not even left any beer in the apartment. I could have used one (or more) at that point.

There was no point in trying to call her. It was Friday night. She was out somewhere. I could look for her, but that would only cause a scene. There was only one thing left to do.

I sat down, and for the first time since Rob's death, I cried.

Chapter 4:
Orlando

Suggested Listening:
"It Must Have Been Love" – Roxette
"Goin' Through the Motions" – Blue Öyster Cult

For all have sinned, and fall short of the glory of God.
Romans 3: 23 (WEB)

THERE WERE not many benefits to my job. The constant travel ensured that I did not have time to spend with my friends. Mike stopped by with medicinal beers when he could, but these visits were generally spent listening to me whine about Jenny. The long hours while I was on the road meant that, by the time I got back to the hotel room, I had no energy to do anything but down the six-pack that I had made sure to buy. The weekends were spent doing laundry, paying bills, and doing other chores that had accumulated while I was away.

Three months had passed since Jenny's letter ripped into my life. We spoke a few times a week; sometimes getting together for coffee, other times over the phone. We talked about counseling, about what it would take to get her to move back in, about honoring our vows. Let me rephrase that: I talked about that stuff. She mostly talked about the logistics of our pending divorce.

Don't get me wrong; the conversations were civil, even loving. She knew that she had hurt me, and I knew that she was not taking this step because she was having fun doing it. There was significant pain on her side, too. For one thing, her parents were against the idea.

Her father did not want her living at their house because she had a house to go to: her husband's. (That was one of the only times he referred to me as anything other than faggot.) She was temporarily living in the apartment of her friend, Diana. But even though Diana let her share her apartment, she was totally against Jenny's actions.

"You have a wonderful man who would do anything for you," Diana lectured, according to Jenny. Diana thought that she had a relationship like that at one point, but the guy that she was dating walked out on her after he found out that she was pregnant. "Matt is in it for the long haul," Jenny quoted Diana as having said.

Even her long-time friends from South Buffalo were on the fence about where to lay their allegiance. They wanted to support their friend, but they also knew me, and they could see that I still had the intention of making things work.

The only one who seemed to be all for Jenny was her friend Sara, so Sara was the only one Jenny listened to. Sara would tell Jenny that she was doing the right thing any time Jenny seemed uncertain, or her resolve wavered. Sara went out of her way to suggest that Jenny wasn't doing enough to get me off her mind. She suggested guys for Jenny to date. She would make sure there were one or two single guys nearby whenever they went drinking.

I had been to counseling with the priest at Chapel who married us. He had me handwrite a complete marriage history to get the full story based on some writing prompts. Of course, Jenny was supposed to complete the same history independently, but she never did. After two or three sessions, and no expression of interest from Jenny, the priest told me that there was nothing he could do, and suggested that I pray.

In the meantime, she had moved to an apartment of her own that was two blocks from mine. I would drive past it whenever I could, hoping I could catch her outside; dreading that I would see someone else parked in the driveway.

It was during this scenario that I was told of a retreat through work. In early March, Marine Midland Bank would be having a national meeting of all the auditors in the country in Orlando, Florida to work out a national audit program. Since I was hired, the bank had purchased two other banks that did the same thing we did, but their audit programs were all different. The bank needed to introduce a unified audit program, and they decided to do so by bringing together all the employees for an all-expenses-paid, week-long stay at a golf resort.

Better yet, the auditors were encouraged to bring their spouses! At the bank's expense!

"I don't think it's a good idea," was Jenny's response when I told her over some coffee and pie at Perkins.

"It will be perfect," I countered. "We will have our own bungalow. I will be gone all day at meetings, so you can go off with the other wives to the pool, or to Disney, or wherever. Then we'll catch up at dinner and we can go to clubs or just hang out with my coworkers. You know most of the wives, so that won't be an issue."

"But what about sleeping arrangements? This is not going to get me back into bed with you, Matt."

"Okay, fine. I'll sleep on the couch if that is your biggest objection. Look, I think this could be what we need. Some fun. A chance to reconnect. You get a week of vacation at worst. I get a week-long chance to get you to fall in love with me all over again. What have you got to lose?"

She took my hand and dejectedly said, "I don't want to give you hope, Matt. I've made a decision—the hardest one in my life. I have to be true to it."

"Why? Why are you convincing yourself that we can never make this work?"

"Because…" Her voice trailed off. She looked out the window before turning back toward me. "Because I couldn't make my vows work. Either way, I let myself down. If I don't come with you, I've given up on my marriage. If I come with you, I've given up on my decision to take my life into my own hands.

"Right now, I am responsible for me. If I do good, it's because of me. If I fail miserably, it's because of me. When I was with you, I never knew if it was me failing, or you failing, or us failing. If it was you failing, I couldn't do anything to stop it."

"Luckily, I never mess anything up," I said, trying to lighten the mood.

A small smile briefly passed her lips. "I don't know." She looked away again. "Everything I do lately is wrong."

"Then trust me in this one thing." I took her hands in mine, and got her to look at me. "Come with me on vacation. Sleep in my bed. Make me your husband for one week. One week! We will either fall back in love, or we won't. At the end of the week, I will ask you again to move back home. If nothing changes in Orlando, you go back to your life knowing that you tried."

"Matt…"

I kept going. "How can you make a life-changing decision like ending your marriage without at least trying once to save it? You know it will be something that eats at you later in life."

A deep sigh. Weakly, she agreed.

This was the first time that Jenny had ever been on an airplane. Leaving the endless winter of Buffalo, the blast of warm air hit us as we got off the plane. The palm trees in the distance lined the cloudless skies as we drove in our rental car to the resort. After a few miles with the wind in her long blond hair, her heart softened and she smiled at me. "This is nice, Matt. Thanks for making me do this."

We got to our bungalow, which was bigger than any apartment we had ever lived in. There was only one bedroom. Standing in the doorway, I asked her, "Am I putting all of our stuff in here?"

Hesitating, she said, "Yes. But, Matt, just because I'm sharing the bed does not mean anything is going to happen."

"I'll take that chance." I dropped the suitcases on the bed, and took her hands. Looking me in the eyes, she wrapped her arms around me, buried her head in my chest, and cried.

Knowing better than to push anything one way or the other, I simply guided her out of the room and to the door. "Let's go take a look around," I suggested.

The days were filled with meetings. I was expected to be at the lodge by 7:30 for breakfast with my coworkers, followed by meetings from 8:30 to 11:30. We were on our own for lunch from then until 1:30, with the expectation that we would find our spouses and have lunch with them. But the spouses tended to get together, and go shopping or to a park or something all day, so no one was back at the bungalows at lunch. So we would hop in someone's car and go somewhere ourselves. Meetings then went until 5:00, at which point employees and spouses were to meet at the lodge for dinner at 6:00. From then on, everyone was on their own.

A few nights, someone would rent a video, and we would go to their bungalow with beer and snacks and watch it with them. One night, everyone went to a dance club until midnight or so.

When we got back to the room, Jenny and I would get into bed and talk for a few minutes before going to sleep. The conversation was just a casual discussion of what we did, comments on the wonderful food, or reminiscing about the beautiful weather and scenery. I did not bring up anything about marriage.

Friday was the last day of meetings. We would be staying the night at the resort, then catching whatever flights we had booked on Saturday. A few people chose to pay for one more night out of their own pockets, and were not going home until Sunday.

After the Friday morning meetings wound down, I wandered to our bungalow to see if Jenny wanted to go to lunch with everyone. The spouses had decided to remain back until after lunch that day, with the theory being that they would begin packing for the next day.

As I walked into the bungalow and announced myself, Jenny came walking out of the bedroom wrapped only in a towel and drying off her hair. I audibly gasped when I saw her. It had been months since I had seen my wife in any sort of a sexual way. And here she was, still wet from the shower, with her long legs flowing out from the flimsy covering.

"Oh, Matt. I didn't know you'd be back so soon," she stammered, embarrassed. "Give me five minutes to get ready."

She noticed that my eyes had not left her. A sly smile crossed her face as she put down the hair towel. "What are you looking at?" she teased as she unwrapped the towel around her body.

"Am I allowed?" I pleaded as I walked toward her.

"Please," was all she said as she guided my hand between her legs and her tongue down my throat.

We did not make it to lunch that day. The afternoon meetings were much more interesting. Jenny and I begged off from going to see *European Vacation* at my coworker's bungalow that night as well.

I guess it stands to reason that, because this is only chapter four of a book, and because you still have a good hundred pages or so in your right hand, that the trip to Orlando was not the magic solution that I hoped it would be.

This started to dawn on me on the plane ride home. The buoyant smiles that had appeared throughout the week were going back into hiding, as each mile drew us closer to Cheektowaga. As we began our descent, Jenny just stared out the window, not listening to the inane chatter that I was trying to distract her with. The same inane chatter that had her laughing earlier in the week. The same inane chatter that we had as we lay naked in each other's arms just hours earlier.

As we stood awaiting our luggage at baggage claim, she took my hand and spoke the words that I had feared. "You know I'm going back to my own apartment tonight, right?"

I guided her away from the rest of the passengers, many of whom were my coworkers. We found two seats near a baggage carousel that was not in use.

"What about last night?"

She pulled her hands away from mine angrily. "I KNEW I should've said no to this damn trip. I KNEW this would happen." She calmed down. "Matt, I warned you before I accepted the invitation not to get your hopes up.

"I know I led you on, especially yesterday. Damn, we both needed that! But don't you understand? That was a physical event. Animal. Instinctual. I wasn't thinking, and neither were you. I was afraid of this."

"Then skip yesterday," I suggested. "We had a blast the rest of the week. Hanging out, heading to clubs. Just laughing with each other. At each other. Doesn't that show you how good we are together? And how much better we could be if we just gave it another try?"

"And if we lived in an all-expense-paid resort with endless sunshine maybe that would be the case. But I have to go back to work on Monday, and so do you. Where are you going this week? St. Louis, I think you said?

"And then there are the bills. Did you catch up on the electric bills yet? What about your student loans? Did you ever call to get the deferment?

"We just lived a week of fantasy, Matt, and I can't think of anyone I'd rather have spent it with. But this?" She waved her hand at our surroundings. "This is reality, babe. This is the world I live in, even if you don't. It's a world of doubt, of feeling like I'm drowning. I can't bring you down with me."

"Did you ever think that I'm drowning without you?" I countered testily. "That my faith in us can keep us afloat while you find yours? You never surrendered your life to our marriage. You were able to surrender your body to my care last night. You trusted that I would take you where you wanted to go. But that same surrender, that same trust, you've never given me as your husband. As your life partner.

"I surrendered my heart to you long ago. I've left it in your care even during your bout of uncertainty before we got married. You did your best to heal it when Rob died. Even now, I'm sitting here with it in my hand hoping that you take it again. It's not the giving of my heart to you that hurts. It's when you won't accept it."

"Then keep it, Matt. Some other woman will take it and protect it fiercely. She will guard it with her life. I just got through using it. Playing a game with it. And you still want me to have it?"

"YES!" I almost screamed.

"Then it is up to me to crush it now. Forever. I'm going back to my apartment tonight, Matt. To live in the reality of the situation that I created. Thank you for a week of fantasy. I'm sorry, Matt, but it's over," she said as she walked back to the baggage carousel where our bags were the only ones still on the belt.

Chapter 5
The Downstairs Neighbor

Suggested Listening:
"Jezebel" – 10,000 Maniacs
"Right Next Door" – Robert Cray Band

Count it all joy, my brothers, when you fall into various temptations, knowing that the testing of your faith produces endurance. Let endurance have its perfect work, that you may be perfect and complete, lacking in nothing.
James 1: 2-4 (WEB)

As my dad neared his 70th birthday, he was diagnosed with emphysema. Both he and Mom smoked their entire lives, like most people of that generation. But now, Dad's smoking caught up to him, and he was on an oxygen tank at all times. And, of course, he had to stop smoking.

All of my siblings and their spouses smoked as well. Once Dad was diagnosed, each of them made it a point to refrain from smoking in his presence. They would either forego a cigarette completely if they just stopped by for a quick visit, or excuse themselves for a few minutes on longer visits.

This was a courtesy that was not provided by my mom.

She continued to smoke in the house, even when Dad was in the room. He asked her on numerous occasions to please stop smoking with him, or at least in front of him. She considered it his problem, not hers, and continued her pack-a-day habit unabated.

During one particularly eventful family get-together, my sister-in-law Cheryl made a comment to Mom about her smoking in front of Dad, when everyone else made it a point not to. This did not sit well with Mom. Cheryl felt that, at the least, Mom was disrespecting Dad's attempt to get better. At the worst, Cheryl suggested, Mom didn't want him to get better at all.

Mom erupted at Cheryl that she needed to stay out of things that were none of her business. After all, she wasn't even a part of the family (even though she had been married to my brother for over 15 years). My brother, at this point, defended his wife and told Mom that if she did not apologize, they would leave.

"Then leave."

"Fine. We won't be back until you apologize."

"Then it was nice knowing you."

That was the end of that particular family get-together.

From that day on, Mom forbid Dad (or any of us) from ever talking to my brother again. (Of course, all of us did.) Any comments from my sisters or myself trying to talk sense into her were met with outlandish stories about how my brother and his wife were always plotting on stealing the inheritance for themselves, and how they said terrible things to Mom when no one else was around. Evidently, Cheryl was a witch. Funny—I had never seen that before (or since).

Despite everything that Mom said, the one who felt worst about the situation was Cheryl. Cheryl tried calling Mom on a number of occasions to ask her to pick up the phone and talk to my brother. Mom would hang up as soon as she heard Cheryl's voice, and would grab the phone from Dad and hang it up if she thought Dad was talking to Cheryl. One time, she hung up while Dad was talking to me, thinking I was Cheryl.

§§§

And as all of this was happening with my parents and siblings, my attempts to repair my marriage were failing.

The Orlando trip had been for nothing. While I thought that the good times had rekindled something that would make her want to fight for us, there was nothing on her end. She did not move back in. She did not want to come over for more discussions. She would not come with me to counselling.

Luckily, Mike was always nearby with a six pack. We'd down a few, then go catch a band somewhere. If I was lucky, I'd pass out before I started wondering where Jenny was. Other times, I'd sit in my apartment and listen to depressing songs until I passed out. Marillion's "Kayleigh" was a favorite.

I just can't go on pretending that it came to its natural end…

One day, I got home from work a little early. Jenny's car was parked out in front. She no longer had a key, and she was not in the car, so where was she? I started up the stairs to my apartment. As I was passing the door to the landlord's apartment downstairs, I heard her laugh. She must be visiting with them while waiting for me, I thought. Except that I wasn't supposed to be home for another hour or more. I went into my apartment without a second thought. If she was there for me, she never came to my door.

One night the following week, I was sitting in my apartment eating dinner when I heard her downstairs again. This time she was leaving, and there was a man's voice in the discussion as well.

I called her the next day. Trying not to be confrontational, I asked her if she was at the apartment the day before. The long pause and the sigh told me that I was not going to like what came next.

"I didn't want you to find out about this before I told you, and I was going to tell you soon. I'm dating Pete," she said, with her mouth as far away from the phone as possible. I could see her in her apartment, looking at the floor, not wanting this conversation. Pete Cooper was the landlord's son who visited his parents almost daily.

"That's a kick to the stomach," was all I could muster. "How long has this been going on? Since we moved in?" That last part was just spiteful, and I shouldn't have said it, but I had to lash out a little bit. You can only hold in so much.

"It's been since I moved out," she confessed. At this point, I know I took the phone from my ear and collapsed into a kitchen chair. *That explains a lot*, went through my mind. Putting the phone back to my ear, she was continuing her explanation. "You were the one who told me to have the Cooper's fix it. And you know Pete's a plumber, so don't you dare go giving me any bullshit about me looking for it."

"So you were fucking him before you moved out?" I asked.

"No, you asshole! If you were listening, I said that he just asked me to dinner after I ran into him at the Blarney Castle. I left because I took him up on the offer when you were in Atlanta for the week. Nothing happened, but I knew I had crossed a line in our marriage. It was not fair to you, and I moved out. I've seen Pete three or four times since then."

"So what about Orlando? I thought we were rekindling something."

"Oh baby, do you know how badly I wanted that to work? How much I wanted to be your bride again? But I can't say that I ever felt the way I should have, that week. And that is the problem, I can't say that I have ever felt the way I should have about you. About being your wife."

"What does that mean?" I asked, because we were finally getting somewhere.

"I don't know what it means. I don't know what it is supposed to feel like. Loved, I guess? Special? Is there supposed to be a tingle or a thrill or a…feeling when you touch me? When you kiss me? I feel safe, and I know how lucky I am to have a man who adores me the way I know that you do. But it's not enough somehow.

"So when Pete asked me to dinner, I turned him down. Of course I did. I'm a married woman for God's sake. But I was flattered, and I felt it. After so long, some excitement! Some danger! Some mystery! When he asked me a second time, and then a third, I gave in. Just to the date. Nothing else happened!

"Sweetheart, I love you because I know you. I know what you like and what you don't, I know how to hurt you and how to heal you. But we can't get there, wherever 'there' is; because of me, because of you, because of money, and for a thousand other fucking reasons that drive me insane."

She paused to listen, but even I knew that now was not a good time to speak. Her voice quieted and she continued, "I knew that if you found out about the date, I would hurt you. I couldn't risk that.

"It's a fantasy, Matt, I know that. I know that I am hurting you, a GOOD man. How screwed up am I? I know that I am hurting the man who loves me, and I still want my good times."

"So come home. Stop hurting me. You are forgiven. You are loved."

"Oh Matt, you sweet fool," she responded. "It's too far gone. Plus with him downstairs so often, do you really think that is a good idea?"

"I didn't think it was too far gone in Orlando. We picked up where we left off, was my opinion. With proper support, we can make it work." No response. Then it clicked. Two plus two suddenly equaled four. "Did you sleep with him?"

The extra second it took for her to deny it was all the answer I needed. "No." Simple. No explanation. Soft voice. In my mind's eye, I could see her praying for me not to push the subject.

"Somehow, that did not sound sincere," I muttered slowly.

Then came the explosion. "My GOD, Matt, why do you do this to yourself? Yes, I slept with him. Okay? Is that what you wanted to hear? Do you want details? Will that get you to go off in another 'poor, poor me' rant? Does it show you what a better person you are than me?

"Give it up, Matt, for your own sake. I'm gone. I'm going to keep hurting you, because you have yourself set up for something that is just not happening. I walked out to try to save you from this, but you keep coming back for more. Just stop it, Matt. Move on. I love you, but let me go. Find yourself someone who will love you like you deserve and like I can't. I just can't. I'm sorry."

And with that she hung up.

After that phone call, she did not keep her relationship with Pete a secret. Far from it. She would show up at the house with him, making enough noise when they left that I'd be sure to hear it. When she had to talk to me for some reason, she would mention him. But most glaring of all was that she let him stay overnight frequently and, even though her apartment had a driveway, he always parked his work truck on the street in front.

And I would torture myself with this information. Many were the nights after Mike left that I would drive to her apartment at one or two in the morning just to confirm that Pete's truck was there. I would then go back to my apartment with a fresh six pack, put on some more depressing music, and drink until I passed out on the couch or in a chair.

I guess I wanted to prove to myself the reality of the situation. In retrospect, it is obvious that I was just finding new pain to numb.

One day when I got home from work, Pete's dad was fixing something in our apartment. He was a great landlord, and would frequently let himself into our (sorry, *my*) apartment to upgrade something, or to fix things that I didn't know needed fixing. He looked at me awkwardly when I said hello.

"Hey. I guess you know about Pete and Jenny by now?"

"Yeah. It sucks pretty bad."

Pete's dad did not want this conversation, and started making a quick inventory of his tools to pack them away hurriedly. "I am so pissed off at him. He knows better than to go after a married woman—at least, I thought we taught him better than that! Then the dipshit goes and gets up with a tenant on top of that. Anyway, I'm sorry. I'm not trying to get youse guys to leave, but I know the situation here must be uncomfortable. If you need to get away, I would let you out of the lease early so that you don't have to be subjected to what he is putting you through."

I had not even considered getting a new apartment. As far as I was concerned, this was our marriage home, at least until the lease expired in five months. But this conversation put a germ of an idea into my mind. Maybe I *should* escape this area.

After all, I knew nobody in South Buffalo that did not also know Jenny, and they knew her longer. While some of her friends were angry at her and did not hang out with her anymore, most still met up with her at any one of the other myriad of bars around. Chances were good that if I called up anyone, they would already have other plans, a euphemism for "we're hanging out with Jenny." So I would head out to Cheektowaga anyway to see Mike or Pat, or maybe my siblings. Someone with beer.

And that was the other thing. I was drinking. A lot. I was good for a six pack a night. "Sleep" was another name for "passed out," because I couldn't just count sheep and go to sleep. I needed to be self-medicated with a near-fatal overdose of alcohol. I went into work hungover almost every day. When I was traveling, I frequently told my coworkers to go to dinner without me. Then I would go to McDonald's or some other fast food joint, and wash it down with a six pack.

Speaking of traveling, I was gone from the apartment more than I was at it, so why was I paying for something so big? Especially if it was going to be empty most of the time.

So I did nothing, which was the most I was capable of in those days.

One day, three weeks or so after my conversation with the landlord, I heard the happy couple downstairs visiting. While I was not eavesdropping (no, seriously), I heard Jenny say, "Alright, I'll catch up with you later back at the apartment." With that she opened the door to their apartment and left.

I had downed two or three beers by that point, and had a stupid thought and some artificial bravery. This idiot, I thought, needed to know that I still was in love with the married woman that he was dating.

So I "happened" to be leaving at the same time I heard him saying goodbye to his parents.

"Oh, hey," I innocently said as I descended the stairs to the main door.

He tried to ignore me with a simple grunt of acknowledgement as he hurried down the driveway.

"I don't appreciate your hooking up with my WIFE," I prompted as I caught up to him. Stepping in front of him, I continued, "You could have a little honor, and step away while Jenny and I try to work this out. You might be getting it, but that doesn't make you a real man. A real man would have respect for the ring on her finger."

"What ring? Haven't you noticed that she took that fucking thing off a month or so ago? And as far as respect, why should I respect you when she doesn't? Why are you acting so surprised? She calls you desperate. Pathetic. THAT is not a man! I agree with her father. You really ARE a faggot! Now get out of my way before I pound your face into my car door."

I stood there quietly as he got in the car and drove off. Pathetic? I guess I was. I walked back upstairs to mull this one over with whatever remained of the twelve-pack of friends that I had brought home that night.

Jenny was not appreciative the next day when she called. "What the FUCK were you thinking last night? Did you really think that Pete would agree to stop seeing me just because poor, poor Matt ambushed him? My GOD, what an IDIOT you are!"

"An idiot? So I don't have the right to confront the man who is destroying my marriage, when he flaunts it at the only place I can call home? I would be less pathetic to you if I just let him walk in and out of the same building as me with my so-called wife? I should just shut up and take it? What should I do? You know best! Tell me! TELL ME!"

"I'm sorry, I didn't realize just how tough this must be on you. I'll talk to Pete," she offered.

I was sick of the condescending attitude. "Oh, you'll 'talk to Pete.' How fucking thoughtful of you. You didn't realize how this was affecting me because all you give a shit about right now is avoiding reality. This is what you want, so everybody must be on board with it too. If they don't understand, that's their problem. Does your mom think you are doing the right thing?"

"Don't bring her into it!" Jenny screamed.

"No, of course not. She might not agree with you. I'm sure your dad thinks Pete's a real man, huh? The way he's showing the faggot how to treat his woman?"

"They're not happy with the situation, I'll give you that," she muttered.

I'd obviously hit a nerve, so I continued. "And maybe having my wife traipsing around town with her new man makes me feel just a teensy bit awkward when I run into one of your friends. You know—the only people I know around here? And maybe there's no hot girls around here that are willing to put out just because they feel sorry for me. I'm sure you would handle it completely differently if I started screwing Diana or Sara? You'd just take it in stride? You wouldn't have a little conversation with them?"

"That's different. They're my best friends. Of course, I'd confront them. You didn't even know Pete before this. That was the first time you ever talked to him."

"Fine, I get it. I'm a bad person for trying to save my marriage. You told me that I should just let you walk out of my life. Somehow, I don't remember that being part of my vows. I remember something about 'til death do us part.' Something about 'for better or for worse.' Or did I mess that up too? Was it just 'for better' or was that just your vow?"

"That's not fair! This hurts me too!"

"You have a unique way of showing it! I'm sad because my husband loves me, so let me fuck the guy that lives in the apartment downstairs! Look, I'll get out of your life. I'll get out of this town, and go back to Cheektowaga. Then you don't have to deal with me, and your life can go back to 'happily ever after' because you won't have to deal with me. Oh, by the way, you do still have to deal with Pete now."

Changing the subject, she quietly replied, "Going back to Cheektowaga would probably help you a lot. You'd be closer to Mike and Pat, you could see your family. They can help you get over this."

"What about you?" I asked.

"What do you mean?"

"It sounds like you are already over this?"

She broke down crying as she replied, "You'll never understand." With that the phone went dead.

Chapter 6:
Back to Cheektowaga

Suggested Listening:
"Schism" – Tool
"Come Talk to Me" – Peter Gabriel
"Family Man" – Mike Oldfield

Beware, brothers, lest perhaps there might be in any one of you an evil heart of unbelief, in falling away from the living God; but exhort one another day by day, so long as it is called "today", lest any one of you be hardened by the deceitfulness of sin.
Hebrews 3: 12-13 (WEB)

There was one significant advantage to moving back to Cheektowaga. I was now less than two miles from the airport. And I was at the airport almost every week.

That summer, I had moved into a two-bedroom apartment over on Claudette Court, literally three streets south of Chapel. It was a series of corporate apartments owned by a local lawyer. Most of the people in the neighborhood were in similar circumstances, either divorced or single. The apartment was much smaller and a little bit cheaper.

But best of all, I could get my head on straight because I wasn't seeing Jenny everywhere.

Of course, "getting my head on straight" meant drinking more. Much more.

I was now starting to think about getting my life started again. Hitting the dating scene. Letting the ladies know that I was back on the market. Look out, ladies, here comes the fat drunk of your dreams!

There was a single mom that lived across the street. She was good friends with my next-door neighbors, who had invited me over for a cookout when I first moved in. They spent a lot of time that summer out on their front steps drinking, so a lot of the neighbors came by as well.

Camille was at one of Bob and Gary's front porch sessions one night when I stopped by. She was dressed in short shorts, sandals, and an REO Speedwagon t-shirt. She had two kids, aged 6 and 10, was divorced, and trying to get her life together.

Bob and Gary were nice enough to keep feeding me beers. Like I always do, as I became more intoxicated, I became more talkative. It wasn't long before my story started coming out. Camille listened. That was what I needed. She barely commented, simply nodding her head as I described the letter, Orlando, and the landlord's son.

As she was getting ready to leave, she said, "You don't want to hear this, honey, but I was Jenny. Why do you think I'm here? I knew it all. My ex? Today, he is a vice president at some big ass company here in town, and he and his new wife live in a mansion in Clarence. We get along better than ever! You forget about her, honey. Restart your life."

Luckily, the next day was Saturday, because the hangover I had was legendary.

Camille was outside mowing her lawn with her two kids running around. I decided that I was still drunk enough to go over and see what happened.

Today she was wearing short shorts and a Styx t-shirt, along with sneakers. The day was pretty hot, so she was sweating a little. Her glistening skin gave me some ideas that I hadn't even considered until I walked over there.

"Hey, I just wanted to say thank you for listening to me cry in my beer last night. I don't usually unload on people that I just met. You just happened to be the unlucky soul to have to listen to it," I started.

She smiled. "I would have told you to shut up if I needed to. I could tell that you needed to get that out, and I also could see that you were drunk enough to do it, too."

With that, a bear of a man came walking out of her building. "Oh, Frank, let me introduce you to Matt. He just moved in next to Bob and Gary. Matt, this is my boyfriend, Frank."

Oh well, there went that idea.

It was still nice to have some new people to be around. I got together with Bob, Gary, Camille, and some other neighbors once a week or so. Mike would stop by every now and again, and he got to meet everyone.

"Damn, Camille is hot," was his initial assessment.

One Saturday afternoon after mowing the lawn, I was having a cold one with them when Jenny parked in front of my building. I walked over to the apartment as she walked up my driveway. My new friends stopped talking to watch the proceedings.

"Hey. I'm sorry I just stopped by, but I needed to get you to sign something," she smiled at me, looking at the neighbors. "Plus, I wanted to see where you were living and how you were doing. Can we go in?"

So we went up to my apartment. I showed her around the little place for the thirty seconds or so that it took, and sat at the kitchen table. "What do you need me to sign?" I asked somewhat testily.

"It is a document that says that you will not have an attorney representing you at the hearing. That's still the case, right?" she asked as she handed me a one-page document.

"You know I have no money to hire a lawyer. I'm giving you everything. I'm keeping the debt. You walk away with your new life, and I pay for it. That's the deal, right?"

"If you really feel that way, you should get a lawyer," she replied. "I'm not trying to screw you. But that is what you agreed to."

"I wish you would screw me, then maybe neither of us would need a lawyer. The bed is only a few steps away," I joked. She did not like that approach. "Look, I don't want to spend money I don't have on a divorce I don't want. If you go through with this, it's on your dime. I'll take my chances."

"Look, I came out here to see how you're doing," she spat. "Obviously, not too well by the looks of all of those empties. My God, how many is that? Are you okay?" She looked concerned.

"Never better," I grunted as I signed the paper. "Anything else?" I got up and started leading her to the door.

She grabbed my hand. "Listen, Matt, I know you don't believe this, but this is for your own good. You don't know..." With that I kissed her, forcing my tongue in her mouth. She immediately melted in my arms, and I felt her tongue joining mine. She started rubbing my crotch as I put my hand up her shirt.

"Where did you say your room is?" she purred as she started to walk back into the apartment.

"Sorry, I wouldn't want you cheating on Pete," I grumbled as I started back downstairs.

She followed angrily. "You see? This is why it would never work out," she said loudly as she followed me down the stairs. "I never know how to take you. One minute you are this great guy that I'm in love with, then you flick a switch to an asshole who is out to hurt me."

"And yet a minute ago, I could have taken advantage of you. But I know that would only throw you off your mission to convince yourself that you feel nothing for me. It certainly felt like you were feeling quite a bit just then." By this time, we had stepped outside, still speaking loudly.

Jenny noticed the neighbors staring at us. Camille nervously called out, "Everything all right, honey?" as she walked toward us.

"It looks like you replaced me anyway," Jenny noted while looking Camille up and down. Camille was once again wearing short shorts and a cut off tank top.

At the same time that I said, "She's just a neighbor," Camille started walking over to the driveway saying, "There wasn't much to replace, bitch." I got in front of Jenny, looking at her.

"Camille is a neighbor who has a boyfriend and two kids. She is a friend."

From over my shoulder I heard Camille call, "Who doesn't want to see him hurt. So why don't you get going? You see he's in good hands around here."

Wordlessly, Jenny walked to her car. I followed her. She started the engine, looked up at me and with tears in her eyes said, "I'm sorry. I don't know what I'm doing. I thought that maybe us seeing each other would be good for you. I see it wasn't. I'll stay away."

With that she drove off.

"I'm sorry. I was out of line," Camille apologized. "We knew from seeing you walk to your building with her that you didn't want to deal with her. That you didn't know what to do. Gary suggested that I go up to your apartment acting like she was busting in on my man."

Gary laughed, "That would have given her something to think about, you gotta admit!"

Bob shook his head, "She's not hard to look at."

"Who?" Gary asked. "Camille or Matt's wife?"

"Both," was Bob's answer.

"Thank you, all of you," I smiled. "I don't usually have people standing up for me. This has been very tough."

Camille smiled. "It sounds like you were getting somewhere with her before you came out. You should've just fucked her for your own piece of mind. You'd have felt better."

"Or let one of us do it for you," Bob joined in. "I would have volunteered!"

"You would have done that?" Camille asked incredulously. "I pictured you having taste!"

§§§

Not long after this encounter was the annual St. Barnabas lawn fete. St. Barnabas was the next Catholic parish over from Our Lady Help of Christians on the corner of Dick Road and George Urban Boulevard. Every year since my parents moved to Cheektowaga, the St. Barnabas lawn fete was a significant summertime event. As a kid, it meant rides and sugar waffles. As a teenager, it meant a place to hang out with friends. Now, I was looking forward to the beer tent and the mass of female humanity that always showed up.

I went over by myself on Saturday night after mass at Chapel. By the time I got there at 8:30, the lights were coming on. People were packed in, elbow to elbow at the gambling booths and the food concessions. I bought a sugar waffle (always my favorite) and strolled around the grounds, just looking at some of the sights. The teenage girls did not look like that when I was a teenager. One of the first times I noticed myself getting old. And creepy. I moved on.

Eventually, I made my way to the beer tent. This was the most crowded area of the lawn fete. I was walking to one of the few empty spots at the bar when I heard from my left, "Yo, Matt."

At a table against the side of the tent were Bob and Gary. I had not seen them when I walked in because of the crowd. I motioned that I would join them after I grabbed a beer. While I was waiting to be served, Camille walked up to me with her boyfriend. "Hey, neighbor. What ya drinking? You remember Frank, right?"

Frank shifted his beer to his left hand, and stuck out his right for me to shake. As my hand was enveloped by his bear paw of a hand, he said, "Hey man, good to see ya again."

"Yeah, same," I lied, turning back to the bar to try to get served.

Out of the blue, Camille inquired, "Did I ever introduce you to my sister?"

My ears perked up. "No. I didn't know you had a sister."

"She lives on Claudette, too. Four buildings down from mine. She's here tonight. Do you want to meet her?"

"Now, babe, I told you I didn't think this was a good idea…" Frank started.

"Shut up, Frank," I wanted to say, but didn't because he could have ended it all right there.

"Shut up, Frank," Camille scolded. "Matt would probably like to get to know some more people in the neighborhood. Right, Matt?"

"I think she means you look like you need to get laid," Frank offered.

That earned him a slap across the back of the head. "C'mon, honey. Let's see where Chloe has wandered off to." Looking back at me, she confessed, "My parents liked alliteration. My brother's name is Cody."

Sitting next to Gary when we got to the table with our beers was a beautiful woman with long, blonde hair. Dressed in a black tank top, she sat laughing with the others. Camille sat down next to her and whispered something. The blonde stopped laughing and looked at me.

"Matt Christopher, this is my sister Chloe," Camille announced. "Chloe, this is Matt. He lives in the upstairs apartment next to Gary and Bob."

"Nice to meet you," I acknowledged as I sat down next to Bob. Damn, I only brought one beer. I was going to need a lot more than this.

While I was glad to have the company, and even more happy to be staring at a scantily-clad blonde beauty, I really was hoping to have an anonymous evening getting tanked alone in public. I was within walking distance of the apartment, so I could get as drunk as I pleased. Now I had to adhere to social graces like talking and, worse, listening.

"So what do you do?" broke my internal dialogue. The question came from Chloe, who was hiding a smile behind the beer that she was pretending to take a drink of.

"Um, banking. Nothing exciting." I took a real drink of the beer that I was holding.

"What do you mean nothing exciting?" Chloe encouraged. "Dealing with all that money? I've probably never seen that much money in my life."

"What do you do?" I stammered. I wasn't drunk enough yet. My true personality was still showing, and that was not good. I damn near drained my cup, hoping for an excuse to escape.

"I'm a stay-at-home mom. I have two kids who are the center of my world." Chloe started to reach into her purse to look for something, but Camille discreetly elbowed her. "Oh, you probably don't want to hear about them."

I really didn't want to hear about anything. What was going on here? How could I get away without hurting anybody's feelings?

"I'm running a little dry," I noted, even though I had only been there for a few minutes. "I'm going for a refill. Anybody need anything?"

"You buying?" asked Gary.

"I'll take one," requested Chloe. Camille again elbowed her.

I started to get up. "On second thought, I'll come with you," Chloe offered.

"Good luck," I heard Camille whisper. Or at least, I thought I heard.

Now I was really lost. Why in the world would she want to come get a beer with me? I was going to bring her one anyway.

"Camille tells me that you're divorced. I am too. A little over a year."

"Technically, I'm not divorced yet," I confessed. "Just separated."

"Oh, sorry." Chloe looked embarrassed. "Camille thought it was over." She had reached the counter. I ordered two beers and was waiting for my change. Chloe looked over toward Camille and shrugged as she took a sip and waited for me to finish the transaction.

I got my change and took a sip. As we started to walk back toward the table, I realized that I was being rude. This woman was trying to be nice to me, and I was giving her the cold shoulder.

I stopped a few steps away from our table. "I'm sorry," I told Chloe. "I'm just not comfortable being on my own yet." A table had cleared out next to where we were standing. "Would you like to join me?"

Chloe looked relieved. "I would really like that," she smiled.

Over the course of the next hour or so (and a few more refills), I got to know Chloe a little bit better. She had been married for six years ("Six years? There is no way you are old enough to have been married that long!") before her husband, a truck driver, found a girl on one of his trips. She had just had their second child, and all the responsibility caught up to him.

"Plus, he wasn't getting it as much anymore," she confided. Blushing, she hurriedly said, "Sorry, I think I may have had one too many. Excuse me."

With that, she got up to find the restrooms. While she was gone, I got two more beers. I was enjoying myself, and she was not hard to look at. Were my wedding vows still in effect? Not that it was a possibility anyway, but what would the harm be? Did I really have any chance at getting back with Jenny? Chloe reminded me a little bit of Jenny. I didn't know if that was a good thing or not.

I watched Chloe walking back to our table. She was wearing a pair of jean shorts and sandals. Her long hair was pushed to one side of her face, and I noticed that she was wearing hoop earrings. Her deep brown eyes were highlighted by just a touch of mascara, which somehow highlighted her hair. Knowing that I was staring at her, a slight smile crossed her lips as she rejoined me.

"Another one? You trying to get me drunk?"

"No, I just enjoy your company, and I don't want the night to end just yet." Classy.

"So what about you? Why would any sane woman give up on you?"

"Because I'm not all that big of a prize. I mean, maybe I'm TOO big of a prize," I teased, stroking an all-too-prominent beer gut. I took a drink with my eyes gazing down. "Because I'm a drunk. A loser. Because I'm never around. And when I am, I don't listen or notice things that I should."

"Like when a divorcee is making the moves on you? My mom has the kids tonight, and you succeeded in getting me drunk. Camille has been saying that it's time that I got on with my life, and tonight, I see what she means. There ARE some good men out there."

I was shocked. By this time, the beer tent had thinned out dramatically. Bob and Gary and crew had left fifteen minutes or so before, discreetly leaving Chloe and me alone.

Chloe got up and came around to my side of the table. She sat next to me, put her hand on my cheek and quietly whispered, "What do you say?" She kissed me, gently at first, but soon her tongue was in my mouth.

She pulled away and looked at me hungrily. "Want to walk me home?"

My mind raced as we started back to Claudette. Of course, I wanted her in the worst way. She was feeding the fire raging in me by suggesting things that I oh, so wanted to do to her. There was nothing stopping me from a night of whatever delicacies that I wanted.

"What happens after tonight?" I asked as we started up her driveway.

"What do you mean?"

"Is this because you are drunk or because you are interested in me?" I stopped (normally it is the woman saying this stuff, but leave it to me to break the mood). "I mean, long term. At least past tonight."

"Why does it matter? I want you tonight."

"It matters because I can't get hurt again. I don't want to wake up in the morning and find out that this was just a fun night out. I want this to mean something if it is going to happen."

"You are kidding, right?" she sighed. "Wow. I never thought I would be turned down like that. I was afraid that you might think that I wasn't attractive or interesting. But no, I get all stupid over a guy who can't let go of the past. You do know that SHE had no reservations about the future when she got laid by her lover boy, right?"

"You are beautiful, Chloe. Hot, actually. I hate myself already for saying anything. I—I just can't."

"My God, I don't believe this! Fine, have it your way. Go home and jerk off and then feel bad for yourself some more. What a pathetic way to live!"

She stormed down the driveway. After that night, Camille never hung out with me again. Neither did Gary or Bob.

Chapter 7:
Traveling and Live Music

―――――――

Suggested Listening:
"On the Road Again" – Me First and the Gimme Gimmes
"Highway Song" - Blackfoot

―――――――

There is one who is alone, and he has neither son nor brother. There is no end to all of his labor, neither are his eyes satisfied with wealth. "For whom then, do I labor and deprive my soul of enjoyment?" This also is vanity. Yes, it is a miserable business.
Ecclesiastes 4:8 (WEB)

Summer gave way to fall.

Not that it really mattered. Most weeks saw me getting up at four in the morning on Monday to catch a plane somewhere, work until six or seven at night, drink myself to sleep in a hotel room, and get back to my apartment at 11 on Friday night after a three-hour flight delay. Saturday was spent doing laundry and any other chores I could fit in until I could escape to a club with Mike or Pat, or to Wegmans for my very own twelve pack.

Most Sundays, I would crawl out of bed to go to church at Chapel. I would sit in the back—half hoping no one would see me in the state I was in, half hoping that I would see one of the old crew. On the very rare occasion, I would see Marino at a club, but Dempsey and Werner had moved out of Buffalo to start their careers.

If the weather was nice, I would go over to my parents to mow their yard for them, then bring their mower over to my apartment to do my own yard. My lease made it clear that the tenant was responsible for yard care. There was a divorced woman that lived downstairs, and I'm sure that she had a lease identical to mine, but she told me at our first and only meeting that, because I was a man, yard work was my job. One of the first weeks I lived there, I had a two-week trip out to LA. When I came home, the lawn had not been mowed, and there was a notice on my door that if the lawn were not cut by Monday, I would be charged extra rent for the landlord to hire someone. From that point on, I just took care of it.

When I wasn't out of town, I had a good relationship with the folks in my office. But there were few women in my office that were potential dates for me. Our receptionist was stunningly beautiful, and a Buffalo Jills cheerleader on top of it. She loved heavy metal, and occasionally showed up at some of the same clubs where Mike and I hung out. But she was also married with two kids.

A woman across the hall always caught my eye. She always wore short skirts and five-inch heels, and her blouses always showed a good amount of cleavage. I knew her name was Mary, but she was in a completely different department, so I never had an opportunity to work with her. But my desk was near the copier and, as some sort of administrative assistant, she made a lot of copies. I would have been more productive, and maybe promoted, if I hadn't spent so much time staring at her when she made copies.

None of my coworkers were single women. In fact, there was only one married woman in my department. So whenever I went out of town, I was usually either alone or with men.

On the trip to LA, I went with the only woman in our office, Michelle. On the plane ride there, I was nursing a nasty head cold. By the time we landed, my head was so congested that I could not hear. The rental car reservation was in my name, so I walked up to the counter, pulling out my credit card and my license, while Michelle waited nearby.

Not hearing a word of what the counter person was saying to me, I proceeded through the transaction by memory. I had done this so many times, I knew what the questions were, in what order they were asked, and the best way to answer them to get out of there as quickly as possible. I was doing well until one unheard question brought Michelle up to the counter in a bit of an agitated state. The transaction continued, and eventually, I walked away with the keys to our rental car.

On the drive to the client, my ears popped, and I could hear again. I asked Michelle what got her so angry at the rental car counter. Evidently, I answered the question "Will your wife be driving the car?" with a yes. Michelle responded that his BUSINESS ASSOCIATE would also be driving the car. Wow, touchy!

None of this helped me get over Jenny.

She had pretty much stopped calling me, and she never came back to my apartment. If she did call, it was some sort of an update about the divorce proceedings, or to warn me that a document was coming, and what I supposed to do with it. The divorce was targeted for some time around the New Year.

So it was sometime in November that I boarded a plane for Charlotte with my coworker Tim. Upon getting to Charlotte, we drove two hours to Asheville and got to work. It was immediately obvious that this job was going to be a bear. The few records that the company gave us did not agree to anything, and the people were antagonistic. The company, we found out, was in financial trouble, and the bank wanted more work performed than usual. When we checked in with the loan officer and told him what was going on, he increased our workload even though it was unlikely that we could comply. "Just do your jobs," was what we were told.

The week progressed slowly. The company fought us every step of the way, and the loan officer kept adding work for us to do. Then, each night at five o'clock sharp, Tim packed up his things so that he could get to dinner. Unfortunately, he always went off to dinner by himself because he had the rental car. I was left to walk across the street to the mall, where I would eat something at the food court, and pick up a twelve pack from a convenience store nearby. In the morning, I would meet him for breakfast hungover, ready to bang my head against the wall that this job presented.

On Thursday night, Tim told me that he had found an excellent club not far from the hotel, and that we should eat dinner there that night. I was fine with that. I needed something to do. For whatever reason, after not hearing from her for weeks, I had received a number of phone calls that week from Jenny, and talking to her each night about the divorce was taking away the joy of the buzz that I was medicating myself with.

Tim drove us about three miles to this huge country and western club. Although there was a dining room, Tim went into the club portion, bellied up to the bar and ordered a beer. The bartender was a very good looking blonde woman with a well-practiced smile. "What'll you have, baby-doll?" she drawled in my direction.

"Do you have a menu?" I implored, hoping that Tim would get the hint.

"We don't serve food out here, darlin'. If you're hungry, go on in to the dining room over there."

"He'll have a Labatt Blue," Tim ordered for me. "C'mon, loosen up Matt. You've been tense all week. I thought you should get drunk WITH someone tonight rather than drinking by yourself."

"I just got some shit going on at home, is all," I started to confess. "Sorry if I haven't been a party all week."

"Not a problem, Matt," Tim brushed me off. Looking past me, he abruptly announced, "I'll be back in a minute."

Tim rushed off through the gathering crowd toward the entrance. My beer was delivered by a guy in a cowboy hat. "Are you staying for the show? If so, the admission is $7. I can add it to your tab."

I looked around for Tim. I wonder if he knew about this. His beer was sitting there nearly full.

"Is my colleague here staying?" I asked the bartender.

"Don't look like it," he grumbled. "I don't see no ticket."

"Then I guess I'll go to the dining room," I decided, handing him a fiver for the beer. "Let him know where I went when he comes back."

I walked slowly to the dining room, looking for Tim among the crowd. The wait for a table was 20 minutes so I waited at the bar in the dining room. Tim still hadn't arrived when the table was ready.

Still alone when the waitress came to take my order, I started to wonder what was going on. I was stuck without a car in a country and western bar in a small town in North Carolina.

Now I like all music, but C&W is definitely near the bottom. My brother is a big fan of older country acts like Merle Haggard and Waylon Jennings. That was not what was playing this night. I was listening to, I guess, Garth Brooks and Randy Travis? Alabama?

Although the music was not exactly to my liking, and my colleague had mysteriously disappeared, I did enjoy my steak. After washing it down with three beers, the waitress was looking for me to free up the table for some new people, and probably more tips. I was just wondering how the hell I was going to get back to my hotel room without a ride.

After paying my bill, I wandered back to the club, and paid my $7 in the hopes that Tim had returned. By now, it was after 9 and the club was packed. An opening band was finishing their set to a largely indifferent crowd. The crowd was varied, mostly people in their late-20s and early-30s, some wearing cowboy hats, but most dressed like me in jeans and a nice shirt.

After searching for Tim among the crowd in vain, I went back to the bar where Tim had ditched me. I figured I might as well get hammered there. I had already blown my $34 per diem, so what was another few beers at $4.25 apiece?

After a half hour break, the main band of the night came on. I found myself enjoying them, even though I did not recognize a single song. They had an excellent fiddle player who had a number of solos, and the guitarist could play slightly heavier than I would have expected in a country song. By the time they took their first break, it was nearly 11.

By now, I had kind of figured out that Tim had abandoned me. This being in the days before cell phones, there was no way of contacting him. My only chance was to try his hotel room. I had tried this from a pay phone at the bar earlier in the night, but there was no answer. Now I figured that I would try again, and if he didn't pick up, I would call a cab.

"Hello," the voice on the other end of the line responded groggily.

"Tim, where the fuck are you?" I pretty much screamed at him. This was both out of frustration and drunkenness, but also because it was the only way to be heard above the throng.

"Oh, hey. I was just on my way to get you, Matt. Stay there!" The phone hung up.

Having had enough of country music for one night, I wandered out of the club. Standing there in a long-sleeved dress shirt, the cool North Carolina night felt nice. The night air also made me realize that I had upward of six beers, and my head was none too happy about it.

As I started to realize that my steak was in danger of ending up in the parking lot, I started to go back into the club before being stopped by a very large man at the door.

"Sorry, but once you leave you can't return. House rules," he pointed at a sign next to the door.

"I just need to use the facilities," I pleaded.

"House rules. Go find a gas station. There's one a block south of here."

I walked back out to the parking lot, now being watched by the beast at the door. Tim was on his way, and I needed a john. If I lost my dinner in the parking lot before Tim got there, I would probably get an unfriendly visit from Bruno the Bouncer at the door. Maybe even local law enforcement looking for a little excitement. A Yank in the drunk tank might help pass the time in the absence of any real crime. If I waited until Tim got there, our rental car would need special attention before we got to the airport tomorrow. And I didn't think that waiting until I got back to the hotel was an option.

Luckily (in a warped sort of way), Tim made the decision easy for me by not showing up. After a few minutes, I wandered over to the parking lot of a nearby office building, walked around the back, and deposited the remnants of a steak dinner and way too many Labatts in the grassy knoll behind an accounting office.

Feeling a little better after a bit, I strolled back toward the club. It had now been at least a half hour since I called Tim, and the hotel was only three miles away. He should have already shown up while I was behind the office building. If I missed him, I would have to find a pay phone and call again. I might have to do that anyway to get a taxi if he hadn't shown up yet.

As I was making my way between the parking lots, I saw a car that looked like our rental car (or at least what I remembered of our rental car) pulling into the lot of the club. Walking toward it, I saw Tim getting out of the car with the blond bartender from earlier in the evening. He was wearing jeans and a t-shirt. The last time I saw him, he was in a suit.

"Matt, you remember Jill, don't you?" Tim inquired casually.

"Hey, sugar," Jill smiled in my direction. "Thanks for a great night, Bob," Jill waved in Tim's direction. "Don't forget to call me, okay?"

"Bob?" The look on my face told Tim what I was thinking.

"I told her I was Robert Smith, a musician from Pittsburgh that was recording tomorrow with his band, the Cure. Hey, she bought it!" he exclaimed. When he saw how pissed I was, he faltered "I tried to see if she had any friends for you, but she's not from around here either."

"You should have told me you were leaving. I would have gone with you back to the hotel, and you could've done whatever you wanted. Or left me the car and went to the hotel in her car."

"She doesn't have a car, and we were into it pretty heavy in the parking lot. I don't think she would've been okay with me running in to get you."

"So you left me here for like six hours while you got a little action?"

"We kind of fell asleep," he admitted. "Sorry. Hey, thanks for waking us up, though. She needed to be home by midnight, or her dad would have flipped!"

"It's almost one," I pointed out.

"Oh well, it's not like I'm gonna see her again. When she asked for my phone number, I gave her the phone number for the Pittsburgh Pirates box office!" It turned out that this was his standard M.O. when meeting young ladies during his travels.

Now in the car and on our way back to the hotel, I realized that I was probably in better shape to drive than he was. His speed alternated between 70 and 20 on the road back to the hotel, but it was the veering between lanes that frightened me most.

"What were you drinking?" I asked, gripping the door handle as he took a turn at about 50 mph.

"We split a bottle of Jack." With that, he reached into the back seat to produce an empty bottle as evidence. Not a small bottle either. "Oh, and she had some weed."

After finally getting back to my room, and collapsing on the bed at 1:15, I awoke to the wake-up call at 6:30 still in my jeans from the night (morning?) before. A shower and a cup of coffee in my room made me feel human again. That, and the four aspirin.

Remarkably, Tim was already at breakfast in the lobby restaurant, packed and ready to go. Some toast was all I able to stomach, while Tim ordered eggs, bacon, and hash browns.

A long Friday morning at the company finally gave way to quitting time, and we made the two hour drive back to Charlotte for our plane. Luckily, the delay was only one hour this time, and we took off at 7:15.

While we were away, Buffalo had received one of the earliest snowfalls on record. That Wednesday night, about 14 inches of snow had fallen, followed by another four inches on Thursday. When our plane landed at 8:30, my first order of business was brushing off my car in the airport lot. Then I had to rock it back and forth to get through the drift that was placed there as the plows went through the rows. I drove first to Wegmans for a twelve pack of something to take the edge off.

This being the first snowstorm at the new apartment, I assumed that I would also need to shovel the driveway to pull my car in. After all, I was the man and I had to mow the lawn. Imagine my surprise when I went to pull in the driveway and found it already shoveled! Right down to the concrete! On her side!

She was nice enough to shovel her half of the two car driveway. She did not shovel my side of it, however. Actually, instead of shoveling my side, she used my side to throw the snow! Rather than throwing it on the lawn to the left, she threw it to the right, onto my side of the driveway! Now, instead of having to shovel a foot of snow, I had to shovel two feet of snow!

I finally walked into my apartment after 11 with my suitcase and my beer. The apartment was as cold as the outside, and I soon found out why. Every window in my apartment was wide open! Little piles of snow sat on my kitchen table and my rug, along with a letter from the landlord dated the previous Monday morning. The letter informed me that they were going to paint the windows that day, and would be leaving the windows open to help get rid of the paint smell by the time I came home from work. Sorry for any inconvenience this might cause.

Luckily, my furnace was working overtime all week to try to make up for the open windows!

But the week was over, at least.

Chapter 8:

Diana

Suggested Listening:
"Hard Luck Woman" – Garth Brooks
"Pictures of You" – The Cure

Let no man say when he is tempted, "I am tempted by God," for God can't be tempted by evil, and he himself tempts no one. But each one is tempted when he is drawn away by his own lust and enticed.
James 1: 13-14 (WEB)

Some people (me) don't learn their lessons.

Back when Jenny and I were still together, the New Year brought only thoughts of celebration. The coming year would be our first as a married couple, and deserved special recognition. Plus, we had never thrown a true party before, one with alcohol and food and music and noise. We invited everyone we could think of to our little Ashton Street apartment, and sure enough, most of them showed up shortly after eight o'clock on December 31.

One of those to show up was our upstairs neighbor, Diana. Jenny had gotten to know her in the two months that we had lived there, and they developed a strong friendship. Diana had stopped down a few times to play board games with us, and the two women had gone Christmas shopping together. Diana and Jenny had exchanged gifts with each other.

Diana was a beautiful single mother with a five-year old daughter, who was the result of a long-term romance from high school. Diana and her boyfriend were going to get married as soon as he finished college for his finance degree. After graduation, they decided that it would be better if they lived together until he got a job, at which point they would tie the knot.

But, unexpectedly, Diana ended up pregnant. Her family, a tight-knit group of Irish Catholics (as were many of the families in this area), made sure that Diana had no intention of getting an abortion. But Diana's boyfriend had no such upbringing and demanded that the pregnancy be terminated. Diana made the decision that she loved her baby more than her boyfriend and moved back home for the support that she would need to bring up a baby alone.

Diana never spoke to the guy again. Supposedly, he moved to New York City where he worked for a venture capital group. Who knows, I may have worked with him at some point in my career with the bank.

Once her daughter got to be a toddler, Diana decided that she needed some privacy to her life and moved to an apartment down the street. The same apartment that, a few years later, Jenny and I made our first home.

That New Year's Eve, Diana came downstairs before the party began to help Jenny and me get ready. Once all the accoutrements were in place and the guests started arriving, Diana excused herself to go and get ready.

By the time she returned, the party was in full swing. I was in the living room with Rob Becker and Mike Wolf, listening to music and talking. Jenny was off somewhere being the hostess.

Around ten, I heard some loud voices out in the kitchen, but I did not pay any attention to them. Mike was concerned (plus he needed another beer), so he wandered out there to see what was going on. The voices escalated.

"Get out of my face, asshole!" I heard Vince shout.

"Leave the lady alone," Mike responded. "In fact, why don't you get the fuck out of here?"

"I'm not leaving. I'm just trying to have a conversation with Diana here, and my fucking sister tries to get me away from her."

"You weren't 'having a conversation,'" Jenny replied. "You were groping her. No means no, jackass, and I heard her say it at least twice."

I had come out to the kitchen by this point. Vince was in Jenny's face and standing in the doorway nearest to the front door, being held there by someone I did not know. A few other people were standing by and holding Mike in the opposite doorway. Mike looked ready to kill Vince if he had the chance.

Diana was at the kitchen table crying. No one was near her as the excitement played out. I walked over to her to see if everything was alright, taking a seat to her left.

"Just leave," Jenny suggested to Vince.

"Fine, I don't need any of you assholes," he shouted as he loudly slammed the door.

Unfortunately, we had not taken the bottle of beer from him before he left. Seconds later, we heard the bottle shatter outside. Luckily, he was too drunk to hit the front window when he threw the bottle. Instead, it just hit the front of the house to the left of the window and shattered.

Mike went back into the living room with Rob and a few other guests.

"Sorry, everyone," Jenny apologized to everyone, feeling that somehow this was her fault. She pulled me aside.

"What happened?" I asked her.

"Vince came here drunk. He wasn't even invited. He saw Diana out there in the kitchen and asked her to fuck him. When she said no, he started grabbing her and trying to kiss her. Luckily, Jim saw what was happening and started to intercede, but Vince pushed him away and started grabbing her again. That's when I came in here. Between Jim and me, we got him off of her. When Mike got involved, they started going at it. We had to separate them."

Jenny gulped down the half-glass of wine that was in her shaking hand. "I'm going to go clean up the glass on the front porch. I don't want anybody getting hurt. Could you go and see if Diana is okay?"

I went back in and sat down next to Diana again, who had regained her composure by this time. "Can I get you anything?" I offered.

She smiled weakly. "No. I'm going to go upstairs and straighten up." Her mascara had run from her crying, and her hair was disheveled. "I'll be back down in a few minutes. I don't want to miss the ball drop."

When she came back down a little while later, I noticed her. I was used to seeing her in jeans or sweat pants and loose-fitting blouses whenever she visited. The woman standing at our apartment door was someone different.

Diana was wearing a short blue dress. The front of the dress was low cut and exposed some very impressive cleavage into which hung a gold cross. The blue strappy heels that she wore matched the dress wonderfully. She had reapplied her mascara, and pulled her long hair back into a ponytail, which revealed a pair of dangling gold earrings. "How do I look?" she asked self-consciously.

It was that image that was burned into my mind whenever I saw her from that point on. Once Jenny and I moved from that first apartment, I rarely saw Diana anymore, although she and Jenny remained best friends.

§§§

Mike's band Cristal Myst had been together for two or three months around the time of my disastrous Charlotte trip with Tim. Featuring a

Billy Sheehan disciple on bass, Mike was finally in a band that was on the verge of becoming professional. With the Becker's youngest sister Marie as the lead singer, the band also featured a keyboard player and a drummer, and they played cover songs from Heart, Pat Benatar, Scandal, and Led Zeppelin in a style that emphasized the skills of Mike and his new bassist. Using the stage name Randi, Marie quickly became the centerpiece of the band for both her strong vocals and her warped sense of humor in her between song banter.

Cristal Myst had played a few dive bars the past two weeks and were scheduled to play a dive bar in Lackawanna the Friday I came back from Charlotte. I had told Mike that if I got back at a reasonable hour from the trip, I would try to make it.

Lackawanna is the first suburb south of Buffalo, stretching along the Lake Erie shore. It was the home of steel mills throughout much of the 1900s, with the city actually named after the Lackawanna Steel Company of Scranton, PA. An area of just over 6 square miles, residents voted in 1909 to secede from the town of West Seneca (which is actually to the east). Bethlehem Steel took over Lackawanna Steel in 1922, which expanded the plant into one of the largest in the country. At its peak, the plant employed over 20,000 people. Lackawanna thrived into the 70s, when the steel plant began massive layoffs until its closure in 1983.

The steel mill property sat on the water, and blocked any access to the waterfront throughout the 80s. Worse, the land was deemed a brownfield by the government, meaning that there was known or suspected pollution due to hazardous waste. It was also discovered that the plant had processed uranium shortly after World War II, and questions arose as to the subsequent clean-up of those activities. While recent years have brought redevelopment to the area, at the time, Lackawanna was an area of above average unemployment and was considered to be one of the rougher parts of the area. That meant a lot of bars, though.

One of Lackawanna's most famous residents was Father Nelson Baker, a Roman Catholic priest who was responsible for building a "city of charity" that included a hospital, an orphanage, elementary and high schools, an infant home, a home for unwed mothers, and a basilica. The Roman Catholic Church has been attempting to get Father Baker canonized for sainthood as a result of his charitable acts.

As a kid, I knew none of this. I only knew "Father Baker's" as the threat that the parents would use when you were misbehaving. My parents would tell me that other parents frequently dropped their unruly children at the orphanage. So whenever we heard Mom or Dad say, "let's go see the boys at Father Baker's," we knew to straighten up. The threat always worked.

Our Lady of Victory Basilica was built in 1926 by Father Baker and is a Catholic parish and a National Shrine. The basilica was built on the site of the old Saint Patrick's parish church, which had been destroyed by a fire in 1916. The basilica cost $3.2 million ($44 million in today's dollars), but, because of Father Baker's influence in the community, was completed without incurring any debt. Constructed of marble, the structure features two spires, a dome 80 feet in diameter and 165 feet high, and seating for 1,200. At the time of the construction, the dome was the second largest in the world, smaller only than the dome of the US Capitol building.

In 1999, six men who had been raised by Father Baker removed his remains from the nearby Holy Cross Cemetery. The remains were re-interred in the basilica in a ceremony attended by over 6,000 people.

Another prominent citizen of Lackawanna was Ron Jaworski, an NFL quarterback in the 1970s and 1980s. The Lackawanna High School football stadium was named after him. But because he played for the Philadelphia Eagles and Miami Dolphins (two of my least favorite teams), we will not say anything else about him.

Unfortunately, by the time my flight from Charlotte got in and I got back to my apartment (and shoveled myself out), it was well past eleven. Rather than get ready for a night on the town after my week from Hell, I stayed home with my twelve pack.

Mike was on the other end of the phone when it rang the next afternoon. "Dude, I don't know how to tell you this, but Jenny was at our show last night."

"So? She's allowed a social life, I guess. Was she with lover boy?" I asked sarcastically.

"No, that's why I wanted to tell you myself. He wasn't there, but Pat was."

"Okaaay," I said, trying to figure out where this was going.

"Dude, he went home with her!" After a pause, he continued, "Matt, Pat fucked your wife!"

Somehow, this struck me as funny. I didn't laugh, but I pictured the scene. Pat had done a lot of things in his life, but this one seemed like a reach, even for him.

"I hope he got a blowjob too!" was all I could think to say.

"You're not pissed?" Mike asked, a little too incredulously. With that, I heard two guys laughing hysterically on the other end of the phone.

"What's going on?" I demanded.

In the background I heard Pat yell, "We thought that would piss you off, you dick."

It turned out that Jenny had heard about Mike and his new band, Cristal Myst. When she found out that they were playing so close to her apartment, she decided to go watch their show. There she ran into Pat, who was also there checking out his friend's new band. Pat and Jenny started talking and had a pleasant conversation. Jenny told Pat that she had broken up with Pete because "he wasn't a real man." She told Pat that she was only going to date "real men" from that point on. Mike joined them at the bar at the end of the set.

"I hate to say this," Mike confided, "but she looked HOT. I don't remember her looking that good when she was married to you—I mean, living with you. Sorry." Realizing that this was probably not what I wanted to hear, he continued his story.

After the show, Mike and Pat thought it would be funny to make up a story where Jenny chatted up Pat, who took her home and showed her what a "real man" was. Bastard that I was, though, I didn't play along.

So Jenny really broke up with Pete? I wondered if there was any hope of getting back together. Against my better judgement, I picked up the phone to Jenny.

Rather than document the embarrassment of that phone call, let's just say that the part about breaking up with Pete was just another part of the joke on me. Let's also just say that it ended with another "Give it up, Matt," and a dial tone when she hung up on me.

A few weeks later, Cristal Myst was playing at the same Lackawanna club. Being a Saturday, I was able to make it. While I wanted to see Mike play, I was also secretly hoping that Jenny would show up again. Although I had talked to her numerous times, I hadn't seen her in person since the fiasco at the apartment.

I showed up early to hang out with Mike and the rest of the band. They were expecting a decent crowd because their prior show was well received. By the time their first set ended, there were more than 100 people in the bar. Not a bad draw for a dive bar that was supposed to hold like 50. The band sounded excellent, and the crowd was really enjoying them.

During the break, I pushed my way up to the bar to grab another beer. From a seat at the end of the bar, I heard a familiar voice call my name. Sitting with three other women that I did not know was Diana.

She came running over to me. "Oh my God, Matt! How great to see you! Let me buy you a drink." She gave me a hug. She looked great in a pair of tight jeans and a satin blouse with a few too many buttons undone. I couldn't resist a quick peek at the tan beauties not quite offered for my viewing pleasure.

We chatted for a moment about how we were, and what we were up to. The drinks came: a Labatt for me, some sort of mixed drink for her.

She turned serious. "I feel so bad for you, Matt. I hate what Jenny has done to you. She told me about Orlando, and how badly you tried to get her back. It seemed so romantic."

"Answer me a question, Diana." My previous Labatt consumption had allowed me to speak more freely than I may have otherwise. "You're her best friend. What is going on with her? Honestly. Don't be afraid to hurt my feelings. What went wrong?"

"I wish I knew, Matt," she confided. "She lived with me for a while and I still don't know. I don't think she knows. She's been on her own for, what, six months? I've asked her that question a hundred times and got two hundred different answers. She's confused, honey," she said, earnestly looking me in the eyes. Taking my hand, she continued, "She's miserable, Matt. She wants you, but she doesn't want you. The whole thing with Pete was her way of acting out. When you didn't notice it, she tried to push it further. Then she went too far. Now, she's stuck with a guy that she doesn't really like, but she feels like she can't go back to you because she broke her vows.

"And now, it sounds like you've replaced her with your neighbor and…"

"What do you mean?" I laughed. "Oh my God, Diana. If you knew what I've been through." I went on to tell her the story about Chloe.

"You mean you passed up another woman because you were still married? Holy shit! I have never heard of a guy passing up a piece of ass when it is offered to him like that. And you did it because of her?"

"It was the right thing to do," I said proudly. Then, when I noticed the slight frown that crossed Diana's face, I followed with, "Wasn't it?"

"No, Matt. I don't think it would have made any difference. She's too far gone at this point. Plus, I really think that she wants you to be happy. If that means banging some broad at a lawn fete at this point, I think she would understand.

"Besides, she thinks that you are with that woman's sister anyway. What was her name? The way she stood up for you, Jenny thinks that would only happen if she wandered into someone else's territory."

"The funny thing is, Diana, Camille was never even a thought. When Jenny came over, I hadn't even met Chloe yet. That whole incident was a misunderstanding."

"I shouldn't say this, but you misunderstood something too, Matt. Do you know why Jenny stopped by that day?"

"Yeah, she needed some document signed."

"And you think that's all? Matt, she…"

Mike came by right then. "Who's this hot number you're hitting on, Matt?" By the smirk on his face I could tell Mike knew full well who she was.

"You remember Diana, don't you?"

"Of course I do. She still owes me a little something for saving her at your party," Mike flirted. "You can come backstage with me to pay up. It'd be more fun than hanging out with this loser."

"Not tonight, Wolf. I'm protecting her honor. And Lord knows she needs it from you!"

Some laughter and small talk ensued for five minutes before Mike went back to the band. Diana and I stood and watched the second set.

As it wound down, Diana said, "Well, I've got to be getting home. Tell Mike that I thought his band was excellent."

"What were you saying earlier about Jenny coming over that day? Before Mike interrupted?"

Diana looked flustered. "I shouldn't have said anything. Forget I mentioned it."

"Wait a minute, you can't bring something like that up and then leave me to wonder about it."

"I'm sorry I brought it up. Ask her about it, and maybe she will tell you. I promised her that I wouldn't. She's not going to be happy that I told you as much as I did." Looking around, she noticed, "It looks like my friends abandoned me earlier. I guess they thought that you were an old boyfriend or something."

"I wish." It came out as a flippant remark, meant to be self-deprecating and uplifting for the hearer. But it hit some sort of emotion in Diana.

"Really?" An awkward pause. "Have you ever thought of me romantically? That would be kind of weird, what with your wife being my best friend."

"Soon-to-be-ex-wife," I corrected.

"I mean it, Matt. Have you ever thought of me romantically?" she repeated.

Trying to take the Mike Wolf approach to women, I responded, "Romantically or sexually?"

Surprisingly, Diana didn't hesitate. "Both."

"I remember that blue dress you wore on New Year's Eve. The heels. The cross that hung between your breasts." I made it a point to stare down her blouse. "I thought, what a lucky guy that Jesus is."

She broke into laughter. "That's sacrilege!"

"That wasn't as sacrilegious as some of the other things that went through my mind that night." Another quick glance, meant to be noticed, followed. "Or tonight."

"Like what?" she whispered.

"Like this," I said as I brushed her hair back and gave her a gentle kiss on the lips.

"That's it? Not something like this?" she asked as she kissed me long and deep.

She immediately regretted it. "What am I doing?" she said as she started to gather her purse and look for her keys.

"Wait a minute," I implored. "Now I'm confused again."

"I can't do anything with you, Matt. You're married to my best friend!"

"A minute ago you were telling me that Jenny was never coming back to me. That I should bang some broad at a lawn fete. Now you're worried that, what, you might hurt her feelings? Fuck her feelings! She obviously didn't think of mine when she went out on her little rendezvous."

"I'm not some broad at a lawn fete! I'm her best friend and I still have to face her."

"Tell me something," I demanded. "If Jenny wasn't in the picture, would you want to come home with me now?"

She laughed, "I might not wait until we got home."

"Then why are you walking away?"

"Maybe for the same reason you walked away from the lawn-fete girl. It's not right." A tear formed at the corner of her eye. "I'm sorry, Matt. I really am." She rushed out the door.

That was the last time I ever saw Diana.

The phone call that I received the following day from Jenny was seething. The fact that I would try to make a move on her best friend was the last straw. She had been delaying setting a final court date because of her uncertainty. This incident sealed the deal. If I couldn't be faithful to her, then there was no hope left.

"I'm calling my attorney tomorrow to set a court date, you scumbag," she screamed as she hung up the phone.

Chapter 9:
Divorce Day

Suggested Listening:
"Can't Fight It" – Bob Mould
"I Tried" – Jeff Healey Band
"That Was Yesterday" – Foreigner

He answered, "Haven't you read that he who made them from the beginning made them male and female, and said, 'For this cause a man shall leave his father and mother, and shall join to his wife; and the two shall become one flesh?' So that they are no more two, but one flesh. What therefore God has joined together, don't let man tear apart."
Matthew 19: 4-6 (WEB)

I HAD NEVER BEEN in a court of law before. Or since.

It's a lot like what they show on TV. When you are the defendant, it is intimidating!

I didn't have to be there, of course. The same thing would have happened whether I showed up or not. But I felt that since my name was on the case (*Christopher vs. Christopher*), I should at least see what the hubbub was about.

I did not have an attorney. I was immediately called to the stand.

Sitting next to her lawyer was Jenny, in dress pants and a silk blouse. She had obviously been crying. It didn't matter what I wore. As the defendant, I could have shown up in ripped jeans and a t-shirt, and I still would have been just as guilty of whatever I was allegedly guilty of now. But I was in a suit and tie because I wore them every day for work. I had, of course, taken off for this spectacle. After all, everything that I had worked for up until this point in my life was on trial.

The judge first reminded me that I was entitled to counsel, and that counsel was encouraged. Once I acknowledged this, I was specifically asked if I waived my right to counsel, which I did. The judge then asked me three or four generic questions, such as if I was Matthew Christopher, and where I lived, and what I did, and was I married to the defendant on the dates listed in the complaint. Having confirmed all of this, the judge had no further questions, nor did Jenny's attorney. I was dismissed.

But rather than be allowed to watch the rest of the proceedings, I was asked to leave the courtroom.

Shortly thereafter, our marriage was found to be guilty of Irreconcilable Differences by the Family Court of the State of New York, who pronounced our marriage terminated. As the defendant, I guess I was the bad guy.

Unsure of what to do, I hung around outside the courthouse for a while. It was December in downtown Buffalo, and the wind off the lake suggested that winter was on its way. People came and went while I stood there wondering what had just happened.

At some point, Jenny walked out of the courthouse with her attorney. She saw me standing there immediately. She pointed me out to her attorney, who had obviously told her not to go near me. She sent him on his way, but not before he eyed me up and down like the lowlife that I was just judged to be in a court of law.

Jenny slowly walked up to me. "How are you holding up?"

"Better than you, by the looks of it. Are you okay?" She had obviously been crying. Somehow, I managed to not shed a tear yet.

"That was the hardest thing that I ever had to do in my life. I had to testify that you were somehow this horrible person who I could no longer live with." This sentence was interrupted several times with sobbing. "Oh, Matt. I am SO sorry it ever got to this."

I hugged her. "I am too, sweetheart, I am too."

"Matt, I had to tell a story, on the record, of some horrible person. My attorney was clear that I couldn't just say that I was unhappy, or that I made some mistakes. I had to make sure that the judge knew that the divorce was the only sensible solution for me. 'Cause otherwise, he might recommend counselling or some other arrangement."

"And that would have been bad, why?"

She ignored me and continued. "My attorney practiced with me before we came to court today. I couldn't say that you drank sometimes, I had to say you were a drunk. We didn't have disagreements over stuff, we fought. That was the word I needed to use. He said," her voice cracking, "to make it sound like I was scared to be around you."

She forced her tears back, composing herself again. "I had to make it sound like you cheated on me when you were out of town." She looked at me guiltily. "I know you didn't, but when he asked me if that were possible, I answered that it was. I told the court that my affair with Pete was because I didn't trust you when you were out of town.

"I made you out to be someone that I know you aren't. Oh God, can you ever forgive me?" she asked as she broke down again.

I was fuming as I held her. I knew there was no sense in feeling this way, though, since everything that she said was what I was on trial for. Not legally, of course, but in her mind at least. And I knew that she wasn't lying. To her, at least, this was a version of the truth. It had to be for it to have gone this far. There must be a grain of truth in every lie for it to be believed.

After thirty seconds or so, she composed herself. With an attempt at a laugh, she said "So what are you doing the rest of the day? It looks like you're off to work."

"No, I took the day off. I figured I'd need to get drunk, and I was right. I need to hold up my reputation."

"No, Matt, don't. You need to get on with your life, baby. You need to get over this, get over me."

"You're right. I think I'll go find some skank to fuck me out of this. I always have!"

"That's not what I meant, and you know it!" Her tone softened. "Okay, I deserved that, I guess."

I couldn't hold back my anger any longer. "Really? You think? You go into a court of law and, on the record, start concocting stories about me, and then find it, what, hurtful I guess, when I show some sort of emotion about it? About being called a violent drunk? A cheat? An adulterer? I'll give you the drunk. But I have not touched another woman since I said 'I do.' And God knows I could have!"

"I heard about your little martyrdom with that girl at the lawn fete. That's on you, Matt. I would have understood if you went home with her. Don't go trying to pin your 'holier than thou' behavior on me."

"Then what DO you mean? Well?" I was pissed. "I did everything I fucking could to keep us together. To honor 'til death do us part.' 'For better or for worse.' My mind is clear that I can stand before God and say that I honored my vows. I'm definitely guilty of not WANTING to honor them more than a few times! But I did! I tried to make this work! And yet, I'm the defendant. It was ME who was on trial. I couldn't even stay in the courtroom to hear about all of these heinous crimes that you testified that I committed against you.

"And you tell me to get over you? How do I do that? I GAVE you my life. Somehow, you handing it back to me now means that I know what to do with it?

"Yeah, I gotta get my shit together, no doubt. I'm drinking too much, I know." My composure, my strength, gave out right then. "What am I supposed to do?" I started crying as I turned and walked away.

"Matt! MATT!" Jenny stood calling.

I stopped and regained my composure as best I could. As I wiped my eyes, Jenny walked up to me.

"Listen, this isn't easy for either of us. I'm sorry I assumed that you were stronger than me today. Both of us have a lot of healing to do. A lot of forgiving to do." We stood there awkwardly for a minute trying to figure out what to say or do next.

Two broken people standing on a street in downtown Buffalo on a Tuesday afternoon in December.

Jenny broke the silence. "I have been hoping that you would have started trying to get over me by now. Obviously, I tried getting over you already."

"Yeah, where is Pete?" I asked, honestly wondering where he was in her life. "Is he treating you okay? I might be your ex now, but I still want what's best for you."

"Pete was an idiot," she spat. "He's out of my life, thankfully." She stopped. "You deserve an explanation. The truth. Finally. But you are not going to like it, and I'm scared that you'll hate me even more than you do now."

"I don't hate you, Jenny. Believe it or not, I still love you. I might be hurt by what you say, but I won't hate you. Please tell me. It might actually start some healing, finally understanding why all this happened."

A deep breath. "I never liked you traveling. I had never lived alone, and all of a sudden, I'm alone five days out of the week. I never found a way to cope with the loneliness. When I lived with my parents, there was always someone around, and I remember how it used to piss me off. My parents, my brothers, my sister, I wanted them gone. I never realized how much I counted on having someone around, even if they were annoying me.

"So when you were gone, I would leave. I needed something to do, someone to do it with. I would go to see my mom. But my dad was always there giving me shit about something. And it really didn't matter anyway because you still weren't there when I got home.

"So one night I went over to Sara's. Didn't tell her I was coming or nothing. I just showed up. I was driving around, and I just showed up." Tears again made their appearance and rolled slowly and silently down her face. "I had been crying, and she was worried about me. We went to Blarney Castle over on South Park to grab a drink. I told her a few things I shouldn't have. I was pretty low when I got there, and then I started drinking. That didn't help either."

"What did you tell her?" I asked.

"That I was miserable. Lonely. I know I said that I thought I had made a mistake getting married." She looked at me nervously. "I was drinking, Matt. I didn't really think those things. My God, I was SO in love with you, but missing you so much. The hurt came out, not the truth.

"And you were right, that night I was telling you about it. Sara should have supported me by telling me to get back with my husband. But she said that I got married too young and, at that point, I knew she was right. It… sounded so… right." She gazed off into the distance, as if hearing Sara's voice again, giving her advice for the first time. After a few seconds, she continued.

"Pete was at Blarney Castle that night. I said hello to him on my way in. After I had bared my soul to Sara, told her about my messed-up feelings, she encouraged me to go over and talk to Pete. She said it would make me feel better. He bought me a drink. Sara was looking to get chatted up by some Romeo at the other end of the bar who was eyeing her up all night, and I was getting in the way. So I went over to Pete's table, while lover boy came over and put his moves on Sara. After a few drinks, Sara said her goodbyes to her boy toy, and rescued me from Pete. As I was leaving, he asked me to dinner. I said no, but it felt so good to be asked. Like I still had it.

"By the time I got back to the car, I was already starting to feel guilty. Sara told me not to be. She said that you were probably out doing the same thing wherever you were. The worst part is that I couldn't argue with her. That I somehow wanted to believe her.

"That weekend, you and I got into that argument when I told you what Sara had said. Of course, I didn't tell you about Pete buying me drinks. But you were off somewhere the next week anyway, and Sara now had it in her head that I needed to get out more often. So quite a few nights when you were gone, the two of us hit a bar somewhere. I got a lot of free drinks, but nothing else, I swear to God.

"I saw Pete a couple of times, and each time, he invited me to dinner. What was the harm? So one night, when you were in Atlanta, I took him up on his offer. We went to Jacobi's for pizza, and we stayed afterwards and danced. You never took me dancing, Matt! You always listened to that awful prog rock shit. How I wanted you to take me dancing! We stayed until it closed. He wanted to go back to his place after, but I said no. But it was all I could do to decline."

The cold December air sent a chill through me. I really didn't want to hear the rest of her story, but I knew that I had to. That this was important, even if it was going to be painful.

"I went to work the next day after only two hours in bed. And I didn't really sleep anyway 'cause I felt so guilty that I was so tempted. I should have been shocked or ashamed, but I was tempted. Even through the guilt, there was an excitement.

"That night, rather than go to Sara's, I went to Diana's. I had been avoiding her like the plague for weeks, mostly because I knew what she would say. I told her everything, and, damn, did I get an earful! That I should be ashamed of myself, that I had no right flirting with another man. Believe me, no one knew that more than I did, but I did not want to hear it. I told her that I didn't know if you were cheating on me. 'You know how much Matt loves you, Jenny,' she said. 'You're only trying to justify what you did.'

"Well, that was enough of that! I just walked out on her. But she was right, and I knew it. I knew that I had crossed a line that I could not turn back from."

"Why couldn't you turn back? You know we could have worked it out."

"I had crossed a line, Matt. I broke a vow. To God AND to you. You might forgive me, but I couldn't face God."

"Look, if there's anything I learned from going to church is that God is the one that WILL forgive you."

"But I still broke the vow, damn it! And I still had to face Him either way. I knew what I had done, and I always would know. You might forgive me, and God might forgive me, but I could not forgive me. Not then. Maybe not ever. So I wrote the note that night, and moved out. I didn't actually file for divorce until the next week. I wanted you to have it, though, so that I could not back out of my decision. Mom let me stay the night, but dad told me that I had to go back. But by now, I couldn't go back, so Diana took me in."

"Why did Diana take you in if she was so angry with you?" I wondered.

"Probably because she thought she could talk some sense into me. She always thinks that.

"Anyway, at that point, I figured that I had nothing else to lose, so I started seeing Pete more regularly. The week after Thanksgiving, I went back to Blarney Castle hoping I would see him, and he was there. I gave him my work number and we started getting a little more serious."

"You slept with him."

"Yes, I slept with him. Then you asked me to go to Orlando with you. There was no way I could ever pretend things were somehow normal in our marriage, even though I wanted to. I just couldn't do that to you. In my mind, I hoped that you would never find out, or that you would just go away, or find someone else, and that I wouldn't have to tell you. That I wouldn't have to hurt you."

"So what happened with Pete? I thought that you were getting serious with him."

Tears welled in her eyes again. "I haven't seen him in months. I stopped seeing him about a month after Orlando. I was feeling guilty about what I was doing, and I was thinking about your offer to come back. Really thinking about it. But I couldn't get past the vow that I broke. And he started treating me different. It turns out that he had been dating some girl the entire time that he was sleeping with me. I never told anybody. I lied to Sara and to Diana. And to you. I couldn't take the 'I told you so's' and the sermons reminding me about the mistakes that I had made.

"By the time I came to see you at your new apartment, I hadn't seen him in a few weeks. I had realized what I had left behind and I was hoping that I could get you to take me back. Regardless of my mistakes. Maybe even because of them. That's why I came over. I didn't need that thing signed that day. I could have mailed it to you. When you started kissing me, I so wanted you to take me to bed like you offered. Had you just kept kissing me, and not walked away, we could have started again."

"Why didn't you say so? Then and there?"

"Because you had been drinking again. Christ, there were like 50 empties in your apartment that day. You were drinking when I showed up."

"I had been mowing," I protested.

"And you were so mean to me," she continued. "Grabbing me and then turning me away! I remembered then how hot and cold you run when you drink. So nice and loving one minute, then a complete ass the next. I never knew when you were going to snap. I didn't want to get humiliated. But I did anyway."

"Why didn't you just tell me when you got there that you wanted me back? Before I started kissing you? I had been begging for you to come back for months. Why did you think that I would turn you away then?"

"I was on your turf now. It sounds stupid, but this was your new life. You had friends other than me waiting for you outside. You didn't need me. There was a hot girl in shorts, looking at me like I was an intruder. I thought you had moved on from me finally, like I had told you to do. Like I had hoped you would. Now, seeing it, I thought that I would mess you up again by dropping that bombshell.

"Think about it. If that was your new girlfriend staring at me, and I came over and just casually announced 'hey, babe, take me back,' what would that have done to you? What would you have done? And I know I couldn't have taken it if you had rejected me in front of her."

"You could have told me that you wanted to get back together anytime you talked to me since Orlando. I know I asked you dozens of times."

"I know. You don't think I regret that now? But I was too stupid. Too stubborn. Although, at the time, I thought that I was being smart. That this was somehow helping you get over me. That I was getting over you."

"Why did you go through with all this then?" I asked, pointing to the courthouse.

She wiped away the tears on her cheek, but they were quickly replaced with new ones. "I thought that woman next door was my replacement."

"I told you she wasn't."

"You already had insulted me with that comment about Pete. You had turned on me already, and she sure looked like I was intruding on something." She started crying freely again. Once again seeking refuge in my arms, she cried, "Why were we so stupid, Matt? Why did it get this far down the line before we had this conversation?"

"As much as it pains me to say this, I think this is for the best." Although those words came from my lips, I didn't believe a word of it. "Maybe I am the one who was too young. I might technically be an adult, but I sure don't know how to act like one. I played a big role in this mess, Jenny. I know I did. I could have been a man, and made this better somehow. I don't know how, but a man would have been able to hold on to his wife. But I'm not much of a man, I guess."

"You are an amazing man, Matt. I just didn't know what a good man looks like." Once again, she looked nervous. "Do you really want to see me happy?" she asked slowly, drying her eyes again.

"Yes, I really do,"

"Then I will tell you. Matt, I'm seeing a guy, and it feels like it is long term." Her face lit up as she was speaking. "I've been seeing him about two months now. Diana has met him, although I told her that I just started seeing him. She likes him, and she has pretty good taste." Jenny smiled as she added, "She thought you were pretty great too!"

Her smile at this point told me that she had reconsidered the incident at the bar. "I'm sorry about that. I got pissed off about her because I felt what you must have felt when you found out about Pete. I was so JEALOUS. The possibility of you banging a neighbor didn't bug me half as much as the thought of you doing my best friend. Diana told me the whole thing, and now, I wish you two would have hooked up. But then?" Jenny growled in dissent.

"Right now, I would give anything for another night with you. I'd give 1,000 nights with her for just one night with you." This restarted the waterworks with Jenny. She buried her head in my suitcoat.

Slowly, she gathered herself again and straightened up. Wiping her eyes, she sighed, "I guess we should be going. Getting on with our new lives." She stuck out her hand. "Friends?"

Putting my hands on her shoulders, I said, "Friends" as I kissed her forehead gently.

"Wish me luck?"

"Good luck, Jennifer Keller. I assume its Keller now and not Christopher. I'll see you around, okay?"

"I love you, Matt, and I always will. Don't you ever forget that."

Those next steps back to my car were the hardest I have ever taken.

When I got back to the apartment, I took off my wedding ring for the first time in years. After holding it in my hands for a moment, staring at it and thinking of all that it represented, I kissed it and put it in my bedside drawer.

Then I opened my first beer of the day.

§§§

Mike and Pat had already known that their presence would be required that night. Although a large part of me just wanted to get stupid drunk by myself, even I knew that I needed company that night. Not that I didn't get stupid drunk before they showed up!

About seven, two cars pulled up in front of my apartment, and three people brought up two cases of beer. Good friend that he was, Mike had gone up to Canada to bring real Labatt!

Mike and Pat came into my apartment along with another guy who I had met briefly, a guy that Mike knew from Canisius by the name of Marty D'Angelo. I had met him a few times at school, and he had been at the Cristal Myst show the night I ran into Diana.

"Hey, I'm sorry to hear about your divorce," he commiserated as he walked in.

"I hope you don't mind that I brought Marty," Mike said. "It's actually one of the last nights that he is in town before he moves to New York."

"Yeah, I got a job out there as a bartender," Marty offered. "I'm trying to get a book published, and I figured I'd have a better shot out there than in Buffalo."

"We need to get drunk," was Pat's decision.

So we did. The music was loud, heavy, and tended to be about the subject of getting laid, getting drunk, and doing it again. Ozzy, AC/DC, Dio, and the Scorpions became my counselors that night. We told bawdy stories about our conquests, even the ones that didn't happen. *Especially* the ones that didn't happen.

"Hey, remember that night you ended up in the bedroom with Gina?" Pat prompted. Of course, I went into a graphic story of everything that had only happened in my imagination.

And so it went until nearly eleven. By then, I was nearly incoherent. We had finished off one case, and were making a significant dent in the second. Mike and Pat were getting ready to pack it in.

Marty wanted to stay behind, though. Throughout the night, he stayed above the fray, and kept getting me to talk about how I was actually feeling. To actually expose some of the pain. After Mike and Pat left, Marty and I kept talking until at least one-thirty. That was the last thing I remember about that night, looking at the clock.

The next morning, the alarm rang for work like it always did. I promptly ran into the bathroom to puke. I jumped into the shower to try to get my bearings. Only partially successful, I wandered into the kitchen to make coffee.

The mess was like you read about, with beer bottles and food wrappers everywhere. That was when it hit me. What happened to Marty? He did not have a car. He had come over in Mike's car. He was not in the apartment (believe me, it was small enough that I would have noticed).

It was too early to call Mike, so I went to work wondering what the hell happened last night. My boss, God bless him, knew why I had taken the day before off, and was very understanding of my condition that day. Nothing got accomplished, and he sent me home at three. "Just don't repeat yesterday," was his only warning.

Believe me, I couldn't touch another beer if you had paid me at that point!

When I got home, I called Mike. "Hey, what happened to Marty last night?" I asked. "He stayed behind, and then wasn't there in the morning."

"He left with me. What are you talking about?"

"No, he stayed behind. I talked with him until one-thirty."

"Matt, you passed out at like ten-thirty. We dragged you to bed, and the three of us left." He sounded worried. "We knew you were bad, but not that bad. Dude, I think you need to get some help."

Chapter 10:
Losing My Religion

Suggested Songs:
"This Wreckage" – Gary Numan
"Homesick" – Soul Asylum

My God, my God, why have you forsaken me?
Why are you so far from helping me, and from the words of my groaning?
My God, I cry in the daytime, but you don't answer;
in the night season, and am not silent.
Psalm 22: 1-2 (WEB)

I write this book in my 50s. At this age, I have memories. Experience. Some might even say wisdom. But my struggle to enter the world of real adults continues.

And I have been reminiscing about a building of all things.

Built between 1969 and 1972 at a cost of $50 million, the Marine Midland Center is the tallest building in Buffalo, and the largest private building in New York State outside of New York City. The four-story base straddles the south end of Main Street above ground, atop a two-story underground parking garage housing 465 spaces. With more than one million square feet of office space, the tower reaches 38 floors into the skyline. On a clear day, this building is visible for 20 miles.

Upon entering the building from the city-block-sized plazas on either side of Main Street, a visitor ascends the escalator to the lobby, where the main bank branch and the commercial banking office are located. After checking in with security, you are guided to one of the two elevator banks, one for the lower floors (7-24) and express elevators to the higher floors (24-38). Floor 24 is the Executive Suite, where the world headquarters of Marine Midland Bank are located, and is accessible from all the elevators so that the bigwigs could go wherever they wanted quickly.

When I worked there, this was my morning routine. Of course, I wasn't important enough to have one of the underground parking spaces, so the journey above began with a trudge from a waterfront parking lot five or six blocks away. My office was on the 28th floor.

Our department occupied one half of the floor, with the examiners in cubicles to the left of the door. The loan officers got the window desks, so we would frequently visit them in an attempt to see some remnant of sunshine on the few days it appeared. Otherwise, we were high enough to be seemingly among the clouds on the many rainy and snowy days that Buffalo is known for.

But like all things in life, change happened.

In 1998, Marine Midland Bank re-branded itself as HSBC Bank to reflect that it was owned by the Hong Kong and Shanghai Banking Corp. This was the end of the bank that was founded in Buffalo in 1850. The building was renamed One HSBC Center. In 1999, the executive offices were moved to New York City.

HSBC Bank, as it was now known, operated in Buffalo until 2011, when it sold its remaining branches to a competitor. Upon the expiration of its lease in 2013, HSBC moved all its remaining offices out of the building and out of Buffalo. Over the preceding years, many of the other main tenants—such as the Philips Lytle attorney group and the Consulate of Canada—also moved their offices out of the building. Now named One Seneca Tower and still the tallest building in Buffalo, the building is 90% empty and, at night, sits mostly dark.

I have also been thinking a lot about time lately. I never thought I would grow up. I never really wanted to. Now that I'm here, and I realize that there is not as much time in front of me as there is behind me, I'm forced to consider how to make what time is still left to me as good as I can make it.

And I realize where I have wasted time. Not all time, really, but specific times.

So as I consider this point in my life, the sight of a once proud building mostly dark against a city skyline is emblematic. A once important building is reduced to being inconsequence. The lights fade. Someday, here on Earth, all I will be is a story my kids tell their kids. A name on an ancestral tree. Unless there is something more…

§§§

Rob decided to join me at the bridge in my dreams shortly after the divorce. I guess he thought that I needed a little comforting. But I had more to tell him than he might have bargained for.

You see, I was thinking about time then as well. I was too numb most days to realize that, but ultimately, that was the gist of it.

A friend was taken away because of selfishness and nonchalance. A marriage was torn apart from neglect because it was taken for granted.

Time was marching on, relentless and uncaring, changing whatever it touched. It wasn't going to grant me an opportunity to go back. It takes down buildings, it takes the lives of kings, the skills of athletes, and the dreams of youth. Not to mention friends and wives. It wasn't going to give me any special treatment.

And I realized that time answers to only one master, who alone is above time, beyond time. That master, of course, is God. He created time, as He created everything that time marks.

Now 26 years old, time was no longer my friend. Where once it allowed me to get my driver's license, drink beer legally, and get married, time had recently been cruel to me. And I thought Rob should know.

"Hey, Matt. You're not looking too good tonight. I'd offer you a Mick Dark, but I don't think it's a good idea. It looks like you've had more than your share already. Sorry about Jenny, but there is a different future for you now."

"You know, Rob, I lost both of my grandmothers in the past five years," I started, ignoring his remarks. *"My father has been turned into an old man, constantly attached to an oxygen bottle and unable to drive. Marino and Werner and Dempsey and all of our other Cheektowaga crew are adults now with their own lives and stories. All I can think of is that time is behind all of this. Time has turned my loved ones into memories.*

"And because time has done all of this, doesn't that mean that God was behind all of this? The all-loving, all-caring God that I thought I had learned about from Father Paul with his damned free will. God is the one directing all of this, isn't He?

"You went away. Forever. Leaving only another memory. Another casualty of time. Of God. And now your memory haunts me in my dreams like this. To burn inside my brain.

"Then Jenny leaves me. This time, the memories are not pleasant. The person is still there, but the wife, my love, is not. The pain remains to haunt me, when I drive past

her apartment at two o'clock in the morning to see who is staying the night, when I am alone. This does not feel like the work of time. This feels like the work of God.

"But why? I am a good Catholic. Even hungover, I go to church every Sunday. I pray when I need something. I put $10 in the basket when I can afford it. I've been faithful, haven't I? And yet, God directs time to do His bidding.

"To make matters worse, in the church's eyes I'm not even a good Catholic anymore. To them, I have committed a mortal sin and so I can no longer take communion or serve in an official capacity. Now that I need people most, I'm an outcast. Most damning, literally, is that my soul is doomed.

"Unless I apply for an annulment, of course. Just pay the church some large amount of money that I don't have, and they could arrange it so that my marriage never happened. My soul would be as good as new."

Rob just stood there, leaning over the bridge, looking forward as always, just taking it all in.

"Do you know how many nights when, three or four or five beers into the evening, sitting alone in a hotel room a thousand miles from home, that these thoughts have been entering my mind? The unfairness of giving my allegiance to such a God. What did I get for all my time at Catholic school, the numerous Saturday nights at the back of the church with youse guys deciding who was going to buy the beer that night? I was faithful. Why wasn't He?

"For that matter, why wasn't she? When I heard the full story behind Jenny's affair, I was okay for a while. After *all, my absence fueled much of her unhappiness. I walked away from our discussion outside the courthouse understanding her actions, somehow sympathizing with them. I was implicit in the crime, so the judgement against the defendant seemed reasonable. Guilty as charged, your honor.*

"But now that a few weeks have passed and she is out of my life and the ring is no longer on my finger, some things still don't add up. I was faithful. Against my will admittedly, but faithful nonetheless. And the absence was not even my doing. It was required to make a living, to earn the things that we both desired: a house, kids, a working vehicle. I know that we never spoke about what we wanted out of the marriage, but that's what every married couple wants, right?

"And Monday morning rolls around again, and a new hotel, and a week with another near-stranger while my loved ones continue to live their lives without me. Then Monday night, and my head hits the pillow in an alcohol-induced haze, you and your damned dreams come."

"You abandoned me, too, Matt. Don't forget that. Before you ever stepped foot on a plane."

I ignored his remark and continued. "And by Friday, when the plane is inevitably delayed and my car is buried under a foot of snow in the parking lot, when I finally return to an empty two-bedroom apartment, then I'm allowed to return to my life. What is left of it anyway."

Rob placed an empty bottle with its mates in the former six (now three) pack. A thought crossed my mind.

"I've been abandoned. I'm on my own." Then, "Who

am I worshipping? And, more importantly, why?

"Think about it," I asked Rob. "Where would I be if I had never stepped into a church? How could it be any worse? Couldn't it have been better?

"What if I had chosen to ignore some of the commandments along the way? To have chased women for the sake of pure physical enjoyment rather than in pursuit of the happily-ever-after that I thought I had? I may have gotten laid more. I might have some of the stories that Mike Wolf and Pat Hartmann told me at my divorce party. I don't even care if those stories weren't true: I want that.

"What if I had chosen to not love my fellow man? I could have ignored your pain, your calls for help. The fact that I did ignore them is brought to my attention frequently during these damned dreams. But, really, what more could I have done? Listened to you? No one is listening to me now. No one cares.

"No one, it's obvious, including the One that I was told by Father Paul is always there.

"Come to think of it, He obviously let you down, too. You were Catholic. You prayed, just like me. And yet, there was no answer. Just like I'm getting no answer now."

"Sometimes the answer is 'no,' Matt. Sometimes the answer is 'not yet.' I did not know that. You should. Especially after these 'damned dreams.'"

Once again, I ignored him. "Then Mike goes off and does a show on Saturday night, and could not be bothered to get together to hear me whine. And Pat has a date. And my sisters are busy with their families. So there is nothing to do but another trip to Wegmans for another twelve pack of Labatts as the only answer."

"Is this really where you want to go, Matt? I went there, and look what happened. Look around, Matt. There is a way forward. But you continue to look behind you."

"One of my favorite classes at Canisius College was a logic class, Rob. One of the textbooks was written by Lewis Carroll, you know, of Alice in Wonderland fame. Somehow it qualified for one of my religion requirements.

"The more logically I look at my circumstances, the more obvious the situation becomes. I pray, but get no answers. You prayed, but were ignored. Jenny prayed, and still walked away from her vows.

"God created time. Time stole loved ones.

"God is in charge of all things. You and Jenny were taken from me.

"I am alone.

"Logically, this leaves only one of two conclusions. One, God is against me for some reason. Or two, there is no God."

"Matt, don't do this. Explain where I fit in to your little logic exercise. If I'm gone, why am I here?"

Again, I chose not to listen. An inconvenient fact. I continued, "The first possibility seems unlikely. I can't think of a more dedicated Catholic than me. I was an altar boy in elementary school. I have the mass memorized. My Catholic and Jesuit schooling is impeccable. Despite my best efforts, I did not have sex before marriage, or outside of the bounds of marriage. He can't find anything in my life *that warrants the punishment He is doing out.*

"That leaves the second option. Which, at the end of the day, makes more sense anyways. I've never seen God. No one ever has. It always seemed a little like a fairy tale. A being that knows everything, and exists everywhere? Even Tolkien didn't go to that extreme in his books. Other civilizations believed in gods that were not real. The Romans and the Greeks each had hundreds. So why should this God be any different?"

"Matt..."

"Goodbye, old friend. I finally think I know what you have been trying to get through my brain all this time. I appreciate it."

But he didn't let me go that easily. "That is most definitely not the message I've been bringing. Actually, the message is the exact opposite. You'll get the message at some point, when you are ready to listen. To understand it. Today is not the day.

"You can turn your back on God, Matt. It hurts Him, but that is evidently what you need to do right now. That is Father Paul's free will in action.

"Just remember that God is not turning His back on you. He will always be there, always calling you home. Remember the story of the Prodigal Son? We learned that one in grade school.

"Listen when you don't think anyone is there. When something doesn't make sense, He is the reason. You cannot escape your heart, Matt, and that is His home.

"You may be exercising your free will right now, Matt.

> But God has a plan.
>
> "This is not the goodbye that you seem to think it is. I'll be around. He'll be around." Rob picked up his half-empty six pack and wandered into the mists to the side of the creek as the alarm clock sounded.

So, by myself in some random hotel room in the outskirts of a city that I never wanted to visit, I decided that God had nothing to offer me if He existed at all. And in my mind, God became god, Jesus became a mythical figure that slightly deranged people discussed at the risk of my derision, and church became a building whose parking lot slowed down traffic when it was emptying on a Sunday morning.

Once I made this decision, life became so much clearer. I no longer had to worry about abstaining from sex outside of marriage. Now all I had to do was find someone who was willing to partake in it with me.

I no longer had to pray to a god who did not listen. I had friends and family for that.

I no longer had to behave ethically at work. I could accept bribes and gifts if I ever got promoted to a position that would be important enough for someone to bribe or give a gift.

And I no longer had to forgive. Jenny or anyone else. I could let their hurts fester as long as I wanted. I could imagine revenge scenarios and wish them harm. I could relive everything that was ever said. I could look back in anger.

I was now so much better off.

§§§

Mike and Pat just took my new-found freedom from god in stride. They knew there were other issues that I was dealing with. Like drinking.

They were concerned with my not remembering my divorce night.

They chalked it up to the emotions of the day. After all, neither of them had ever been through something like that, and they could give me a pass on it. But they were much more diligent when we went out.

One of the things that they tried was to talk about any sort of goofy thing that would get my mind away from reality. And so began a long-running tradition of conceiving movies with Mike and Pat that didn't exist, but should. This tradition started because Pat and I were convinced that we could make better porno movies than those that we had seen.

At the time, Pat was dating a woman named Joy, so our first movie was going to be called *Over-joy-ed*. We did not consider any sort of plot, just stilted dialogue that would be uttered during the sex scenes.

Numerous such films were considered on subsequent nights. *I Was a Teenage Bugger-Boy for the Nazis, The Adventures of the Idaho Potato Farmer Girl,* and *Spanky McSpunky* were just a sampling of the many masterpieces conceived and outlined in various drinking holes around the area. But thanks to a lack of pen, paper, and memory, these classics never saw the light of day.

We soon turned our talents to the horror genre. This was much more fruitful. We noticed that, while most household tools had been used to slaughter someone in some horror movie somewhere, we found a criminal shortage of deaths by kitchen cutlery in cinema. We set out to change this with our all-time classic: *Night of the Bloody Fork.*

The opening scene is in a cutlery store on a rainy night. The camera pans past a broken front window and past the chef's knives, many of which are dangling from their displays. Suddenly, the camera catches sight of a trail of blood on the floor. Following the trail through the fine silver tableware section, we see the body of the owner slumped over the counter. With a start, the owner pulls himself up from the counter with a gasp, turns a frightened look to the camera, and clutches his chest where we see a single serving fork (with spurting blood, of course) emanating from his heart.

Several murders follow, each using a fork of some variety: a fondue fork, a pitch fork, a tuning fork. The murders are all different: some men, some women, some at night, some in broad daylight, some in good neighborhoods, some in the inner city. Police are stumped. They cannot figure out any connection between the murders other than the use of a fork of some variety.

One particularly dramatic scene, as conceived by me, acts as the emotional and artistic centerpiece of the film. In it, our detective, a classic gumshoe named Dirk O'Malley, speaks to a prostitute under a street light on a rainy night. Although we clearly hear the questions that the police officer asks, we only hear the prostitute mumble her answers. The mumbles signify the hopelessness, the silence, of the poor, the unclean, the desperate. That, and I couldn't figure out good clues that she could provide Detective O'Malley. But the effect would be dramatic.

After the Mumbling Prostitute scene (as it came to be known), there is another murder, this one on a country road. Unlike previous murders, the victim was stabbed by a knife rather than a fork. Police are stumped as to the change of tactic, and several scenes go by as they try to figure it out. There are arguments that this is not the work of the same killer. They are ready to call it the work of some other lunatic when they are provided with the answer in the form of a letter to the detectives. The murder happened at the fork in the road!

The End!

That's the genius of this movie, as we saw it. The viewer is left to find their own answers. What happens next? Does the killer see his life going in one of two directions, perhaps one to good and the other to further evil? Or perhaps, he has tired of figuring out more fork allegories, and is looking to branch into other tools. After all, there have been no good horror movies (to my knowledge) featuring weed whackers. Or perhaps, we decided that there were some girls at the bar that were more interesting than a movie that would never exist!

Regardless, I could now spend more time pursuing such trivialities now that God (I'm sorry, god) was out of my life.

Chapter 11:
Back to Perkins

Suggested Listening:
"Disintegration" – The Cure
"King of Wishful Thinking" – Go West

I adjure you, daughters of Jerusalem,
by the roes, or by the hinds of the field,
that you not stir up, nor awaken love,
until it so desires.
Song of Solomon 2: 7 (WEB)

I was left with a car that was reliable but had a rusted-out floor and no muffler. I still had the savings bonds that I was buying through payroll deductions at the bank, but these did not mature for years.

But I was also left with a line of credit that Jenny and I had taken out together. Jenny had run the balance up substantially when she left because she needed to buy a car and furniture for her new apartment. The bank would not take her off the line or limit advances because we were still married. One of the first things that I did after our divorce was finalized was to close this account, which meant paying it back.

So I had another bill to add to my rent, my student loans, and the credit card given to me by the bank for expenses (which I had to pay back in full each month). My salary, once a source of comfort, was now not enough to cover the new load of debt.

While we were going through the divorce, I didn't think it would be a big deal. When we both had real jobs, we were making payments relatively easily when we were together, so how hard could it be if we were apart? Plus, by not arguing any of the points of the settlement, I could make believe that none of it was happening. I would just agree. None of it seemed unfair.

And I was very good at making believe nothing was happening. And when I no longer believed it, I just ran to Wegmans, Tops, or any out-of-town convenience store that sold my medication of choice cold and in easy-to-carry quantities.

I had not considered that part of the reason we were able to make the payments each month was because we had two incomes. Now that my salary had to cover everything, I realized the mistake that I had made.

My job was going well, but there was no promotion in sight, nor was I scheduled to get a raise anytime soon. I could quit buying the savings bonds, but that only saved me $25 a pay. I was never in town to truly look for another job (keep in mind that this was before internet job boards and social media).

So, with no other good options, I decided to go back to Perkins.

I had worked at Perkins for more than four years, all throughout my time in college and for a good six months after graduation. I had left on good terms, so there should be no obstacles from that end. I had enjoyed my time there, and the hours were flexible. I was always home at some point Friday night (even when Friday night became Saturday morning), and I was never asked to fly out on Sunday, so if I could get some weekend shifts, I would at least make some extra money to help cover expenses.

A quick visit to the restaurant when one of my old managers was working, and I had a second job.

I began working the dinner shift on Saturday and the breakfast shift on Sunday. This was perfect for me because it allowed me to sleep in on Saturday if my Friday night flight got in late, and it gave me time to pack Sunday night.

I had worked all-nighters back when I was in college. Those shifts were memorable. Most Saturdays, a group of people would come in from seeing the *Rocky Horror Picture Show*, dressed as their favorite character. Always polite and friendly, they would generally break into some scene from the movie, frequently singing "Time Warp" to the rest of the patrons who had no clue what was going on, or why these people were dressed as they were. Usually, around five in the morning, the Cheektowaga cops would come in, frequently sitting with a bunch of hookers who also got out of work at the same time.

The new shifts were not nearly as entertaining. With one exception.

We had a number of guys who came in each day and sat at the counter for hours at a time: the "counter creatures" as they were affectionately known. These were guys that evidently had no home life or were avoiding it for some reason. They were mostly harmless, just seeking interaction with other humans in an otherwise lonely world. The waitresses enjoyed talking to them, mostly because they knew that they were good tippers. But some of the waitresses actually felt sorry for them. A story made its rounds that one night a waitress had set up one of the counter creatures with one of the hookers that had gotten off early.

One particular counter creature, let's call him "Ted," was a scientist of some variety, and said to be very wealthy. He only came in when a certain blonde waitress would work, and then he would request to sit at a table in her station, where he would stay her entire shift. She never minded, because he always left $20 or more in tips. All she had to do was be friendly and bring him coffee every 15 minutes or so.

This Saturday evening, as the waitress's shift was close to ending, there was a scream in the dining room, and she came flying in the back followed by another waitress. The manager and the busboy were soon seen escorting "Ted" out of the building. A few minutes later, two Cheektowaga cops came in back to talk to the manager and a number of the waitresses.

"Ted" had been proposing to the waitress that she should go back to his place to earn better tips, an offer that the waitress quickly rejected. It was at that point that she noticed that one of his hands was out of sight. The scream was when she noticed where it was.

"Ted" was no longer seen at the restaurant.

I quickly discovered that the waitresses were one perk to the new job that I had not considered. I had forgotten some of the crazy stuff that had gone on during college. Now, with my own apartment and no fiancé or wife to stop me, the good times were just waiting to start.

I also quickly discovered how many of the waitresses used to work with Jenny, and still hung out with her occasionally. And how they had told the rest of the waitresses about the new guy. I would be flirting with one of them when they would ask me if it was true that the girl I hooked up with after I left my wife chased Jenny out of my apartment. Or how hard I had made it on Jenny by trying to stick her with all the bills. Or how I had hit on her best friend.

One waitress, Katie, didn't get involved with any of the gossip surrounding me. While she was a very pretty girl in her early twenties who worked every Saturday evening, she was not the skinny, hot chick that seemed to be the standard issue Saturday night wait staff. She was going back to school for her master's degree. She frequently sat in the breakroom studying while I tried my best to make my moves on the blondes and the college girls and getting rebuffed accordingly. She did not want to be bothered, so I did not bother her.

One particular Saturday night, after I had been there for two months or so, she was again at her books when I took my break. Being later in the evening, none of the other cooks or waitresses were there.

"Mind if I join you?" I inquired politely (although if she had declined there would have been nowhere else to go).

"Suit yourself," she replied without looking up.

A few moments of awkward silence followed while she studied and I ate. One of the other waitresses came in the back to use the restroom. Upon leaving, she said to Katie in an icy tone, "Any time you want to come off your vacation, we can use your help."

"I've still got five minutes," she shouted to the departing waitress. "Bitch," she muttered, forgetting I was there. When she realized her mistake, she put down her book, and looked at me somewhat angrily. "You're always hitting on her, Mr. Studley. Why don't you get on my case, too? It might score you some points with her."

I didn't know how to respond, other than a few half-hearted "ums."

"I'm sorry. That was uncalled for. You are one of the few people around here who gives me any space. I appreciate that, and I should not have said anything. It's just so frustrating sometimes, listening to those whiny teenagers."

"No problem," I sighed. Changing the subject, I inquired, "What are you studying for?"

"Nursing. At D'Youville."

We spent the next five minutes making small talk until her break was up. She told me that she tried living at home with her parents, which made neither of them happy. She figured that the waitress job would help her make ends meet now that she had moved out.

My shift ended at 11, and I was looking forward to stopping at Wegmans to meet six new twelve-ounce friends (for sleeping purposes, of course). I went into the breakroom to punch out and to change. When I came out of the restroom, Katie was sitting and putting on mascara in a hand-held mirror. In jeans and a sweater, she looked a whole lot different than in the frumpy waitress uniform! My expression of surprise and mild lust was noticed.

"Yes, there is a woman underneath that waitress uniform," she teased.

Not wanting to admit my crime, I countered with a simple "Goodnight."

"Wait, aren't you going out with us?"

"I wasn't invited anywhere. Where are you going?"

She sighed. "That's just like Jill! She doesn't invite everyone. I'm meeting Jill, Yvonne, and a few of the cooks at Otto's. Tag along."

"I don't know. I gotta work tomorrow."

"So do I, you wuss. C'mon," she implored. "From everything I've heard, you could use a night out."

"What have you heard?" I asked, surprised.

"I'll tell you at Otto's," she joked, grabbing her purse and walking out the door. "See you there!"

I had never gone out with this crew, and I was very uncomfortable doing it this time. Only being there twice a week, being significantly older, and a pretty major loser (as my reputation preceded me), no one really wanted me there. I decided that I would go for a drink, hang out with Katie and then head home. I could still grab a six pack and be back to my apartment by midnight. I changed my mind while sitting in Otto's parking lot, and headed instead to Wegmans and bought a six-pack. I changed my mind again on my way back to the apartment and decided I might as well go. It would be unfriendly to Katie if I didn't go after she went out of her way to invite me.

When I walked into Otto's, the group at the table quieted down and stared at me. "Um, hey, Matt. Grab a seat," Jill hesitated. "We didn't know you were coming." There were seven people sitting around a table for four.

Katie got up from the table at that point. "Why don't we get another table and bring it over?" Unfortunately, there were no empty tables anywhere to be seen.

"That's all right," I offered. "I'll just grab something at the bar. Anybody need anything?" Upon hearing nothing, I wandered off, fully intending to go home. Halfway there, I decided that this little high school prank didn't warrant my hurt feelings. I had a better job than most of them could ever aspire to, and, other than a misstep in my personal life that I was working my way out of, I didn't need any of them. I was well respected at my real job, and had numerous business people that I could now call associates.

Wait a minute, did I just show some confidence? No, because I still only had two true friends. I decided that I did need them after all.

So I went to the bar to order a Labatt, which I now intended on taking back to the overcrowded table and drinking, even if it meant having to wedge in a chair in the middle of an aisle.

"I'll take one, too," Katie requested, suddenly standing at my side.

"Make it two," I yelled to the bartender.

"What a bunch of stuck up...I don't even want to say," Katie spat. "They didn't want me here tonight either, but Yvonne invited me, so Jill couldn't really say anything."

"Are we at work or in high school?" I inquired, to Katie's great amusement.

"Let's do them a favor. Let's find another table," she suggested.

"Fuck 'em," I countered. "Let's go back and make them have a miserable night."

Laughing, we went back, grabbed two chairs, and positioned them at the head of the table next to each other. We then proceeded to ignore them and talk amongst ourselves.

I found out that Katie was the oldest child of three, that her dad had worked for more than 20 years at Republic Steel until it closed and was now a cashier at Tops because that was the only job he could find. Her mom, needing to pick up extra income because of her husband's underemployment, went back to work as a secretary at an insurance office.

Katie had her degree in history from Penn State, where she had received a substantial scholarship. But, like many of us at that point in time, she could not find a job that would support her, so she moved back home with her parents once she graduated. The extra person in the house added stress to an otherwise stressful environment. Once she started the Perkins job, she was able to get her own place.

Worse, Katie had to start paying back her student loans. Unless she went back to school. So D'Youville it was. Of course, she had to take out more student loans to go to D'Youville, but at least she did not have to pay anything back yet.

My beer was almost gone, and I wanted to get back home. It was after midnight, and I needed to be up at six to shower and get back to work. I started making suggestions that it was time to leave.

"Don't you want to know what I've heard about you?" she asked.

"Okay, I'll play. What have you heard about me?"

"Buy me another beer and I'll tell you," she smiled.

So we spent another hour or so talking. This was the best I had felt in a long time. Here was a woman who actually wanted to talk to me, to know more about me. I had no interest in this woman earlier tonight, but

I quickly realized that there could be something here. But I had no hope of this going any further. I had been disappointed too many other times.

The next day at work, she thanked me for a nice evening. Then she said something totally unexpected. "I don't normally do this, but would you be interested in going out to dinner with me sometime? Just us two?"

"Where were you thinking," I joked, not knowing how to respond. "Perkins?"

"Actually, that would be funny, if we showed up for a date and asked to sit in Jill's section." Katie was relieved that I broke the awkwardness with some humor. "But maybe somewhere else. You make the call. After all, I had to ask YOU out," she teased as she walked away.

So the next Friday night, after a few mid-week phone calls from Kansas City to set something up, I met her at Danny's, a pub across the street from the Airport Bowling alley in Cheektowaga. Danny's is famous for its chicken wing soup, as well as all sorts of other good Buffalo bar fare.

She was dressed in tight jeans and a sweater, and a pair of three inch heels. Realizing now for the first time that this was meant to be a date, I started getting a little nervous. I found her to be pretty, and I thought she was an interesting person that I greatly enjoyed talking to, but I was not sure about romance. After trying to get a date for so long, I finally had one, and I didn't know what to do! This was the first woman that I had been out with since my divorce.

Katie picked up on that immediately. "You seem nervous. You haven't been out much recently, have you?"

"It's that obvious?"

"Let's just say that you are not the typical Don Juan."

We seated ourselves in the corner and ordered beers. "You know, if it makes you feel any better, I have never asked a guy out before," Katie confessed after the waitress left. Changing the subject nervously, she continued, "She didn't leave any silverware. First mistake. Sorry, I'm going to be judging her. She will not get a tip if she doesn't measure up to my standards!"

"Why me, Katie?" I wondered, after taking a drink of my Labatt for courage. "I've obviously messed up one serious relationship pretty bad. I can't say that it wasn't my fault. Between my travel, my drinking, and my messed-up finances, I'm not much of a prize."

Katie looked at her beer. Quietly she said, "Do you think that I've got it so together? I've messed up a ton in my life too! You just didn't get an advanced scouting report on me like I did on you."

Her eyes raised to meet mine. "I had a fiancé a little over a year ago. We were going to get married this past June. He was a wonderful guy named Mark. I met him at Penn State, and we fell in love. He was in Pre-Med. We had dated since sophomore year. In senior year, we got an apartment together. My parents are very religious and did not like that at all!

"We graduated together, but he went on to Harvard to get his doctorate. That was fine, I was willing to wait. Before he went off, he proposed to me. He was going to get his first year of medical school out of the way while I stayed home, got a job, and planned the wedding. Then the two of us would move to Boston to get an apartment while he finished up.

"Then, early that November, an old boyfriend called me up out of the blue. He was in town for business. I should never have agreed to meet him, but I went to a bar downtown where he was staying. I could have said no, I could have went looking like a slob. But I dressed as hot as I could. I guess I wanted to feel wanted. Make him realize what he didn't have.

"After a couple of drinks, we said goodbye and I started to walk to my car. But I let him walk with me. We were downtown, after dark, and I was a little scared. As I was getting ready to get in my car, I turned to say goodbye, for real this time.

"I ended up in his hotel room." She took a long drink. "When I got home the next day, my mom told me Mark had called twice the prior night. I knew immediately what I had done."

"It's okay, I don't…"

"No, let me finish, damn it! This is the first time I've ever told anybody this. Please let me get it off my chest."

"Sorry."

"Mark came home for Thanksgiving break. We went to his parents' house for Thanksgiving dinner. After dinner, we went for a walk with his dog. I told him what I had done. How I had cheated on him. I did not expect him to forgive me, and I got what I expected. He took back the engagement ring that night. I never even got to say goodbye to his parents."

Tears had filled her eyes and a moment of silence followed. "Okay, you can say something now."

Luckily, just then the waitress came back to take our order. When I told her to come back later with two more drinks, Katie laughed uneasily while wiping away a stray tear or two. "Mistake number two," she quipped. "When your guests are in a serious conversation, leave them alone."

In response, I took Katie's hands, looked her in the eye, and kissed her hands. I didn't say a word; it was one of the only times that I have ever been at a loss for words. I knew I couldn't say anything to make her feel better, so I had to find some way to let her know that I was listening and that I cared.

She took her hand and put it on my cheek. "That, Matt Christopher, is why I chose you. By not saying anything, you affirmed me in a way that no one has been able to do in a long time."

The conversation from that point on was nowhere near as deep. My alcohol consumption was greatly diminished (only three Labatts). Laughs replaced the tears.

As we left the restaurant and walked to the car, I touched Katie's elbow. When she stopped and turned to me, I kissed her. This time there was no doubt. Unlike with Chloe, when I did not know if I could break my vows and face rejection, I had no such boundaries. Unlike with Diana, when she did not want to break a friend's trust, Katie had no such reservations.

"Come home with me," I asked.

To my surprise and delight, she did.

Chapter 12:
The Dating Scene

Suggested Listening:
"Cinderella Search" – Marillion
"Wasted" – Def Leppard

I said in my heart, "Come now, I will test you with mirth: therefore enjoy pleasure;" and behold, this also was vanity. I said of laughter, "It is foolishness;" and of mirth, "What does it accomplish?" I searched in my heart how to cheer my flesh with wine, my heart yet guiding me with wisdom, and how to lay hold of folly, until I might see what it was good for the sons of men that they should do under heaven all the days of their lives.
Ecclesiastes 2: 1-3 (WEB)

I wish I could say that I had found my true love.

But Katie and I were not soul mates. The traveling was a problem. Like Jenny, she did not appreciate being left alone throughout the week. Her parents did not like me the one time I met them. Katie told me that they were always comparing me to Mark.

Another issue was her roommate. The first time I went to her apartment, I was greeted by a man with long hair. "You must be Matt! Ooh, I am SO excited to meet you. I'll tell Katie you are here. Can I get you anything?"

"Um, no," I stammered, confused. "Is this Katie's apartment?"

"Oh, I'm sorry," the long-haired man lisped. "I'm Katie's roommate, Nate. Oh, here she is now."

He left the room as Katie came into the kitchen. "Get out of here, Nate. I told you to leave him alone."

"I couldn't help it, you little whore. You get all the good-looking guys," he pouted as he left.

"I'm sorry about him," she apologized. "He didn't try to hit on you at all, did he?"

"Soooo, he's your roommate?" I inquired.

"Yeah, I didn't mention him because a lot of guys would have been creeped out if they knew I lived with a guy. Don't worry, though. He's obviously gay, so he has never slept with me. He's a childhood friend, and we both needed roommates to make ends meet."

"I figured that out pretty quickly," I carefully noted.

"Was it the lisping, the hand gestures, or just the fact that he's a flaming queen?"

"I heard that," was the response from the other room. "I'm not always the queen!"

"Should we get going?" Katie asked as she started to the door.

"Don't do anything I wouldn't do," was heard from the other room. "And believe me, I do it all!"

Another time, I decided to surprise her by just dropping by the apartment with some beer. Because I was coming straight from work, I was wearing a suit. Nate answered the door when I rang the bell.

"Well, hello handsome!" was the greeting I got when I saw him. "You clean up nice! I do love me a man in a suit."

"Is Katie home?" I quickly asked to let him know the reason I was here.

"No, she is out grocery shopping. But you are more than welcome to come in if you want. She won't be home for a while, but I'll keep you company."

"Um, just tell her I was here," I replied as I started to back away.

"Don't worry, I'll be gentle."

"I think you have the wrong idea. I'm not gay."

"Only because you've never met the right guy."

"I've been married before. I know I like women."

"I've had married men before. In fact, I've had a guy that got a divorce because he discovered men."

I was now very uncomfortable. "Just let Katie know I was here."

Two hours later, I got a call from Katie. "I'm sorry about that. I didn't think he'd try to steal my boyfriend. He is such a slut!"

And it also turned out that Mark was not totally out of the picture—at least not in her mind. She would often slip up and call me Mark. I heard his name at least once a day.

Not that Jenny was out of my life or off my mind either. I often found myself comparing Katie to Jenny. Never out loud, obviously, but frequently in my mind. Katie was much more serious and organized than Jenny. A goofy remark about something that Jenny would find hysterical would leave Katie staring at me like I lost my mind.

And because Katie was the only woman other than Jenny that I had ever made love to, I certainly made comparisons in the bedroom. And I found out that I liked making love to a woman that I loved more than to a woman who I liked. Oh, don't get me wrong. It felt great! But waking up to a woman that is not in love with you can make for an uncomfortable morning. Almost as uncomfortable as not having anything to say to the woman that you just shared an incredibly intimate moment with.

It ended one January night when my flight back from Memphis was delayed nearly four hours due to a big snowstorm in the east. My connecting flight out of Newark was cancelled, as was another through DC. I was able to get on a flight to Chicago at the last minute, but had a three-hour layover in O'Hare. I walked in the door after 1 AM.

Katie had come over at eight, thinking that I would be home. She had a key to my apartment, so she let herself in. While she was waiting for me, she went outside to shovel the six inches of snow off the driveway. It was while she was outside shoveling that I tried calling the apartment to tell her I was running late. Not connecting with her at her apartment or at mine, I tried her parents' house. They were less than pleased to hear from me, and icily told me that she was at my apartment. At that moment, my flight to Chicago started boarding.

Once in Chicago, I called my apartment again. When I told her that I would be home after midnight, she got angry. "I've been here for hours. I shoveled for you so that you didn't have to. And yet, you still can't get home at a reasonable time."

"It's not like I'm doing this on purpose. I want to see you as soon as possible. Believe me, I've had a hard week. It'll be good to see a friendly face."

"Well, I'm not sticking around. I can't stay up that late. I have homework to do tomorrow, and I can't be falling asleep doing it. I'll see you at work tomorrow. Do you start at four?"

The next day at work, she was cold to me. As she was leaving, she pulled me aside (I still had another hour on my shift) and said, "I'm not coming over tonight. I didn't finish my homework yet."

She did not work Sunday morning, although I did. Upon punching out at four, I tried giving her a call to no avail. She called me about ten that night after I had gone to bed (I needed to get up at four the next morning for a flight).

"So where are you off to this week?" she asked, knowing full well that I was heading to Baltimore.

"Baltimore. You knew that."

"Yeah, I just wanted to give it one more chance. Look, I can't take this. You're never here. I get to see you a few hours a week if I'm lucky. This is going nowhere. I'm not getting any younger, and I don't want a long-distance relationship."

"Well, it's not something I love either. But I don't have much choice. It's my job."

"And it's my life. And I need to live it."

So with a few apologies and some regret, she returned my key, wished me well and moved on with her life.

I can't say that it was the worst thing that could have happened. We liked each other's company, but nothing that rose above that. We made a smart move by putting it aside sooner rather than later.

It helped me immensely, though. I was feeling better about Jenny not being in my life, now that I knew that there was life after her. I had not spoken to her at all through my brief time with Katie, and I didn't miss it. I felt free finally. I also knew that there were other women who would give me a shot. And I was ready to find them!

But not here. Mike wanted to go to a bar on Sunset Bay. I hadn't been back on the beach since Rob died. I couldn't get that out of my mind.

"Stop it," I told myself. "You're going to have fun. Besides, it's a beach bar. There will be music. You can listen to Actor and have a few drinks. You have a ride home." So, reluctantly, I went.

Mike Wolf was in full rock regalia when he picked me up that evening: torn jeans, snakeskin boots, his hair sprayed tall. These were his people after all.

Now, I loved the 80s. Pretty much everything about it: the music, the freedom (at least for me), the relative peace and prosperity of the country, the beer. One thing that always eluded me about that decade, though, was the men's fashions. I loved the women's fashions, especially at the bar scene: high heels, big hair, tight acid washed jeans. Even leg warmers!

I couldn't pull off any of the men's fashions at the time, though, which clouded my judgement on just how awesome it could have been.

I was topping the scales at this point at 250 pounds, pretty much limiting my wardrobe from any of the tight jeans or form-fitting shirts of the day. My limited budget prevented me from picking up a pair of snakeskin or ostrich-skin boots. And, even in my mid-20's, the receding nature of my hairline prevented a decent mullet. Forget about the teased-out, long and sprayed big hair sported by Mike.

Watching him prepare for a night on the town was fascinating. After a long shower, he would blow dry his hair in front of the mirror, teasing it and getting it just so. Then came the hair spray. Aqua-Net was his brand (as well as the choice of most of the hair bands at the time). One full application used at least a quarter of the can. Then another primp and tease, and another full application. A final adjustment, and the whole thing was doused with another full application. At this point, you could barely see through the resulting mist in the apartment. My banker hair was not moving for the night, as the second-hand hair spray was enough to plaster it to my head.

Although she didn't come with us that evening, Mike was dating a petite blond girl at that time. She would frequently get ready for the night with him, so take the above hair spray party to festival-like conditions. Breathing was optional on those nights.

Today, the topic of global warming is divisive, with scientists claiming that it is the result of carbon emissions from our vehicles and from burning coal for electricity. I propose that the biggest damage to the ozone layer occurred in the 1980s, while the hair bands and their ilk kept the Aqua-Net company afloat with their aerosol cans of hirsute perfection.

Music blasting, Mike and I drove through the Southtowns and down the New York State Thruway to Angola.

Sunset Bay is located about 20 miles south of Buffalo along Lake Erie. Consisting of a beautiful beach, cottages for rent, and a number of clubs, Buffalonians had been going to Sunset Bay for generations. My sisters had rented cottages there (once they had moved out of the house, of course). I went there every summer when coworkers from Perkins rented a cottage (I was not allowed to go with them). I would show up in the afternoon to find most of them still asleep, empties (and bodies) strewn around the trashed living room.

There was a club on the beach (ingeniously named Sunset Bay Beach Club) that had live music every weekend. One of the most popular bands on the scene at the time was Actor. Featuring Jessie Galante, a beautiful blonde woman with one of the great rock voices, Actor played mostly cover songs. But not always the same moldy-oldie chestnuts. One of their signature songs was Head East's "There's Never Been Any Reason," for example. They had recently released an album of all original songs. And if you didn't like their music, you could always just stare at Jessie.

Mike insisted that I go with him this particular Saturday. "You need to get out. I know you like Actor. I met the guitarist a few weeks ago at a Cristal Myst show, and he told me to find him and hang out with him. There will be all sorts of people there. Probably some girls who would spend some time with you." Of course, he meant all sorts of happy people, not people moping around and feeling sorry for themselves.

"Yeah, and I'm just going to go up to some stranger on the beach and ask what? You want a piece of this?"

"No, but what else are you going to do? Do you think anyone is just going to show up on your doorstep and offer herself to you if you stay home? You need to get back in the real world, Matt."

"You're not going to the real world, Wolf. You're going to the beach. You belong there because you have long hair and are in a band. You're a rock star. Women in bikinis can sense an accountant geek like me from miles away. I don't belong there."

"Us 'rock stars' are people just like you, Matt. You know more about music than half of the posers at the shows. Talk music. You know you have that in common with everyone there, and I think you'll be amazed at the level of conversation you can have with them. Possibly even the geek-averse bikini chicks."

Once there, I went to the bar and ordered my first Labatt. Mike went off talking to some people. I made sure to get lost in the crowd. I didn't want to be here. The girls in their bikinis, tight jeans, and high heels were ignoring me as they always did.

You see, Mike's premise was flawed in one significant aspect: in order to show off my encyclopedic knowledge of music, one has to have a conversation with someone else. Which means people needed to respond when you said "hello." None of the young ladies that I approached did so.

But this was my first time hitting a club since the divorce. Since Katie. I had quit Perkins shortly after we broke up because it was too awkward seeing her. She ignored me as best she could, which made the other waitresses happy. "Your girl is ignoring you Matt." "Looks like you got dumped again, Matt." Plus, six months of extra income had allowed me to catch up on my finances. That meant that I was free this Saturday night.

Kim Mitchell's "Go For Soda" starts playing.

A girl walks up to me. Laurie. One of Mike's friends from Canisius that I had met one or two times at his shows. Tight jeans, five-inch heels, a DD chest that her bikini top was struggling to restrain. She grabs my hand and pulls me out on the floor. Wait a minute, that was a line from a Springsteen song. No, it was really happening. She's in my arms, slow dancing to a Heart song coming over the speakers.

"Buy me a drink," Laurie says as the song ends. She takes my hand and leads me to the bar.

As we walk hand in hand, there are at least half a dozen guys eyeing her up, giving me the silent thumbs up for being with her, wishing they were me.

A vodka tonic and another Labatt later, we walk outside onto the beach, the warm sand spilling into my sneakers. One of the band members walks up to us. Laurie introduces me. "This is Matt. Make sure youse guys take care of him." The guitarist calls out to the bartender, "This guy's with us. Give him whatever he wants."

We walk over to the table where the rest of the band is hanging out. Mike is there already. I am introduced to the rest of the band. We talk. We laugh.

Beer is consumed. A lot of it.

The band plays.

Laurie dances.

I get a long kiss.

The night ends.

The morning broke through my hangover. I was alone in my apartment in Cheektowaga, with my head pounding. Luckily, the bathroom was close by as last night's dream emptied into the filthy toilet.

But it happened. What did she say when we left? I knew her name, but she didn't give me her phone number. I knew there was a reason why, but I'd be damned if I could remember it.

I saw Mike the next night when he stopped by. "You and Laurie definitely hit it off."

"That was a sympathy date," I corrected him. "She didn't even leave me her number."

This surprised him. "Really? The way you two were going at it, I thought for sure I'd be hearing some good stories tonight. It's the only reason why I came here; I wanted to hear you describe her tits!"

"What was that about? It made me feel good to walk around with a hot chick, and even better to grope her a little bit, but why did she talk to me at all?"

Mike looked guilty. "I told the guys in the band about you. I wanted you to have a good time. They must have said something about you to Laurie, but I doubt the band set you up or anything. And whatever happened with her was not something that I had anything to do with, either."

"I guess I appreciate the gesture, but I'm okay."

"Really?" Mike turned serious, something that he rarely did. "I was hoping that this wouldn't come up. Do you have any idea how much you have been drinking lately? Do you even know how you got home last night?"

"Yeah, you drove me home."

"No. Laurie did. You passed out on her before Actor even finished their second set. She actually had some fun with you before you passed out. She really enjoyed talking with you about music. She loved your weird taste in bands. You guys really hit it off. She asked me if she could drive you home. She told me that she was hoping that you woke up once you got home. She was going to try!

"But she couldn't wake you up. She literally got your keys out of your pocket, helped you stumble upstairs to your apartment, and made sure that you got in bed. She called me this morning to apologize to me for not sticking around. She felt that someone should have, but she wasn't interested in babysitting. Last night or any other night.

"If this were the first time, I would have laughed it off, but you know damn well that this has happened before. You got better for a while with Katie, but now you're worse than ever. Dude, you need to get it together. If you had just stayed this side of blacked out drunk, you might have a new start with someone."

"And yet you always show up with beer. Or to go out. If I'm that bad, why are you always drinking with me?"

"Would you hang out with me otherwise?" Mike got up angrily. "I try to get you out of the house so you don't drown in your own fucking tears. So instead you drink yourself silly on the beach instead of in the house. Pat and I try to give a shit about you, but you don't give a shit about yourself. We don't want to see you like this." He waved his arm around the mess that was my apartment. "Like this," he said as he punched me in the gut. "How many pounds have you gained since the divorce? Fifty?"

"So because I'm gaining weight, I have a problem? I don't eat well on the road. Most of the other auditors have weight problems, too."

"It's not a WEIGHT problem, Matt! It's a DRINKING problem! Do you even eat when you're on the road? You're always telling me about picking up beer on your way back to the hotel. You've told me many times about being hungover at the job."

"I get bored! I get lonely!" I pleaded.

"Then do something at night. I would love to travel like you do! Why do you think I'm in a band? I want to travel the world!"

"What am I going to do on the road?" I responded angrily. "I don't go to places like Paris, France. I go to places like Paris, Tennessee, population a thousand at best. Not to New York City, or Kansas City, or even Iowa City. I go to the furthest farm town away from Iowa City. I go to places where the people dream of vacationing in Iowa City. Where getting their own Burger King is a sign that they're a big city.

"Where am I going when I am in a town like that? The bowling alley? Who am I going with? My married boss, or the coworker who, by the way, also lives by himself and can outdrink me any day of the week? Better to drink alone and not have to answer to anyone! Including you!"

Mike slowly shook his head. "Listen to yourself. Fine. I'll shut up. Think about what I said." Reaching for the door, he added "I'll see you around."

Chapter 13:
Pen Pals

Suggested Listening:
"House of the Rising Sun" – The Animals
"The Science of Selling Yourself Short" – Less Than Jake
"S.O.B." – Nathaniel Rateliff and the Night Sweats

Listen, my son, and be wise,
and keep your heart on the right path!
Don't be among ones drinking too much wine,
or those who gorge themselves on meat:
for the drunkard and the glutton shall become poor;
and drowsiness clothes them in rags.
Proverbs 23: 19-21 (WEB)

I KNEW THAT I needed to get my shit together. I did not need Mike or Pat or anyone else to tell me that.

What they could not tell me was what to do about it. They just told me what NOT to do. The only thing that got me through. My medication.

Mike did everything he could to keep me from going off the rails. He came over as often as he could, or took me to see bands. One of our favorite spots was a bar on William Street called Desiderio's. They had a large stage that attracted most of the local bands of the day, and, because of the bands, attracted large crowds. Those crowds generally contained a significant percentage of women, and of that subset, a large proportion of good-looking women.

One of the problems that I frequently encountered was my weight. I was huge. I say that I was 250, but I was probably kidding myself. I was fat. Guys who work out are said to have six-pack abs. I could say that I was in better shape than those guys. I had twelve-pack abs, obtained from drinking the aforementioned twelve packs. Canadians might say that I had two-four abs.

Around this time, Marillion had a tour date at Massey Hall in Toronto. There was no local date, and I wanted to see them. They had just released *Clutching at Straws* and songs like "Kayleigh" and "Sugar Mice" were constants in my miasma. I had never seen them before, and Toronto was not a long drive. Mike knew all this, and surprised me one day with tickets to the show.

So one Wednesday night in September, Mike and I hopped into my beat up Chevy Monza, crossed the border, and went to commiserate with Fish and the boys for an evening.

Massey Hall is an old theater in the Garden District of downtown Toronto, on Victoria Street, and is on the register of Canadian National Historic Sites. Built in 1894, this venue seats nearly 3,000, and was a perfect location for this show. Our tickets were in the balcony, which was still close enough to appreciate the showmanship of Fish as he performed the first half of *Misplaced Childhood* in its entirety. The acoustics of the hall, designed for symphonies, allowed every note to be heard crystal clear.

As the last notes of "Incommunicado" faded away, Mike and I filed out of the hall and into the late evening. Finding our car in the parking garage, we got in and I started the engine. However, when I went to turn on the headlights, I got nothing. No headlights, no taillights. As it was pushing midnight in a downtown area, there were no open auto parts stores nearby to pick up new headlights.

We were now faced with two choices: drive nearly 100 miles and cross an international border in a car with no headlights (after consuming some quantity of alcohol) or find a hotel in the downtown area of a major city. As option one seemed silly, we chose option two. Abandoning the car in the parking deck, we started walking up Yonge Street looking for a hotel that a) had a room and b) didn't cost more than $200 for the night.

"Hey, darlin'. You lookin' for a little companionship?" said a nice lady in a short dress and heels.

"I think that tall guy would like a little brown sugar," said her black friend next to her.

"No thanks," declared Mike as we continued walking.

"Oh, and they're American!" said the black lady. "We'll give you a discount if you pay us in US dollars."

"You won't be disappointed," we heard as we walked into the lobby of a Holiday Inn. Finding that they had no rooms that fit our description, we ventured back onto Yonge.

"Oh, baby, you changed your mind! I knew you would," said the first girl as we walked past them again. "Don't tease us like this. We want it!"

But Mike and I weren't going to give it, especially because it included cash which was in short supply for both of us, so we went to another hotel on the next block, where we were greeted by a very effeminate man at the front desk. After we asked him for a room, he responded by asking us where we were from.

"We don't want this place to become a brothel," he lisped when we told him we were from Buffalo. Not having any luggage for this unplanned trip, we went straight upstairs.

I was all too used to hotel rooms at this point, whereas Mike had rarely been in one. I was figuring out which of the two beds I was going to claim, when Mike figured out that they had porn on the TV. "Do you mind if I charge $19.95 to our room? I'll pay you back."

Deciding against Spank-o-Vision, we instead wandered down to the hotel bar. There, in his full drunken majesty, was a Scotsman regaling the patrons with stories of drinking from the homeland. Loud, obscene, and very funny, he was used to telling stories in a bar. His brogue somehow made the stories that much more entertaining.

"Ah, two new lads be joining us. Come, welcome gents. Grab a pint." Two beers were brought to us by the bartender as soon as we sat down. "Where are you lads from?"

"We just came from the Marillion show at Massey Hall," I offered.

"Marillion! Me boys! You may have noticed, lads, but I meself hail from that blessed land of the Scots."

"Like no one would have noticed that," quipped one of the other patrons.

"Quiet, you," admonished the Scot. "Yer Americans, no?"

"Yeah, we live in Buffalo," Mike ventured. "Our car broke down so we're staying the night."

"Just checked in, did ya? Did ya notice the fookin' queen at the front desk? That bloke was eyeing me up, I tell ya."

"Yeah, he wanted to make sure we weren't from around here," Mike noted. In his best effeminate voice, he said, "This hotel is NOT a brothel."

This struck the Scot as hilarious. "What a fookin' queen! I can see him saying that." With that, the Scot repeated Mike's words as an effeminate Scot. "So there's some loose ladies around here, eh?"

"Yeah," Mike responded. "We were propositioned by two of them on our way here. A black one and a white one."

"A black one?" repeated the Scot, suddenly very interested. "So if I go outside that door right now, I could find fookin' Diana Ross and pay her to give the old John Thomas a once over?" Draining his beer, he said, "Sorry boys, but I've got to go find me fookin' Diana Ross."

After he hurried out of there, Mike and I finished our drinks and went to our rooms and slept. Once morning came, we drove our headlight-less car back to Buffalo, and I walked into the office a few hours late.

§§§

I agreed with Mike on one thing. My life was missing a companion. I felt better about myself when I was dating Katie. Of course, part of that was because she did not want me drinking. If I'm honest with myself, that was one of the things that ultimately caused us to go our separate ways.

What I needed was a woman who would not only love me for who I was, but also someone fun that I could party with when the opportunity presented itself. I did not want a teetotaler. I wanted someone who could keep up with me when we went to the bars to see Mike (or any other band) play. If she were with me, I was sure, the stuff in the middle of the week would go away. Although I probably would still have one or two while I was out of town.

My lifestyle did not allow me to meet anyone, though. I was too shy (or drunk) to meet anyone at the clubs when I went out. There continued to be no one at work that was a possibility. So shortly after my confrontation with Mike, I decided to try a new approach.

One Sunday afternoon, I was paging through the Sunday paper. I had been drinking most of the day, if only to consider my options. I thought better while I was medicated. It was there that I saw the answer to my problems.

Classified ads (I told you that I thought best drunk).

One of my problems at clubs was the inability to make comprehensible sentences, yet alone in a manner that would sweep a young lady off her feet. She would also have to see me, a problem when my weight was as high as it was.

As a writer (yes, I still fancied myself a writer even though Mike no longer was interested in using my lyrics), I was sure that I could craft an interesting, articulate, and convincing ad that any available woman would be foolish not to respond to.

The first two ads yielded exactly two responses, both of them ads for dating services.

So I changed my approach. I started answering ads that were already placed. This had a number of advantages. First, I no longer had to foot the bill for the ad. Second, I could respond to only those ads that I was interested in. I was always afraid that the deluge of responses I would receive to my ad would result in a number of women that I would not want to be seen with. Luckily for me, I never had to worry about the mass rejections that I was fearing.

So, one Sunday, I sat down and mailed out ten letters to ten potential lovers. These letters showed off my worldly nature, talking up my numerous travels and suggestions of exotic locales that we could visit on our dates (like Cleveland). They listed my many hobbies, like drinking, listening to music, and partying. And they suggested that I was interested in a long-term romance. Who wouldn't want some of that?

For some reason, I received no responses to those letters. Except for one letter advertising a dating service.

I decided to be more selective. Obviously, I was sending letters to ladies who were not my type. Probably older women who couldn't keep up with me anyway. So the next week, I only sent out five letters. I noticed that many of the same ads appeared the previous week anyway.

This time, I did receive a response. A nice young lady named Tawny (obviously her real name) wanted to meet me for hot, steamy sex. She was nice enough to provide me with a graphic picture of herself, and provided me with a 1-900 number to get in touch with her. And she assured me that she wanted to be touched.

She did not seem like my type, however, so I tried again the following week.

The third time was the charm. In addition to the letter from the dating service and one from Roxy (who, coincidently, had the same 1-900 number as Tawny—must be her roommate), I received a letter from a woman named Stacy, a divorcee that lived in Tonawanda. She was in her early 20s, and was nice enough to provide a real picture of herself and a phone number that did not require a credit card. The picture was of a redhead with glasses as taken by a professional photographer.

So I called her one Tuesday night. She turned out to be just what I was hoping for. She loved heavy metal, she spent a lot of time in the bars of Tonawanda, and was looking to get into a relationship with a stable man who would like to do the same things as her.

I set up a date for us to meet the following Saturday night.

We went to a Red Lobster (ooh, fancy!) not too far from her house. I ordered a Labatt (only to get the conversation started), and she ordered a Genny. I had already had two Labatts before I left my apartment (just to calm my nerves). The waitress brought the beers to our table. Over small talk, I finished my beer before she came back for our order. Surprisingly, Stacy had also finished hers as well. So we ordered our dinner and another round.

Stacy was 21 years old, and had been divorced for nearly two years. She had only been married for six months. Her husband was interested only in sex, and did not work. She had only known him for two weeks when she was married on a drunken dare.

Her family no longer talked to her. She spent most of her time since then trying to get her life back together. She didn't work or drive, but was hoping to find a job somewhere near her apartment because she really needed to catch up on the rent. She was also hoping that I could teach her how to drive.

I was starting to think that I had made a pretty bad decision in asking this girl out. After my third beer, I asked the waitress for the check.

"Why don't we stop on the way home and get a twelve pack?" Stacy offered. "My roommate promised me that she would go out tonight, and we could get to know each other better."

A twelve pack? No arguments about getting drunk? I suddenly did not want to give up on this relationship.

I woke up the next morning in her bed with a killer headache and no idea where I was or who I was with. I quickly realized that I needed to get sick.

By the time I had deposited the remnants of last night in a stranger's bathroom, my head cleared up enough to recreate the previous evening. While there were apparently plenty of highlights, I wanted to forget most of them. Or at least remember some of them. I was locked in the bathroom of some girl that I just met, feeling like I was hit by a bus.

By the time I sheepishly exited the bathroom, Stacy was already up and making bacon and eggs. "Good morning, you lightweight," she teased. "It's bad when you can't keep up with a girl!"

"What time is it?"

"About ten. You passed out about midnight. I really thought you could hold your alcohol better than you did. But, damn, even drunk, you took me for a ride!"

"I need to get home," I pleaded. I needed to pack for a trip the following day.

After breakfast, I made my way to the door. She stopped me before I got there with a long, deep kiss. "Not so fast. You promised me another ride this morning!" She put my hand up her t-shirt with one hand, and started unbuckling my pants with the other. Fifteen minutes later, as she was pulling her pants back on, she asked me to call her when I got back from my trip.

I stopped by Mike's house on my way home to tell him about the previous night. I was still pretty much hungover when he answered the door. I was unsure how I felt about what just happened. I found Stacy to be a really nice girl, but with a lot of baggage. I could see that the lack of a job meant that she probably would need a sugar daddy. Barely able to pay my own bills, I did not relish having to help her at some point pay her rent too.

Then there was the fact that she didn't speak to her own family. I was generally close to my own family (at least in my own mind). I could only imagine the family dynamics and the ongoing headaches relating to them.

But there was also the sex. I actually felt bad about the concept of not seeing her again after what had just happened.

Mike had a different theory. "You are just happy that you might have a new drinking partner."

"What are you talking about? Yeah, I got drunk. So what? She did too."

"That's the last thing you need. If she can pound them like that, she has some sort of issue too. And she got married to someone because she was drunk? That doesn't concern you?"

"I just said it did."

"Because it is something you wouldn't ever think to do. Did you ever think that she might not have done it if she hadn't been drunk? That maybe the drinking was the problem, not the fact that she did it? Could there be a problem?"

I was getting upset. "Look, I know you're concerned about me drinking, and I appreciate that. I truly do, even if I don't like being reminded about it every fucking time I see you. But to tell me that some girl that you never met has a problem? That's kind of over the line, dude."

"You came to me for advice. I'm just telling you what I think. If it's not what you wanted to hear, that's on you."

The next weekend was similar. On Saturday I went to her apartment, and we stopped at the store to get some microwave food and a twelve of Genny. Once again, she stopped me at the door with sex before I drove home very much under the influence.

This incident actually registered with me. I had never driven drunk before, but the drinking was the only thing I had in common with her. (Okay, and the sex.) I knew that if I were to see her again, I would end up downing a few, which usually meant downing QUITE a few. I called her the following night.

"Stacy, I don't know that I can do this anymore. I'm actually kind of scared to see you again. It seems all we ever do is drink. I don't want to go down that road."

"Oh, so I'm the bad influence?" she asked, hurt. "It's not like you advertised yourself as a saint. You were looking for someone to party with, I think your letter said. I'm just trying to be that girl you were looking for. Now all of a sudden, I'm a bad influence?"

"I'm just creeped out at how the other night turned out."

She talked me into coming over to pick her up Saturday night to come to my apartment. She ended up spending the night because, even after my brief epiphany a few days earlier, I was too messed up again to take her home.

A coworker of mine was getting married in the near future. I had been worried about who I was going to take as a date, so that morning, I asked Stacy if she would come with me.

"I don't really have anything to wear," she protested.

"Just wear a simple dress," I suggested. "It's not going to be very fancy, but they should have good food. And of course, an open bar."

"No, you don't get it. I don't own a dress."

"So we'll go get you one."

So that day, we went to a department store and bought her a dress. A low-cut, short black dress and some five-inch heels to go with it. And we went to the wedding, and proceeded to get drunk. Very drunk.

Once again, I woke up in my apartment with my suit crumpled in a corner next to her new dress. I felt different somehow, though. I was still massively hungover. That was familiar. But something had changed.

On Monday, I was immediately called into my boss's office. After shutting the door, I was warned about my behavior the previous Saturday. Specifically, when I left the party drunk and got in the car. My boss had told Stacy and me that he would drive us home. We declined, at which point he insisted. Stacy informed my boss that he needed to "mind his own fucking business." I had called him an asshole, and we left. I remembered none of this.

After signing the warning letter that went into my file, I was given the number for the employee help line for alcohol abuse and was told that I was to call it.

I stopped seeing Stacy that week.

Chapter 14:
Healing

Suggested Listening:
"Separate Ways (Worlds Apart)" – Journey
"No Son of Mine" – Genesis

Death and life are in the power of the tongue;
those who love it will eat its fruit.
Proverbs 18: 21 (WEB)

I continued looking at the personal ads while I was dating Stacy, but no one else ever responded. I stopped sending out letters after Stacy and I parted ways, figuring it was best not to get involved again.

I spoke with a friendly counselor about my drinking. I convinced her that my relationship with Stacy was to blame, and that I had broken it off. She seemed okay with this turn of events, and reported back to my boss that I was no longer at risk. She provided me with a number to call if I ever felt myself slipping into my old habits.

I actually did stop drinking at that point. Not willingly, but I had been scared senseless. That was the second or third time that I had no recollection of something major happening in my life because of my alcohol intake. I wanted to prove to myself and to everyone that I could stop anytime that I wanted to.

Besides, I was out of town so often, no one knew that I was having one or two on the road. To their eyes, I had stopped. Even Mike was happy with the new me.

Waking up (relatively) sober one Sunday, I grabbed the paper to read the sports section and the comics. Bloom County and Calvin and Hobbes were the only reason I got the paper. Even at my worst, I couldn't get through Sunday morning without a cup of coffee and these two friends. After a good laugh, I switched to the sports.

There was an especially lengthy article that morning about ownership of the Sabres and their recent playoff drought. Rumors were circulating that there was going to be a significant shake-up, and the article recapped how the team had gotten to that point. The article started on the front page of the sports section, and continued on page 10. I turned to page 10 to finish the article.

On the facing page were wedding announcements. Looking at me from page 11, beautiful in her simple dress and veil, was Jenny. Except now her name was reported to be Jennifer Whitehall. According to the article, Mark Whitehall and the former Jennifer Keller were married the previous evening in Amherst in an Episcopalian ceremony, and were making their way to Hawai'i for their honeymoon.

Her smile was radiant as she looked slightly to my left. I froze. The paper fell to the ground.

I was over her, damn it! I hadn't seen her in over six months. Since the divorce. I had gotten on with my life. I didn't need her!

I picked up the paper and looked again. She was making a mistake. I knew that right away. Anyone could see it. I had to let her know!

I picked up the phone and called Mike Wolf. He would know what to do.

His mom informed me that Mike was still asleep, as Cristal Myst had played last night. I told his mom it was an emergency.

A groggy "What's going on?" soon responded from the other end of the line.

"Look at page 11 of the sports section," I implored.

"Did the Sabres fire their coach? Dude, you didn't need to wake me up for that," Mike groused.

"Jenny," was all I responded.

"Shit." I heard the phone get put down, and footsteps recede. A minute later, the phone was picked up again. "I'm sorry, Matt. Are you okay?"

"I've gotta get a hold of her. This can't happen."

"Matt, it already happened. You need to accept this."

"No, I don't, you bastard! That is my WIFE," I screamed. And hung up the phone.

Looking desperately in the fridge for a beer and finding none, I grabbed my coat and ran to the car. A quick trip to Wegmans would help me take the edge off while I figured out what my next steps were going to be.

The signs throughout the beer section were definitive. No beer sales until noon. I grabbed a twelve pack of Labatts and took it to the cashier anyway.

"I'm sorry, sir. No beer sales until noon," she informed me politely.

"Listen, bitch, I need this."

Taken aback, she not so politely repeated her previous statement.

"Sell me the fucking BEER, you bitch!"

"Sir…"

"NOW!"

Needless to say, this behavior drew more than a little attention. The manager and a few other people were quickly on their way to the register to assist the poor cashier. Seeing this, I left the beer where it was and started leaving the store.

"It's all right, I'm leaving," I said as the manager approached me. "Sorry, bad day."

The cashier, manager, and a half dozen customers watched me as I made my way out of the store.

My hands were shaking by the time I got back to the car. I slammed it into gear to get back to my apartment.

Mike's car was already sitting in front. Damn, that was fast. I couldn't take him just now, so I kept right on driving.

I made the drive to Jenny's old apartment in less than 10 minutes. Normally, this would have taken closer to 20. There was a car in the driveway. Pulling in front, I walked to the door and rang the bell to the upper apartment.

A woman answered the door wearing a robe. "Can I help you?" she asked warily.

"Yeah, where is Jenny?"

"Are you sure you have the right house, sir? There is no one here by that name."

Pushing past her, I ran up the stairs yelling "Jenny! Jenny!"

The woman followed up screaming at me. "Get out of this house, you crackpot!"

It was obvious that this woman lived alone, and no one else was in the apartment. Realizing what I was doing, I apologized profusely and ran to the car to get out of there.

After two hours of driving around South Buffalo looking for any sign of her, I resigned myself to the fact that I had lost her. Now the early afternoon, I went to a Tops store, and belatedly bought my twelve pack of Labatt.

I called Mike when I got back home. Pat and Mike were at my apartment five minutes later to calm me down. I had already downed two beers and was working on the third by the time they got there.

Although they took the paper from me to remove the evidence of what drove me over the edge, I had already purchased 10 more copies at Tops with the beer, and had them in the car.

§§§

While I was struggling to put my own life in order, I started to have problems with my Mom. One visit, Mom started telling me about Dad's mistress.

Dad had been retired for nearly three years when he was diagnosed with emphysema. He had worked at the same company for over 40 years. His shift all that time, except when he was out on strike, was from 7 AM until 3:30 PM. You could set a clock to his actions each day. He got up at 6 to start a pot of coffee. He would crawl back into bed for 15 minutes while the coffee brewed, at which point he would get up, pour himself a cup and go into the bathroom to dress, shave and wash up. Then he would fill a thermos, pack a lunch and be out the door at 6:40.

In the afternoon, he would be home between 3:40 and 3:45 depending on traffic. If he ever got home as late as 3:50, it would have set off warning bells with me, because I counted on him being punctual in case I had the stereo blasting.

On this visit, Mom informed me, with Dad in the room, that Dad had been seeing a mistress since before they got married over 40 years earlier. He stopped by her house on his way home from work literally every day for a beer and sex. He went there every weekend day, too. In fact, I was told, he missed part of my wedding because he left during the ceremony to see his mistress.

During all of this, Dad just sat there sadly shaking his head. If he tried to say anything, she would tell him to shut up because I needed to know this.

"Mom, that's impossible. I was home every day from school, so I know first-hand that he was home 15 minutes after work every day. I saw it with my own eyes."

"He never worked until 3:30. That was just another lie he told you so you wouldn't suspect anything."

"Even if that were the case, that doesn't leave much time to do what you are accusing him of."

"A guy only needs two minutes to do what he needs to do," she countered. "He never took that long with me. I don't know why she stayed with him that long. She must really be a hoor." (Mom did not have her sexual terms down.)

"And he was at my wedding. We have pictures of Jenny dancing with him." I pointed to a portrait of our entire family taken at the wedding. "Look, there he is."

"That was after he came back from doing it."

"He is in his late 60's. He has emphysema and needs oxygen just to breathe. He had hernia surgery ten years ago and had a testicle removed. It's not physically possible."

"Men can do their thing even without a wiener."

My siblings were in disbelief, until they heard the story too. Only in their versions, Dad actually had the mistress at his own wedding and spent the night with her instead of Mom. Plus, the mistress was the only one listed in Dad's will, and Mom was afraid that the mistress would kill her someday. Never mind that my sister Jackie was the executrix of Mom and Dad's will, and knew that there was no unknown, outside party mentioned in it.

Mom soon had Dad going to counseling to discuss their problems.

Mom quit going after a few sessions when the counselor tried to show her the shortfalls to her accusations. "Your father paid her to not listen to me. She was a quack anyways."

We asked her to stop talking about Dad. None of us believed her. "Fine, take his side. You've been doing that your entire lives." We told her that even if it were true, we did not need to hear it. "You need to know what an awful man your father is." It was becoming a challenge to go to her house, but we needed to because Dad was now not allowed to leave the house. Mom was sure that the only reason he left was to see the "hoor."

The day after I saw Jenny's wedding announcement, it was off to another nowhere town in a part of the country that most people never see to spend a scintillating week with ledgers, agings, and reconciliations. I took a copy of the wedding announcement with me. Upon arriving at the hotel on Monday night, armed with a twelve pack of some swill that I found at the convenience store nearest to the Taco Bell, I promptly called the number I had for Jenny.

Of course, the number had been disconnected.

I called the operator to have her look up Jenny's number. The operator had no record of a Jennifer Keller, Jennifer Christopher or Jennifer Whitehall. I asked for the number for Jenny's parents.

Jenny's dad answered the phone. Hearing his voice, I panicked and hung up. I would try again the following night, and hope that her mom picked up. Each time I tried, her dad picked up. I could not make myself talk to him. The third time, he yelled into the phone, "Quit calling here, you pervert!"

That Saturday, my phone rang. My sister Sara began, "Mom has officially lost it. I am NEVER going over there again."

"What happened?"

"I went over there last night to see Dad. He hasn't been out of the house in weeks. She starts telling me about how Dad has been beating her for the past 50 years. Ever since they have been married, he beats her at least once a week. Usually about sex. She said that I have no idea how many times she has been at the hospital with broken bones and worse."

"When did all of this supposedly take place?" I was shocked at the level of unreality I was hearing.

"Usually at night after us kids went to bed. Matt, you know that house. How small it is? Did you EVER hear anything like that? Did they even argue?"

"No, I never heard anything. And I would have too, if it happened while I was home."

"No shit," my sister responded. "And Mom said that we knew about it because we heard her screaming and begging him to stop beating her. The doctors told her that they had never seen the amount of damage that he inflicted on her in their careers. Matthew, when did she even have a scratch?"

"Wow," was all I could think to mutter.

"And her broken arm? That was a result of him being drunk one night and taking a baseball bat to her."

When I was in kindergarten, Mom had slipped in the snow of the grocery store parking lot and broke her arm pretty bad. She was in a cast for months.

"I was in the parking lot with her when she fell," I corrected. "Dad wasn't even with us. When did he ever go shopping?"

"I told her I'm not listening anymore. I just walked out. Matthew, I can't go back. I can't sit there and listen to these lies, while my father just has to take it."

"What does he say?"

"You know him. He just sits there. He can barely talk as it is, and every time he tries to defend himself, she just tells him to shut up. I'm sorry, but I can't do it anymore."

My next phone call was to my other sister Jackie.

"Danny is over there right now. For whatever reason, he can get her to calm down so that he can talk to dad. Dad has said a few things to Danny." Danny was Jackie's oldest son. He was currently in college studying criminal justice in the pursuit of becoming a policeman. "Dad knows that Mom is just sick, and wants us to try to help her."

So began the weekly sessions with the social worker.

It was during the first session with the social worker, a wonderful lady named Lois, that she recognized my drinking problem. The weekly counseling sessions were for me.

Jackie had taken it upon herself to convince Mom that she needed help. To this day, I cannot imagine the amount of strength it took to tell your mother that she is mentally ill. I know I could not do it. I do not remember the circumstances, but I would not be surprised if I faked being out of town or something cowardly like that to get out of being there.

But Jackie would not go to the counselor with Mom by herself. And being the only other sibling still on speaking terms with Mom, I was the one to have to go.

I have never liked confrontations. I have always avoided fights: at school, with Jenny, with coworkers. My first strategy is to just agree with whatever is being said ("You're right, I am an idiot," "Yes, I should have worked the weekend to get that done"). If that does not defuse the situation, or the situation does not go away by itself, my next strategy is compromise. Only then will I meekly confront the situation.

Can you now understand why my marriage didn't last?

I was going into a situation where we would have to confront a mentally ill loved one with facts that the loved one would not believe or want to hear. And if there was no confrontation, there would be no healing, no resolution. Even with a trained professional in the room, this was not going to be an easy task.

Coming home from work that Tuesday night, I did not want to face the reality of what was about to happen. If I couldn't tell myself the truth, how was I going to tell my mother? I stopped at Mighty Taco on my way home from work for dinner, then on to Wegmans to pick up something to wash it down.

So I had a Labatt with my Super Mightys. Or two. Besides, this was going to take strength I didn't think I had. So I drank a third for strength. And a fourth for luck.

The counselor, I'm sure, picked up on my condition almost as soon as I opened my mouth to speak. Of course, the smell of alcohol on my breath would have been a clue as I introduced myself. On our way out the door, she took me aside and quietly suggested that it might be good to see her privately about Mom. We both knew why she wanted me back.

After two visits with the social worker, Mom was prescribed some drugs that helped her regain some sense of reality. Diagnosed quickly as bi-polar, the drugs brought back the woman that we knew. At least when she chose to take them. Not perfect, but bearable.

The drugs didn't help change things with my brother. Mom still was adamant that his wife was out to get her, and until my brother left her, he was not allowed in her house.

And Sara was not willing to go back to Mom's because Mom would still occasionally let slip some comment about Dad, and Sara was unwilling to deal with those.

While not wanting to confront my problem, I decided to go back anyway. She had handled the issues with Mom in a way that made everyone comfortable, and actually had Mom admit a few things that we never would have believed. Things like her jealousy of his sisters and her disappointment in where her life ended up.

After I got home from the first session, I called Mike to get his two cents, even though I knew what he would say.

"You know what I'm going to say," Mike started after I told him about the counselor's comments. "You have a problem, Matt. Deal with it while you have an opportunity."

So before the next Tuesday appointment with Mom, I had a private session with Lois. I told her about Rob, about Jenny, about all the travel. The sense of loss. A sense, somehow, of betrayal. But I did not tell her about the blackouts on my divorce night, or at the beach with Laurie, or the numerous times with Stacy. She guessed those.

"Have you ever tried writing your feelings down?" she asked. "Journaling? Keeping a diary?"

"I used to write when I was a teenager," I offered. "I was in a band. I was the lyricist." That last part made me proud.

"Write a song, then," she suggested. "Write it about Rob. Write it about Jenny. Write it TO Jenny. See how that makes you feel. But write it sober!"

"I don't think I can write sober. I never did."

"Write Jenny a song, Matt. I want to see it next Thursday when you come back, and we'll talk more."

That night I grabbed a beer, a pen and a notebook. I couldn't face the blank page without at least a little help. But I came up with something:

> <u>THE PROBLEM IS WE'RE STILL FRIENDS</u>
> CHORUS: *The biggest part of love is friendship*
> *And friendship part of love*
> *The problem is we're still friends*
> *You're all that I think of*

There was a time, a time gone by
Of total love, of you and I
We'd laugh, we'd cry, we'd run, we'd hide
We'd fight it out, all side by side
A world of two in which the world was void
A private life which we alone enjoyed
That world was torn by the note that told
Of friendship held but of love on hold

I hurt, I bleed, I cry, I drink
I sit, I wait, I hope, I think
Why you, why me, why us, why him
A passing fad, a silly whim
You're sorry you hurt me, of what you did
You never loved me, you were just a kid
You made a mistake and now we must pay
The love is gone but the friendship will stay

BRIDGE: *So now I get the love secondhand that used to belong to me*
He gets my love, my laughs, my dreams, my world
All the things we made in a world that belongs to you and me
I get a friend; somehow, someway, I lose

I'd give it up, throw it away
Begin anew again someday
A love, a friend, a someone who
Would build a world, a world of two
Just when I think I'm in the clear
That I'm over you and I'll start from here
You call me up as a friend calls a friend
My heart is broke, you will not let it mend

I can say that, to this day, I am proud of that one!

Mike Wolf read it and thought it was good. "Why couldn't you write shit like this for Matthias?" he teased. Cristal Myst couldn't use these lyrics because they were only doing covers.

Lois, too, thought that this was a very good piece of writing. "Did you write it sober?"

I admitted that I had help from my Canadian friend, John Labatt, in composing it.

"Think of how much better this could have been if you hadn't been drinking. How did you feel writing it?"

I told her that it felt good to let out my emotions in that manner. I felt even better reading it the next day once my head cleared. I couldn't wait to show it to her and get her unbiased opinion. I was actually looking forward to my appointment.

"So are you looking for feedback? Acceptance? Approval?"

She found that train of questioning productive, so we went down that path for the rest of my 50 minutes. My homework assignment was to write another poem or story, but this time to commit to writing it sober.

Again that night, I sat down. I had specifically avoided the store on my way home from the appointment so that I had no temptations. And this is what came out:

> <u>THE SWORD AND THE CALLIOPE</u>
> *Again, again, forever more again*
> *Someday I'll fall as often one day I did*
> *And each time, each ride, every time around*
> *The twist of the knife behind their backs they hid*
>
> *Up and down, around, and back to the start*
> *Always forward to a place where I've been*
> *And each time, the wound – this time and the next*
> *Once more flows freely from some unknown sin.*
>
> *Sword of love: feather edged and razor sharp*

> *On carousel of hope you climb aboard*
> *Life works in circles, the end is the start*
> *The heart just healed pierced again by the sword*
>
> *Hope of love, fantasy ride, county fair*
> *Shows upon your face like the blood of a frown*
> *You do it again as the ride starts anew*
>
> *You only get off when the ride shuts down*

Horrible! I read it again the next day and liked it even less. I wanted to throw it out, but I felt compelled to show it to Lois that week anyway. To show her that I NEEDED the drinks to do anything of value.

"This is spectacular," she exclaimed. "And you did it 100% sober? You swear?"

"Yeah, but it sucks," I protested.

"No, it most definitely does not," she countered. "I'm not sure about it as poetry or as a literary work, but it tells me so much about your feelings. Let's look."

We spent the rest of the session breaking down some of my themes, my choice of words. She noticed the repetition, the sense of never changing. The underlying betrayal, the unknown and unknowing guilt. The overt optimism being sabotaged by my own mistrust.

She was especially intrigued with the final line of the poem. I meant it to be taken literally, as in getting off of the ride to go home. She saw the other meaning of me "only getting off" when something good comes to an end.

"Tell me about that line in particular," she wanted to know.

One more time, I was instructed to put my thoughts to paper. The following Thursday, she was the second (after Mike Wolf) to read:

<u>TO AN UNNAMED FRIEND (A PRIVATE FANTASY)</u>
Blue heels, blue dress, blue purse, red lips
That spoke soft words of past loves' shame
Red lips that nursed a glass of wine
Red lips mouthed words of past loves' pain

Red lips, red nails, red tongue, black hair
Which flowed and framed a perfect face
Black hair when stroked made her tremble
Black hair when touched felt like fine lace

Black hair, black lace, black night, white skin
Of me against tan skin of her
White skin inflamed by a real touch
White skin entrapped by her lure

White skin, white sheets, white sun, new day
Focused in newly-drunken haze
New day, New Year party over
New day – a dream, I'm not surprised

New day, new start, new dreams, blue heels
Are what remind me about her
Blue heels stand out in my mind
Blue heels are all I remember

I was starting to get more comfortable with this exercise. I was able to write this one without a single drink, and I (more or less) liked it. Lois liked it, too, because she wanted to know why I chose this subject. Specifically, who *was* the subject?

We spoke at length about some of my aborted attempts at relationships since Jenny, and why they did not work out. Of course, most of them barely even started, but she quizzed me at length about Katie and Stacy, bringing back my previous poem to see if I had somehow sabotaged those relationships.

The easy part was coming to an end. I had lucked out and didn't have a trip in three straight weeks, which was very rare. I think, in truth, my boss knew that I was trying to straighten myself out, and was trying to help me by keeping me off the road. Next week would be the test, though, a trip by myself to some Detroit suburb nowhere near civilization. Lois wanted me to stay sober by continuing my writing whenever I was tempted to get drunk.

This was one of the hardest things that I had ever done. I realized that part of the reason I drank was from the sheer loneliness of the hotel room. I did not like living with myself.

It was also hard to write because I had spent the day poring over financial data and writing an analysis of it. The last thing I wanted to do at night was think and write some more. Especially about the thoughts that I was having. What they said to me. About me.

But each night I sat down to write a verse. The verse turned into two verses, and, by the end of the week an epic poem that remains my favorite. I don't know if it is any good, but I know the effort that went into it:

<u>OPTIONS</u>
A cold and wet, gray April day
Upon which we first met
Just two people, man and girl
No ties – just a casual thing
A night out and a little wine
Some fun and laughs, nothing more
The kiss at the door meant nothing yet
Because your mind, not made up
As to Option Number One
What about tomorrow night?

A very clear, mid-May night – a dance

A prom, hers to be specific
A weak bond – friends, still testing
Not each other for its still too early
But feelings – a sort of
Does she or doesn't she; not unlike
Using a daisy to decide your romantic fate
But what the hell, present her with
The next step: Option Number Two
Will you wear my ring?

Snow falling on a late-December day
Christmas – our first; but of how many?
We didn't know because our link -
Like a toddler learning to walk;
Not strong, but trying and by its efforts
Getting stronger all the time until
He is sure and starts to run –
So was our future and with it
Went the Options presented to us every day:
Is the result worth it?

A warm summer, just-August night
A night apart with friends, necessary
But at times unwanted – but who cares
Because our bond; not quite that of lovers –
Is strong and sure. It will stand the test.
The test this time is of love: all-important
But confident am I that my love is safe
So we sit – friends happy with our fortunes
While Options chosen before by two
Are broken by one

A brisk but pleasant February day:
A day of hearts, flowers and Cupid's bow
Singing, springing to surprise new lovers
Apologies of mistakes offered and accepted
Makes the bond once again secure – our bodies

Offered to each other and accepted with delight
Make it even more so – make the question
With the ring so much easier to ask
Now comes Option Number Three
Will you be my wife?

Now is the time to think: to weigh the good, the bad
Other decisions are not quite so big
Because they affect only your life, because your life
Is still yours and not mine

A new beginning on an October night
The vows have been spoken, a new family begun
Friends from everywhere toast good health
While silver rings on crystal which prompts
A kiss – for all now see the bond
Made clear in white gold rings
Set upon hands which forever shall be joined
And so we depart – happy with our choice
And Options chosen again by two
Become a way of life

The sun has risen on a November day
Many hours ago, but we, ignorant of that
And of many other events outside of our bed
Bask in the pleasures of which only we can give
To each other – at times exceeding our limits
White gold sparkles still on hands
Now busy here, now busy there
Capturing sunlight as if it's ours to give
Options enter not into this
It is just great to be alive

Now is not the time to think, to wonder why
You have made your choice, witnessed by all
And things have still not changed: your life is yours
It is still not mine

We lay in bed on a September night
The passion long since gone and replaced
By words: of anger, of jealousy, not of love
Something must be done because our bond of gold
Like the soft metal itself has been reshaped;
No longer does it sparkle, no longer is it perfect
What has happened we cannot say but
Somewhere we grew apart, the chasm not large
And Options made we will live up to
Of that I truly believe

Again it's night, this time in March
We've been apart four months – I know
Because that is how long I have been alone
But this night, in one sinful thrust
Our bond is torn – as you knew it would
As you feel your adultery pierce your loins
I feel betrayal pierce my heart
And through simultaneous moans I hear
Options laughing and telling me: you ass
Why should you be different?

So now I sit alone and am reminded every day
By seeing them together, discreetly
Seeing knowing glances, hidden smiles – while I wait
For the ax to fall – her life is his, still not mine

It's April again, spring, sun, warm air
Still my bed is empty, hers is not – and rings
Both tarnished and in disuse – and papers
Legal, filed and duly signed – and dreams
Like the bonds on which they were built – shattered
No hard feelings and still we are friends
And upon her hand, which still at times
Touches me and soothes – another ring
Another Option to which she chose

> *Let's hope this time she's learned*
>
> *It will happen sometime: at night*
> *When I'm out with friends or at work, I'll look*
> *And be looking once more in the face*
> *Of love, in the eyes of both friend and foe*
> *Another joke or the real thing – a chance*
> *Which everyone takes, with rewards of happiness*
> *And peace; with penalties of bitter tears*
> *And in that face, I'll also see*
> *Options which I alone must choose*
>
> *Where do I go from here?*

Okay, deep breath. I know that one was a lot. But it was also the key to letting go.

When I presented Lois this epic (it took her a good chunk of our session just to read it) and told her that I was honestly completely sober during its composition, I knew I had made a breakthrough. I was able to tell Lois that I could now forgive Jenny, and that I felt confident that I could face life going forward. Even if it served up some crap along the way.

I also did something that week after my appointment that I had never considered doing until then. That week, with no drinks nearby, no friends or therapist to guide me, no depressing music on the turntable, I alone did it.

I sold my wedding ring at a pawn shop.

And so began the first chapter of Act Two of my life.

Chapter 15:
Act Two

Suggested Listening:
"Cliché" – Fish
"Take Away My Pain" – Dream Theater
"In Your Eyes" – Peter Gabriel

Who can find a worthy woman?
For her price is far above rubies.
The heart of her husband trusts in her.
He shall have no lack of gain.
She does him good, and not harm,
all the days of her life.
Proverbs 31: 10-12 (WEB)

Sobriety took everything I had, especially when I was out of town. The temptation to numb the pain was overwhelming most nights, wherever I happened to find myself. But I remained sober by writing: about Jenny, about getting older, about trying to stay sober. Not everything was a poem. Much of it was just random thoughts that had no organization, no cohesive themes. The majority of it sucked from a writing standpoint. But it kept me out of the convenience store and out of Wegmans.

Mike and Pat were heroes during this time, and I can never repay them or thank them enough. They made sure that we did things that kept me away from temptation. If I went to a bar to see Mike play, Pat was at my side to support me when I ordered a Coke instead of a Coors (not that I ever drank Coors, I just liked the alliteration right there).

Dating was not really an option at this point. I couldn't face rejection to begin with, but I was also petrified of something not working out. I needed to grieve, Lois told me, to come to grips with the loss of Jenny. (And the loss of Rob. I needed 30 years and to write a book to get over him.)

Lois had helped me to see my part in the breakup of my marriage. She helped me to see that the travel was just a symptom of a problem that neither of us ever noticed. She pointed out that we were on our way toward trouble long before I ever accepted that job.

We never were as close as we should have been. While we had our own sets of friends, and we thought nothing of going out with our friends by ourselves, the more serious oversight was when we did have time together.

We made no attempts to develop together. We looked to others, to parents and to friends, to give our relationship context. On Saturday night, we never stayed in and watched a video with some popcorn and talked. We never had dreams for the future. The word "family" meant our parents, siblings, aunts and uncles, not the person next to us in the apartment with the matching white gold ring.

Had I never stepped on an airplane for work, had she never gone to a bar where men hit on her, had we received the best marriage counseling available, we probably would have ended up in the same situation if we did not try to become each other's partner. Soul mate. Lover. Friend.

And we never did try. So she now had a different last name, and I discussed my drinking with a paid counselor.

Understanding this did not make it hurt less, of course. It just meant I knew more the next time I tried to find someone. Until then, I grieved and I healed.

I had two or three "dates" with some nice women that Mike or Pat knew, but none of them was meant to be serious. I appreciated some pleasant female company, but that was about it. While I found no one interesting at that point, I could feel myself, the real me, the one that enjoyed life, returning.

Mike and Pat had found a new watering hole during this period, the Buffalo Brew Pub. Newly opened at Main and Transit in a former strip club in Clarence, the Brew Pub was a casual restaurant that brewed its own beers (the concept of a microbrewery was brand new at this time). Patrons could sit and eat, order a few drinks, play darts, and most importantly, talk at a reasonable volume. Another wonderful feature was the free popcorn and peanuts in the shell, which you were encouraged to throw on the floor. The wings and the beef on weck were very good, but the real treat was the spiedies, chunks of chicken or pork, marinated, grilled, and served on a skewer.

I ventured to the Brew Pub one Friday night with Mike and Pat and a few other friends that Mike knew from Canisius. We all felt that it was okay if I had a beer while I was there, so I had the Brew Pub's signature drink, an Amber Ale. It was delicious, but to everyone's relief, I only had one. And I was fine with that. I had cravings for more, but was able to control it. I was more interested in playing darts and talking to friends. And I found that I had friends who cared about me.

I passed the test: a night at a bar where I came home in my right mind.

We became regulars at the Brew Pub, with each of us scoring our own mugs in their "Mug Club." My mug name was "Tek," so named because I had become a regular at Cristal Myst's weekend gigs, to the point where I was asked to assist with set-up occasionally.

For the better part of six months, I behaved on my field trips into establishments of adult beverages, never having more than two beers over the course of a night. I no longer purchased beer when I was out of town, unless maybe one with dinner when I went out with coworkers or clients (something I did much more often than in the past). My sessions with Lois tapered off to zero as I learned to control my demons by facing them with pen and paper or, better yet, with a friend or three. A human friend, not one in a blue can or a brown bottle.

Summer was rolling around again. One of my favorite things about summer was going to the campsites that my brother and sister had next to each other in the country. In the middle of nowhere, almost literally. To get to the campsites, you drove about 10 miles south of Springville, the southernmost town in Erie County. Taking a turn off Route 219, you drove another ten miles or more down winding country roads and past numerous churches and farms to a small town. Turning at the only stop sign, you drove up the hill. But rather than follow the road, you took the dirt road that forks off at a dairy farm. This dirt road took you about two miles into heavily wooded territory where, between two random trees, were tire tracks. Following those tire tracks for about 1,000 feet, you came finally to my brother's trailer on one side, and my sister's trailer on the other.

Needless to say, this is a summer-only trip.

In previous years, this was an excuse for me to get shit-faced with my siblings and whoever else was there. Sleeping it off in the screened-in porch off their camper, chasing away the hangover with another beer. Sobering up Sunday afternoon while cooking out, and heading back home to pack for another trip to some god-forsaken cow town.

This time, I only went up for the day, packing no clothes so that I was not tempted to stay. Which meant I had to remain sober, so I did not bring any beer. I mooched a couple of Gennys from my sister Sara that afternoon, but my head remained clear until I left after dinner.

Jackie and her family had made the trip to "the land" that weekend, too. While sitting out in the beautiful shade of the many trees gracing the area, our entire family (sans parents) sat and spent some quality time with each other. Mom had been better lately, with her medication keeping her comments in check and somewhat tolerable. Dad remained housebound with his oxygen, although he could now speak much easier. Sara and George had not spoken to them in months, and relied on Jackie and me to keep them informed about Mom and Dad.

Everyone knew about my struggles with the bottle, and were delighted with the transformation that they saw. They had not seen me sit through an entire afternoon relatively sober since I was a teenager. I smiled. Jenny's name did not come up once.

Sara was telling a story about work. "We just hired a new girl to do marketing for us. Matthew, I think she is from Canisius. You might know her."

"Is she single?" was my immediate response. That was always my response to a discussion about a woman.

"I don't know. She just started. That particular item didn't come up in the introduction."

"Is she good looking?"

"I guess…"

"Tell her to give me a call," I suggested.

"Yeah, I'm going to walk up to a new girl at the office, who I barely know, and out of the blue just hand her a phone number. There's nothing weird about that!"

My other sister, Jackie, spoke up. "There's actually a girl from Canisius that works with me too."

"Is she single?" I asked of Jackie now.

"Actually, she is. And yes, she's very pretty. It turns out, we're having an office party at the Lancaster Country Club in a few weeks, and she does not have a date. She's been saying that she is not going to go because she would feel out of place."

"Tell her to give me a call," I once again suggested.

"Do you really want me to?" Jackie asked seriously.

"Yeah, I guess. I mean I was kidding, but I have no problem meeting someone new. And it's only a phone number. She's not a psycho or anything, is she?"

The night came, the weekend went, and I boarded a plane Monday morning to see another area of the country that no one willingly travels to. After a week of spreadsheets and debits and credits, Friday rolled around and I headed home. With it being a beautiful summer afternoon, there were no flight delays, and I landed before six o'clock. As soon as I got home, I called Pat to see if he was going to the Brew Pub and, sure enough, he was. I was to meet him there about eight.

I went to my room to unpack when the phone rang.

"Is this Matt?" came the voice on the other end of the line. "This is Megan. Your sister suggested that I give you a call."

"Oh, um, hi," I stumbled, trying to figure out how to handle this. I had never had a woman call me before, and I suddenly felt more than a little embarrassed. "I wasn't expecting a call. I have been out of town all week, and haven't talked to Jackie."

"Is this a bad time?"

"No, it's fine. I'm sorry, but I don't know anything about you. You said your name was Megan?"

"That's right. Jackie has told me a little about you, so I guess I should tell you a little about myself?"

Jackie had actually given Megan a picture of me from the first grade, which was the only picture of me that she had. In it, I was wearing a light blue cardigan sweater and a clip-on bow tie. Hardly the persona I projected to most women I was courting.

"That picture was so cute that I needed to find out more about you," she laughed.

"Well, if Jackie's given you some background on me, then you know I'm divorced. Are you okay with that?"

"Your ex isn't still in your life, is she? I mean, I don't want to get in the way of anything."

"No, that ship has sailed. She's remarried, and I haven't talked to her in more than a year," I reassured her.

Over the course of the next hour, we learned quite a bit about each other. The conversation was easy, unforced. I could make her laugh. She could make me laugh. The kicker, though, was when the conversation turned to music.

"I listen to a lot of metal," she told me. "I love Dokken, Scorpions, that kind of stuff. I call it 'aluminum metal.' It's lighter than other metal, like aluminum."

"That's cool," I responded. "My best friend is in a cover band called Cristal Myst. They do some of that music."

"Really? I've seen them a few times with my friends. They're excellent."

"Yeah, my friend, Mike, is the guitarist."

"The really tall guy? You know him?"

"Yeah, he was the best man at my wedding. Sorry, I probably

shouldn't bring that up."

"I've probably seen you before, then, if you go to his shows. I've only been to two, so maybe not. Anyway, what do you listen to?"

"Probably stuff you've never heard of," I responded, suddenly feeling very much the geek.

"Try me. You might be surprised."

"My favorite band of all time is…um, Marillion?"

"'Kayleigh?' I have their album. I love it!"

I think I fell in love right there.

"I may have just fallen in love," I said out loud. "I like progressive music in general: Genesis, Floyd, Kansas…"

"I have a ton of that in my record collection," she continued. "I used to work in a used record store, and my boss would let me take part of my pay in records, so I have about 1,000 albums. You'd probably find a lot of stuff you would like."

Our conversation lasted more than two hours. It was pushing nine when we finally said our goodbyes. We had set up a date to meet the following night at the Brew Pub.

Hanging up, I hustled over to the Brew Pub where Pat and a few other friends were starting to worry about me. Over a game of darts, I recounted my conversation with Megan to Pat.

"I haven't seen you this excited about anything in years," was Pat's response. "It's good to see. So I guess you're not coming with me to Septembers to see Cristal Myst tomorrow?"

"You'll have to find someone else to babysit tomorrow, Pat. I've got a date!"

The next night, I put on a pair of acid-washed jeans (look it up, it was not a good look on anyone, yet alone a 250-pound accountant), a polo shirt, and grey cowboy boots. This was the closest I could get to a "metal" look, with the cowboy boots being a very recent (that day) addition.

In walked a 5'4" brunette, with the most heavenly face known to mankind and deep hazel eyes. At first, I thought that she was there for someone else, because I couldn't be that lucky. But she said, "Matt? I'm Megan," and the night began.

I couldn't take my eyes off of her. She had the most beautiful eyes of anyone I had ever met. She wore no make-up, it was natural beauty. Her voice was soft and gentle. She listened, laughed, and had me hanging on her every word.

She did not drink, but she didn't mind if I had one. "I just don't want to date a drunk," was her only warning. Luckily, I had my problem under control before I found her. Correction—before Jackie found her for me.

As the clock neared eleven, she told me that she needed to get going. She had to do homework for school Monday morning. She was a senior at Canisius, not a graduate like Jackie had thought. I asked her to please call me again. "I have to," she laughed. "You're my date to the office party, aren't you?"

I walked her to her car, where I gave her a short kiss. In so many other situations, I would have tried to slip her some tongue, but I did not want to mess this up.

§§§

Fast forward two years.

I had received a promotion at work to credit analyst, a job that reduced my traveling to one or two days per month. The salary increase allowed me to pay off much of my debt, buy a new car, and move to an apartment in the city that did not require shoveling or lawn maintenance.

After getting tired of playing cover songs with Cristal Myst, Mike Wolf had joined a band with two of the former members of Stryder, one of the biggest Buffalo bar bands of the time, who had just broken up. They were working on original songs and practicing for a debut in the fall.

Pat Hartmann had taken a job with Erie County. More interestingly, he had started a long-term relationship with Megan's best friend, Linda.

I had asked Megan to marry me in the most unromantic way possible. On purpose, by the way.

Megan's mom, the absolute, most wonderful woman to ever walk God's earth, loved me, and could see that Megan and I were going to be married at some point. There was no doubt to anyone about us getting married: me, Megan, Megan's mom, all of our friends, all of my family. Her mom, in front of Megan, gave me a family heirloom: a diamond encrusted, platinum engagement ring that had been in her family since the early 1800s. It was Megan's mom's engagement ring. But since Megan's mom was divorced, she saw no need to keep it. "Just break the curse," was all that she told me.

So Megan knew that I would be proposing to her. I knew that if I planned some romantic get-away, she would know it was coming. And where is the romance in that? Plus, being one of the most pragmatic people I have ever met, she would have hounded me about wasting money on a get-away.

So one Saturday morning, I stopped over at her house. Her mom answered the door and offered me coffee. After two or three minutes, Megan came down from her room in sweat pants and a sweat shirt, her long hair in a ponytail. "Good morning," she acknowledged tiredly, while carrying a basket of dirty laundry on her way to the basement.

Reaching in my pocket for the ring, I stepped in front of her. "Megan, will you marry me?"

As only she could do, she took this life changing question in stride. "Let me get this laundry started. I'll be up in a minute," she said as she swept past me and down the stairs.

Megan's mom laughed.

Better men than me might have been shocked by this reaction (of course, better men than me would have at least tried to be romantic), but I expected something like this. One thing I have always loved and hated about Megan is that nothing is too big or too small. During times of life-changing events, she reacts as if it is just another day in the life. Unfortunately, this also means worrying about small things more than she needs.

Coming back upstairs, Megan took the ring, put it on, and took the empty laundry basket back upstairs.

I actually had to call up after her (with her mother standing behind me), "So is that a yes?"

"Yeah. Give me a minute."

Finally, she came down, gave me a kiss and said, "Yes, I will marry you. When do you want to do this?"

For those of you doubting her pragmatism in all things (including marriage), I offer this defense: when it came time to buy my wedding ring, she bought it from a department store. On sale. Years later, I discovered that she had even used a coupon. I was worth pledging her life to, but only at a 10% discount! Even "happily-ever-after" should not cost full price.

We purchased a house in Lockport, and moved in during April.

We chose a date in September for the wedding, we chose a church, we chose our wedding party, we chose our hall. It was decided that, because this was my second marriage (and because the hall would be cheaper), that we would get married in the morning and have the reception immediately following. She did not think my family would want to make a big deal of me getting married again, and most of her family was out of town.

In the end, this decision was lucky. Mike Wolf's new band, Armed and Dangerous, had booked their debut performance for the same night.

It was at the Odyssey, one of the largest bars in the city, and it was heavily promoted on 97 Rock. Mike had already agreed to be my best man (again) when the gig was set.

I had one more business trip to make before our wedding. It was to be a two-day trip beginning Tuesday to Albany. I would then wrap up what I needed to at work on Thursday, take a vacation day on Friday, and be married on Saturday. My flight was scheduled to leave at 6 AM Tuesday.

After dinner that Monday night, the phone rang.

"You need to get to Millard Fillmore Suburban as soon as you can," Sara told me. "Dad's not going to make it."

An hour or so earlier, Mom and Dad were in the garden in their back yard. Mom had always loved roses, and had dozens of them throughout the yard. Dad, meanwhile, kept a small vegetable garden in the yard that he tended while Mom cared for her roses. The light physical activity was good for him, and could be done in short bursts. When he tired, he could simply walk back in the house and rest.

This night, he simply collapsed. The ambulance arrived and brought him to the hospital, where he was met by both of my sisters.

He had passed away by the time I made it to the hospital. I did not have a chance to say goodbye.

My last time with my father was that weekend when I took him for his final fitting for his tux for our wedding. What would I have said to him if I knew it was going to be my last ever conversation with him?

I would have told him how proud I was of him for staying in a marriage for 45 years, especially after mine collapsed in less than three. I would have told him what a great father he was for raising four productive kids, three of whom also had long-lasting marriages and wonderful kids of their own. I would have thanked him for providing a loving and safe home from the sweat of his brow, even when it meant taking second jobs to make ends meet. And I would have told him that I loved him. I don't know that I ever said that. Ever.

Instead, I just said, "See ya Saturday" as he stepped from the car that final time.

I was allowed to see him when I got to the hospital. My siblings had left the room, and in the silence I simply held his cold hand and cried.

I walked back out to the waiting room. Mom had gone outside for a smoke, so I saw her for the first time since I got there. "Glad to see you finally made it," was her greeting. She looked at my siblings and asked, "How much longer do we gotta be here?"

That night, Megan and I talked about postponing the wedding, which was to be in five days. We knew that it would be both a hassle and additional expense, but who would want to celebrate a wedding under these circumstances? Maybe we could go through with the ceremony, but postpone the reception.

I brought this up with my sisters the next day. "Absolutely not," was Sara's response. "You think Dad would have wanted us to mope around? We will have had time to process this, and it would be good for everyone to have fun and to celebrate life!"

Once the funeral ended on Thursday, Megan and I had to leave immediately to pick up out of town guests, and to get ready for our wedding rehearsal and dinner that night. Funeral for my father: 10 AM. Wedding rehearsal: 6 PM. No emotional confusion there!

§§§

That Saturday, in one of the back rooms of the church, the photographer took a posed picture of Mike and me looking at our watches with smiles on our faces. Megan's father walked in to shake my hand and to tell me how happy he was that I was joining the family. The groomsmen straightened their ties and go out to the sanctuary to seat people, joined shortly by Mike and my soon-to-be father-in-law.

I was left alone. Wrong. I still had my thoughts.

I'd been here before. Staring down my future, seeing my dreams come true. Dreams that once turned into nightmares.

My bride breaking my heart. One of my groomsmen drowning. My Dad dying, my Mom losing her grip on reality.

And now, another future was on the other side of that door. Scarier than any horror movie, it sat lurking. Another character in a real-life drama. Having attacked me before, it wanted another shot at me.

The only foe that I had beaten over that time now decided to show up again as well. I wanted a drink. No, I needed one. I could not go out there without one, just like I could not attack the blank page without one the first time. Just one. I swear.

Mike had driven me to the church. On the way, we passed liquor stores. We passed two Wegmans, and three Tops stores. Not to mention a dozen Wilson Farms and gas stations with bright, happy neon signs with words like "Budweiser" or "Genesee" or "Labatt" beckoning to me. But Mike wouldn't stop. "That's the last thing you need."

He didn't know, couldn't know, what I was feeling right then. The unknown waiting to take away my happiness. To knock me down and strip me of my dignity again, my new-found confidence. *Again, again, forevermore again.* Was this the first strike? I could handle wrecking my own life (I was already a pro at that), but I could not ruin Megan's life too. I loved her too much. I loved her SO much.

We had dated for more than two years, falling in love with each other a little bit more each day. There was no suddenly-burning flame between us, which I thought was encouraging. Instead, there was a slowly building ember, sparking at appropriate times, kindling and growing over time to a brightly burning fire. There were white-hot coals in there, no doubt, but we always found new branches to add to keep the rest of the flames alive. Rains had come along the way, and still the fire burned.

So where was this feeling, this fear, coming from? I needed help to find the source. And the only way I knew how to free my mind, to think, to face myself, had names like Jack Daniels or John Labatt, or Genesee. And they were abandoning me, leaving me to myself.

Genesee. Jenny C. Jenny Christopher. Stop it!

There was a stranger named The Future outside that door, awaiting me on the altar. *I'll look and be looking once more in the face of love, in the eyes of both friend and foe.* I had even written about him, but, now that he was here, I couldn't face him. The only face I could envision wore a hockey mask and carried a knife. *And each time, each ride, every time around/ The twist of the knife behind their backs they hid.*

And somewhere, in a room close to mine, my beloved sat with her friends, facing the same future. What was she thinking, she who was more in touch with reality? Did she see the stranger outside the door as a friend or a foe? Did she welcome him or fear him? Or did she not see him at all?

We had been living together for five months, but she had spent last night at her mom's to honor the tradition to not let the groom see his bride until the altar. I don't know how she slept, if she slept. I did not sleep much.

I could use some support now. Some encouragement. Some medication.

Or Dad.

But Mike came back at that point with his perfect hair and his alligator-skin boots. "I just saw Megan. Damn, you are marrying one smokin' hot woman, Matt. She looks beautiful."

And my groomsmen came in laughing at some unknown joke. They put their arms around me. "It's showtime, dude!"

And I walked, supported by lifelong friends, to meet The Future head on.

But The Future was about to get a few shots in before this story ends.

Chapter 16:
Real Life (a.k.a. Becoming an Actual Adult)

Suggested Listening:
"I'm An Adult Now" – The Pursuit of Happiness
"I Walk Beside You" – Dream Theater

Weeping may stay for the night,
but joy comes in the morning.
Psalm 30: 5b (WEB)

Megan and I had followed our quiet marriage ceremony by going to the Armed and Dangerous debut that evening. The entire wedding party showed up, including Mike Wolf who, from the stage, introduced the new bride and groom, the new Mr. and Mrs. Christopher, to a mostly drunk crowd at the Odyssey. The show was packed, and the crowd loved the music.

We set out the next day on our honeymoon: a romantic trip in a rented truck to Lexington, Kentucky to pick up furniture for our house. Making the entire honeymoon even more romantic was that we also got to spend our first week as man and wife at the home of Megan's father!

I've yet to talk to anyone else who has spent their honeymoon at their in-law's house. By the way kids, don't try this at home.

"Great news, Matt," Mike Wolf announced when I picked up the phone six months or so after our wedding. "Our demo got to the manager for Tora Tora and Tangier. He wants to hear more!"

Armed and Dangerous had quickly become one of Buffalo's premier bands. Sporting mostly original songs, their hard rock sound featured tight arrangements, a strong lead singer, harmony backing vocals from the other players, above average lyrics, and no shortage of energy. The guitar leads were split between Mike Wolf and another guitarist, each with their own styles. The shows were workouts between band and audience, with each drawing energy from the other. One of their few covers was a version of "Comfortably Numb" that ended their set every night. The song started faithful to the Pink Floyd version during the first verse, but kicked in during the second verse. At that point, it became a hard rock song, pure and simple. The outro became a guitar duel, sometimes lasting ten minutes or more depending on how it was going down with the crowd. So it usually went pretty long.

The guys had pooled their money early on, and recorded a four-song demo. Professionally recorded and produced, the end result was shopped nationally, and the song "Love Ain't No Crime" was played occasionally on 97 Rock.

"Cool. Congratulations. What does that mean?" I found myself asking.

"It means we're heading out to California, dude! Los Angeles! A week from Saturday. We have studio time at the end of the month in the same studio that Y&T records!"

I guess I was happy. After all, this is the dream of every aspiring rock band. L.A. The Sunset Strip. Record deals. Tours.

But I was definitely not ready for it.

"What about your job?" I asked. Mike had been working as a counselor for a local cerebral palsy organization. "How are you going to live out there? It's pretty expensive."

"We'll figure it out. We're going to start out by crashing at the manager's place for a while. He's done that for a number of bands until they get established. I've talked to my boss, and he is going to make some calls on my behalf with some organizations out there. And we'll be getting some opening gigs with Tora Tora and some of his other bands."

"What about me?" That was not the right thing to ask, and I knew it as soon as I said it.

"I think I've held your hand long enough, don't you? Isn't that why you got married? So that someone else can look after you? Look, dude, I love you like a brother, but we both need to grow up. This is my chance. I was hoping you'd be excited for me."

"I am, Mike, but this is such a huge change. You've always been there for me. It's almost like you're abandoning me, and you know I don't handle that well."

"I'm not abandoning you. I'm chasing a dream. I need your support. You've always had my back before. I hope you still do."

The following Friday, Pat and I had a going away party for Mike at the Brew Pub. Megan and Linda were there as well, plus a cadre of old Canisius friends. Conspicuous in their absence were any of the old Chapel crew, mostly because they had left for greener pastures months and years earlier.

In my spare time that week, I had written a new poem for this occasion. In a broken voice, I read the following to the gathered crowd:

> <u>FRIENDS FOR LIFE</u>
> *Walk away, my friend, and do not look back;*
> *Your path and mine must shortly part.*
> *Look ahead, dear friend, stray not from your track,*
> *Look back in fondness to your heart.*

Each man's life, a road which others do cross
And goodness – how many lives touched.
As you move on – while I will mourn the loss –
Our lives did meet – thanks for that much.

Your road travels now to bright lights and fame,
Your friends left behind cheer you too.
And in the future, when people speak your name,
Think of us whenever they do.

Friends old and new wish you well every day,
And one, up above, would agree.
All of them hurt you're going your own way
But each hoping for what will be.

Walk away, old friend, it is not the end –
Our paths will cross again someday.
Follow your dream and catch your star, my friend,
Make us proud and walk away.

Tears were shed, beers consumed, and the following afternoon, Mike Wolf boarded a plane for Los Angeles, California. And another loved one effectively walked out of my life.

§§§

Two years later, I accepted a job with a small bank in Canton, OH doing the same thing that I was at Marine Midland. The difference was that all of the clients were regional to Canton, so I would be home every evening.

I handed in my resignation at Marine Midland, backed a moving van to our Lockport house, and moved my bride of two years to a new state where we knew no one.

Megan got a job as a bookkeeper for a family owned business almost immediately, and we found a cute little house about three miles from "downtown." The house sat on a one-and-a-half-acre lot backed by fields. Weekdays were spent working, weekends taking care of the yard.

We soon found out that the area was very close knit. And that we were outsiders. Everywhere we went, the first question asked of us was a polite form of "who are you related to?" Finding out we were from out of state, any potential conversation ended. Megan and I retreated to ourselves even further.

With the exception of her mom, very few people from Buffalo would come to visit us. Our only reality check was our monthly (if not more frequent) trips back to Buffalo to see family and friends. But the friends became more distant as we had less in common with them.

Now reading that paragraph, you might think that we were unhappy. That is not the case. We were alone, 250 miles from home. But we had each other. There were fights, there were tears, there were times we did not like each other. But there were some great times, too. We got to know each other at a level that I had never imagined being able to know another human being. Not knowing that it was possible, we found ourselves falling ever more in love.

Being out of Buffalo, I no longer had to visit with my mother. I simply did not show up when I went back to Buffalo. I stopped calling her. And she never bothered to ask me or Jackie, the only sibling with whom she still spoke, for my new phone number when we moved.

She found me through the U.S. Mail, though. One day, I received a very thick envelope that had been forwarded to me from my previous address. Knowing that it would not be good news, I sat down that evening to read the seven pages of vitriol enclosed.

I was told that I was not wanted, and that's why there were ten years between my sister and me. She was very sorry that abortion was not available when she was pregnant with me. She called me a drunk. She blamed me for destroying my first marriage. She expected Megan and I to follow suit shortly. She was waiting, she said, because Megan deserved a whole lot better than me, even though she was no prize herself.

What followed was an invoice of sorts, detailing all the major expenses that she had to pay for in my life on my behalf. She listed hospital visits, and told me how much Chapel School, St. Mary's High School, and Canisius College cost (even though I was still paying back the loans that I took out to pay for the latter). There was the cost of the Ford Fairmont that I wrecked, the cost of my first marriage (including Dad's tux), and gas for the lawn mower that I borrowed when I lived at the apartment in Cheektowaga.

"I understand that you moved again," the letter concluded. "That's so like you. You can't face the truth. You make a mess and you let someone else clean it up. Don't expect me to try to find you. You wanted to get away from me; that's fine. I want nothing further to do with you either. From this point on, I do not have a son. That should give both of us what we want.

"Have a good life.

"I'd sign this Love Mom, but unlike you, I don't want to lie."

I knew our relationship was in pretty bad shape, but I hadn't expected such profound hatred. But now, at least, I could focus on some of the happier things in my life.

§§§

"Are you sure that it's okay that he leaves town next week?" Megan asked the doctor. At 36 weeks pregnant with our first child, we were concerned that the planned trip to Dayton for the following week was cutting it pretty close.

We had moved into a newer house in a neighborhood north of Canton about a year earlier. This house had the benefit of being in a more traditional neighborhood, and we had gotten to know a number of the neighbors and become good friends with them. And because this house became a home, we finally had success in the next step in our five-year marriage: kids.

Megan's pregnancy was remarkable in the complete lack of drama. She felt great from day one. Her only vice was a weekly (sometimes more often) tuna melt at the local Friendly's restaurant in town. That, and one midnight craving for a taco from Taco Bell. Every doctor appointment brought good news: baby growing well, strong heartbeat, mother healthy. The doctor set a February due date.

In the fall, we had contacted a local roofing company to replace the roof of the 20-year old house. We signed a contract for them to begin work in the spring once the weather broke, and went on with our lives. A stretch of warm, dry weather was predicted, however, and the roofer called to start the work earlier. The Friday morning after the doctor's appointment, a crew of three men showed up at the house and started ripping shingles off our old roof. By the end of the day, they had removed all the old shingles and tarped the house. They were set to return on Monday. Weather forecasts predicted sunny skies and temperatures in the high-40s through the following Wednesday.

Now late January, and this rare out of town work trip had appeared for me. We spent the weekend getting the baby's room ready: setting up the crib, unboxing the monitor and making sure it worked, arranging some stuffed Pooh Bears and Tiggers around the room. Contrary to the weather reports, however, Sunday brought with it heavy rains, and suddenly more was predicted for Monday. The roofing company called to say that they would be unable to work on the roof if the rains continued. They had been out to the house earlier to make sure the tarps were secure, and that rain wasn't getting to the exposed wood.

Unable to postpone my trip, and with no doctor excuse to use to get out of it, I hopped in the car and drove the 200 miles to Dayton early that Monday morning. At 5:00, I walked out of the company and checked into the hotel room shortly after. Upon arriving in my room, I immediately called home to see how Megan was feeling. She was still going to work every day, and would be until the day the baby was born. The doctor saw no reason, with how good she was feeling, that she needed to change her schedule.

"Hey, babe. How are you feeling?"

"Matt, we have a problem," she announced. "A pretty big one actually."

She went on to explain that it had rained all day and the winds had picked up significantly. At some point, the winds had caused the ropes holding the tarp on the roof to snap, leaving the wood and the roof exposed. Upon coming home, she went upstairs to get out of her work clothes and to let the dogs out of the crates in which they slept during the work day.

"Matt, the ceiling collapsed. There is water pouring in, down the walls. There's all sorts of insulation in the dog crates. The dogs were soaked from laying where the rain was pouring in. I don't know what to do."

"Did you call Tom and Laurie next door?" I asked. "Get them over there now."

"I don't want to bother them. It's dinner time."

"Get them over there. I'm checking out and coming home."

These being the days before the abundance of cell phones, I had to use pay phones at the rest areas along the way. My neighbor, Tom, answered the phone when I called the first time.

"I'm glad you're coming home, Matt. Be prepared for a shock when you get here. Megan is doing fine, but you have a huge mess on your hands. I'm surprised she was as calm as she was when she called you. Your house is unlivable right now. You'll see when you get here."

I was informed during the third and final call that another ceiling had collapsed. The only saving grace was that the rain had stopped. Tom had called an emergency restoration company and they were on the way over. The roofing company had also shown up, and wanted to keep the restoration company out of the picture, but Tom sent them on their way.

Tom met me at the door when I arrived. Megan had gone next door. The enormity of the situation had finally caught up with her, and the neighbors gently took her next door, where she was having tea with Tom's wife.

Given the time of night, I was unable to see any damage from outside. But inside, even on the main floor, I could see water running down the walls. I was standing on a carpet that was completely soaked through.

Tom followed me up the stairs. The door to the baby's room was closed, and Tom guided me into our bedroom. The entire ceiling was laying on the floor: drywall, insulation, and wood chunks. Water was still dripping into the dog crates from the gaping hole that used to be the ceiling. I could see the joists and the underlayment that made up the roof.

Guiding me past the closed door, Tom guided me to the bathroom where a similar scene awaited. A much smaller room, the damage did not appear as bad.

"Brace yourself, Matt. Go into the baby's room." Opening the door, I understood why he did not want Megan in the house. Why he wanted me to see this room last.

In many respects, the damage was similar to our bedroom. The gaping hole, the water dripping onto an already saturated carpet. But the shock was different.

Instead of laying on the floor or amongst dog crates, the entire ceiling – drywall, wood, and insulation – had dropped directly into the crib. The force of the collapse had destroyed the crib, whose legs and bars were mixed in among the wood chunks and drywall. The water continued to drip where our soon-to-born baby would have lain.

The debris also buried the Pooh and Tigger stuffed animals. A particularly sharp piece of drywall was protruding from Tigger's neck, while only one of Pooh's legs was visible under the pile.

Wordlessly, Tom guided me out of the room and shut the door.

Our son, Derek, was born three days later. Instead of bringing our first-born to his new home, we checked into an extended stay hotel for the first two weeks of his life. Megan, still healing from the incision where the caesarean occurred and unable to drive, spent the entire day with him in a hotel room while I went to work. Once I got home, I took him in his carrier to the lobby to sit with him to give Megan a much-needed break. Her mom was in town, but needed to be at the house all day overseeing the repairs.

We were sued by the roofing company for non-payment of their bill the day before we checked out of the hotel. Upon seeking legal advice, we were told that, because the roofer had completed their work (after the collapse), because Megan had responded in a reasonable and orderly manner when she came home, because our home insurance was paying for the damages in full (to the tune of over $25,000), and because there were no health issues to mother or baby, we had no right to withhold payment.

Two daughters, Lyn and Maddie, followed in two-year intervals after Derek. They arrived in the world with much less drama. A new job offered us the opportunity to move to Pittsburgh. So on a rainy day in June, the five of us piled our lives into another moving van, and headed 100 miles east to the Steel City.

My mother had still never met her grandkids.

Even after the letter she had sent me, I had continued to send her a birthday card and a Christmas card every year. In it, I would include pictures and stories of the kids, updated address and phone numbers when necessary, and a heartfelt plea to patch things up so that she could meet the kids. Most times, I never received a response. One time, I received a letter similar to the previous one, except this one she told me that she didn't want to meet my "brats."

Megan's mom, in the meantime, was ecstatic to spend time with her grandkids. She would often come down to Ohio or to Pittsburgh for a weekend. We stayed with her on the frequent weekends that we went to Buffalo. One weekend, she took our two oldest kids so that Megan and I could have a get-away up in Toronto, where we went to the Hockey Hall of Fame and a presentation of the musical *Lion King*.

We now joke around that our youngest daughter is an honorary Canadian because of that trip!

Megan's mom knew about the problems that my mother and I were having. She could not understand how a mother could turn away from her child so completely. Of course, she knew that there was a good deal of mental illness involved.

She told me on numerous occasions, "Matt, if I ever get a chance to talk to your mother, I am going to tell her how foolish she is acting. I'm going to tell her that she needs to forgive you for whatever you did or didn't do, and to make it a point to get to know her grandkids while she has the chance."

While I appreciated her support, I did not want her getting involved in my mess. So she respected my wishes and stayed out of it.

§§§

In 2003, I read about a new CD that had just been released by an artist that I enjoyed. Newly departed from his two bands—Spock's Beard and Transatlantic—Neal Morse had just released his first solo album titled *Testimony*. There was just one problem: it was a Christian album. While I found him to be a talented and interesting artist, I was not interested in hearing yet another preacher try to get me to believe in his delusions.

When push came to shove, I still believed in a higher being, but not this "God" character that people tried to force down my throat. Megan was raised Christian, and her mom was very active in her local church. We were married in a church. We went to her mom's church for Christmas and Easter services, and we had our kids baptized. I did the minimum I could to keep Megan and her mom off my back. Megan never pushed me to do anything more, but she kept me in line when I got too vocal about my beliefs (or lack thereof).

In other words, I hedged my bets.

But I knew better. Over the years, I had seen the damage that religion had caused. Shortly after I swore off god, Queensryche released their epic *Operation: Mindcrime* album, in which they compared religion to drugs and sex. It quickly became my favorite album. In the 80s and 90s, the world was introduced to the greed of such preachers as Jim and Tammy Faye Baker, Oral Roberts (who claimed that god "would take him home" if he didn't raise $1.3 million), and Jimmy Swaggart. Shortly after moving to Pittsburgh, we were faced with radical Islam as the World Trade Center collapsed and more than 3,000 people died for "Allah." None of this counts the other unreported and under-reported crimes that have been done in "his" name over the years – abortion clinic bombings, beating up gays, pedophilia by Catholic priests, and on and on.

Thanks, Neal, but I didn't want to hear it.

Another one of my favorite bands, Dream Theater, soon released an album that I did pick up titled *Train of Thought*. While I didn't really like the album very much, I still visited their website occasionally to see what they were up to. It was there that I read a post from the group's drummer, Mike Portnoy, about a project he recently completed with Neal Morse. Of course, he was writing about *Testimony*.

Now I was a little intrigued. I liked Morse, and thought Portnoy was a fantastic (if overly busy) drummer. I searched the web a little further for reviews of Morse's album. What I found were very positive reviews of the music, which I assumed would be the case. I was specifically looking for comments on the lyrics.

Most reviewers were like me: not religious and not interested in being preached to. The reviewers were consistent in saying that Morse did not preach. He merely told a story of his conversion to Christianity, hence the title.

Curiosity got the better of me, and I picked up the album.

I agreed with the reviewers. The music was excellent, and I could ignore the references to god as a simple character in his story. Because it was a true story, the lyrics could be appreciated without a preachy feeling. I was less interested in the second half of the second disc, as it drifted to praising god rather than story telling. The best song in that sequence (other than the instrumentals) was one called "Oh to Feel Him" that had an extended instrumental intro (with some classic Portnoy double-kick drums), followed by a complete tempo change into a full orchestra. *Testimony* quickly became one of my favorites.

§§§

Megan's mom passed away on her 65th birthday after a brief illness. We were able to get up to Buffalo with the kids in time to be at her bedside when she left.

It goes without saying that Megan was devastated. She (and I) loved her mother, and knew she was a special lady. But we were not prepared to see all of the people come out to pay respects at her funeral.

She had spent most of her career as a volunteer coordinator of the local Girl Scout council. Hundreds of former girl scouts and their parents came, most offering personal stories of how she had touched their lives in some meaningful way.

She was always involved in her church. Parishioners came to thank us for all of her hard work and the hours that she gave of herself.

She was a caring neighbor. At least five of her neighbors came to tell stories of when she lent them a tool or watched the house for them when they went on vacation.

With three small kids trying to figure out what the loss of their grandmother really meant, and Megan going through the grieving process, it fell to me to be the level-headed one going through the ordeal. Or so I thought. I did not allow myself to shed a tear, believing that would show weakness. I did not want the kids to see sadness, so that they could remember only good, happy things about grandma. Plus, I knew from Rob's passing that grief only brought second thoughts, doubts, and broken dreams.

We interred Megan's mom in a columbarium in the church where Megan and I were married, less than 20 feet from the altar.

That is when god (I'm sorry, God) decided to return to the scene.

Chapter 17:
The Gathering Calm

"Oh to Feel Him" – Neal Morse
"How He Loves" – David Crowder Band

I can do all things through Christ, who strengthens me.
Philippians 4; 13 (WEB)

In December, about a month after Megan's mom passed and amongst the Christmas cards starting to trickle in, was an envelope with my mother's writing on it. Dreading its contents, I waited for Megan to get back from work before opening it. We decided that we would open it after the kids went to bed so that we could respond without having to hold back conversation or emotion in front of them.

I asked Megan to open it and read it first. As she did, I noticed that she did not seem to be getting as upset as I would have expected. In fact, it almost looked like she was relieved. Finishing the four-page, handwritten letter, she said as she handed it to me, "Matt, she is apologizing. She is asking for forgiveness."

In disbelief, I grabbed the letter for myself and started reading it. I was cynical and looking for any sign of Mom being insincere or trying to make me feel guilty about things. But for as hard as I looked, for as much as I could not believe it, the letter was an apology for her behavior since

Dad's passing. It ended with a simple statement.

"I know that I do not have the right to ask this of you after all that I put you through, but I would hope that you would find it in your heart to forgive me. Love always, Mom."

According to the letter, she was getting ready to send out Christmas cards and was going through her desk about two weeks prior. Doing so, she found some of the old birthday and Christmas cards that I had sent her in previous years. Opening one of the more recent cards, a picture of the three kids fell out, and she looked at it "as if for the first time." She described the feeling of a voice telling her that those were her grandkids, who would love to meet their grandmother. She felt this voice telling her that all it would take was for her to reach out in love, and that she could start anew. The feeling returned the next day, and she went back to the desk to re-read all of the cards, and noticed how the kids were getting older. The voice suggested that there was still time.

I called my sister, Jackie, the next day to tell her about the letter. She was amazed that Mom had done it. Being the only sibling that Mom still talked to, Mom had not mentioned anything about the letter to Jackie, nor had she asked Jackie anything about me or the family.

"There's only one explanation," Jackie opined. "Divine intervention. Megan's mom talked to Mom like she always said she wanted to."

Jackie's words sent a chill through me. I had no argument for her, but what she suggested was not possible. There was no god. Jackie was a believer, I was not. But she was not one to suggest that everything was "god's work" or "god's will." So for her to suggest divine intervention meant that she really believed it.

After hanging up, I went back to the letter. I was taken aback at some of the language Mom used.

The letter began, "I have been acting foolish. I don't know how I turned away from my child so completely." Later in the letter, she wrote, "I realize that I need to make it a point to know my grandchildren while I still have the chance." Reading the description of the voice Mom imagined, I could hear Megan's mom lecturing as she promised that she would if she had the chance.

Still, it was just coincidence in the wording. The timing. The fact that it occurred at all. This wasn't divine intervention. Sorry, Sis.

Regardless, that Friday evening after work, I cautiously called Mom. Megan sat by my side on the couch and held my hand as we tentatively caught up with each other and, weakly, forgave each other. I promised that I would bring the kids around to meet her the next time we were in Buffalo.

I cried in Megan's arms after the call ended. I had a mother again.

§§§

The very next morning, the phone rang. "Matt? It's Jenny. Sorry to call you at home, but I wanted to talk to you about something. Is it okay? I understand if this will cause a problem."

I had not spoken with Jenny in more than ten years. She had run into my brother and his wife at the grocery store one day, and asked for my phone number.

Jenny had always been a thorn in the side of my relationship with Megan, for obvious reasons. Megan kept the grudge with Jenny in the foreground, where I had done my best to bury it over the years. My thoughts about Jenny, when they came at all, had been reduced to those of sadness and of lost youth, mixed with regret. Megan's were of a woman who had badly hurt the man she loved. The call was so unexpected and unusual, I chose to bear Megan's ire to see what Jenny wanted.

"I was wondering if you would be interested in filling out some paperwork so that I could get our marriage annulled," she said. She went on to explain that she felt a calling to get involved in the Catholic Church again, and could not because of her divorced status.

"I'll pay for the whole thing, and it would only be filling out some forms. You don't ever have to talk to me or see me again. But it would allow me to get back to being involved in the church." Then, for no good reason that I could see, she asked, "How has your faith been lately, Matt?"

"If all you want from me is some forms filled out, send them my way and I'll take care of them."

"You didn't answer me, Matt. How has your faith been lately? Have you been going to church? Praying?"

"No, I haven't been. I'd prefer not to talk about it if you don't mind. What have you been up to? Where do you work?"

"I'm surprised at you, Matt. I've always held out hope that you would stay true to your faith. God could certainly use a good man like you."

"True to my faith?" I exclaimed. "Why would I want to do that? My world fell apart, and I'm supposed to praise the bastard that is causing all of the destruction?"

"Matt, don't…"

"First Rob, then you," I continued, now on a roll. I was not going to have another opportunity to talk to her, to tell her how I felt, to tell her what she did to me all those years ago. To release some of the pain that I had carried for all those years. "You'll never know how bad you hurt me. How long it took me to get over you. To trust someone with my heart.

"You know I tried drinking myself to death. To numb the pain. To forget. You, Rob, every kid that ever put me down, every woman that ever said no to me. Fuck 'em all, I'll show 'em. So I'd get blackout drunk. Then the next morning, the memories would be back, you'd be back, but this time with a hangover. And the only way to stop the pain, to stop the voices from telling me what a loser I am, to forget the fact that today is going to be more of the same, is to get shit-faced again.

"But I got my act together by myself. BY MYSELF! Your god went along on his merry way, and left me alone to pick up the pieces. And I did. By myself!

"You think that I'm going to worship the cause of all of that? No ma'am. I said goodbye to him a long time ago. I've been fine on my own, thank you very much."

"Don't blame that on God, Matt. You can blame me for my part, I don't care. I'm a big girl. But don't blame God. He has been there all along."

"Oh yeah, where?" I demanded. "At the graveyard? The courthouse? The beer store?"

"Yes, He was there Matt. He was at the altar with your new wife."

"Yeah, a few days after he took Dad away from me," I interrupted.

Ignoring this, she continued, "And when your kids were born. I heard some little ones in the background when you answered. And I noticed an out-of-town area code, so you must be doing okay at work. And has your weather been as nice as ours recently? I could go on, but I don't know your circumstances. All I know is that you have been blessed in so many ways that you don't even realize.

"So He has been with you, Matt. Whether you want to believe it or not."

She wished me well, sent me the paperwork she needed me to fill out, and hung up.

I don't know if she ever got the annulment.

§§§

We had seen Trans-Siberian Orchestra the previous Christmas with the kids. While we loved the music and the spectacle that their music brought to the Christmas season, the ticket prices made us rethink that particular event this year. Still wanting to do something music-related with the kids as a special Christmas tradition, we noticed that a local artist, B.E. Taylor, was putting on a Christmas concert at a church nearly across the street from our house. And the ticket prices were much more family-friendly.

Orchard Hill Church was familiar to us as the local polling place for elections. But it was this little A-frame building that couldn't have held more than 300 people. I wasn't sure where there was room for a Christmas concert.

Upon arriving there with the family on the appointed night, we noticed that the cars continued up the driveway. At the top of a hill at the end of a curvy road and hidden behind a stand of trees, was a huge facility where everyone was entering. We had never seen this building before. Over the door was a banner that read "Welcome to Orchard Hill Church." When I mentioned to one of the volunteers that I thought the A-frame at the bottom of the hill was the church, I was informed that was more of a community center for the church. The building we were entering was the actual church.

We walked into an auditorium that sat over 1,000 people. At 7:30, B.E. Taylor and his band took to the large stage, and the sound and lights were like any professional show that I had seen before. I wondered where they had the mass.

The band played for over two hours, doing some traditional Christmas songs in a unique format. "We Three Kings" ended with a rap (of sorts) by the guitarist (who also happened to be the guitarist for the progressive rock band Crack the Sky). "What Child is This" ended with a sizzling guitar solo. A percussion line from the local high school marching band came out for "O Come O Come Emmanuel." A full gospel choir joined him onstage for a number of songs.

But some of the other songs made me remember that there was another message to Christmas. B.E. sang "Mary Did You Know" and "O Holy Night" so beautifully and passionately that I realized his singing was heartfelt, and not an act. His between song banter reflected his awe at the gift that was this Jesus guy that Father Paul and all the other priests talked about. I wondered if B.E. could be talking about the same guy. Father Paul never seemed to go on about him the way B.E. was.

After the concert, B.E. and his entire band were available in the lobby to meet and to talk with. I wanted to meet him, and personally thank him for the excellent show that we had just witnessed. Upon meeting the family, B.E. said to me, "What a beautiful family God has blessed you with." After taking a picture with the family and thanking him for the wonderful show, he replied, "God bless your family this Christmas."

§§§

I kept having strange little experiences like that.

The Apple iPod was introduced to the world in 2001, but sales did not really take off until about 2004. It wouldn't have mattered anyway because I have never been an "early adopter" of any sort of technology. I still like my pen and paper, for example. I always print out important memos that have been emailed to me. "Paperless" to me means "less paper," not "no paper."

So it was closer to 2005 before I jumped in the water to buy my first iPod. I hesitated because it was going to be the third and fourth time changing how I listened to my favorite songs. I had at least three versions of certain albums, such as Genesis's *Seconds Out,* already (both Megan and I had it on album, and then we bought it again on CD). It took me weeks to transfer even a portion of my approximately 1,000 CDs to the iPod, and even then I only transferred certain tracks.

But I quickly saw the genius that it was. It was a radio broadcast of only songs that I liked without the commercials. With the shuffle feature, I never knew what was coming up next. And every now and then, a song that you had completely forgotten about appeared out of nowhere.

The first time this happened was while I was out of town. In a hotel room in Milwaukee, I was visited by one of my dreams of Rob Becker. I had not had a dream of him in months, but this one came at a time when Megan and I were going through a bit of a dry period. Not happy about my conversation with Jenny, and her working 60-hours-plus a week at work, and me being on the road frequently again, our limited time together was spent running errands and trying to have meaningful conversations about the kids and the never-ending issues surrounding them. While we still loved each other, I can honestly say there were many times in that stretch that we didn't like each other.

Rob was succinct in his message to me that night.

"God chose this woman to be your partner in this life, Matt. You are only good together."

"I appreciate the input Rob, I really do, but you don't know how hard it is sometimes to listen to her worry about some tragedy that hasn't happened yet, and probably won't because we are addressing it like five years before happens. I think sometimes she goes out of her way to find stuff to worry about."

"Could she be reaching out to you, Matt? Trying to connect with you? Is it really so bad? Remember, 'a man leaves his father and mother, and is united to his wife, and they become one flesh.'"

> "Yeah, and you know so much about relationships, don't you?" I regretted saying this as soon as it left my mouth.
>
> Rob finished the Mick Dark in his hand and started to walk away. "I'm not offended, Matt. I want what is best for you. WE want what is best for you. You will see. I'll be around."

The alarm went off and I awoke, feeling awful, like I had betrayed a friend. I could not apologize, which somehow made it worse. I got out of bed, showered, dressed, and went about my day.

The day was uneventful except for the fact that it was to be the last night at the hotel. Tomorrow my coworker and I would check out and head home. That always meant that we would have a fancy dinner, rather than a meal at a chain restaurant. We had been planning on going to a seafood restaurant that the controller of the company couldn't stop raving about. His description of the crab alfredo had me thinking about it all week.

But at nine in the morning, my partner for the week received a phone call from our boss, and it was decided that he would be catching a plane home that night rather than the following afternoon. I was suddenly left to my own devices. I no longer wanted to have a fancy meal, so, like during the Marine Midland days, I grabbed a six-pack and hit the Taco Bell drive-thru after dropping my coworker at the airport.

By myself in the hotel room, three beers down, I felt very alone. Not liking the feeling, and mad at myself for once again resorting to alcohol for comfort, I instead thought about doing something that I had not done in years: write.

I fired up my computer and found myself staring at an empty screen. I had no ideas to put to paper (or screen). Grabbing my iPod, I put in the ear buds and hit play. I had shut off a song earlier in the day, so the first line of lyrics I heard were:

You broke the boy in me but you can't break the man

And my mind raced back to a brown Pinto in a church parking lot in the rain in August, and a ghost singing the wrong words of John Parr's "St. Elmo's Fire (Man in Motion)" to me while I held the keys to the car in my hand. And to my discussion with that very same ghost the previous night. And to all of the times that I had dismissed the real-life version of that ghost when I had a chance to be a friend.

Words came, and were recorded on the computer screen. The words were sad, confessional. Not thinking, the words kept coming, mostly jumbled and incomplete thoughts, streaming through my fingers for more than two hours. Somewhere near midnight, emotionally drained, I hit save and went to bed.

When I got home, Megan asked me how the seafood restaurant was. I told her what had happened, that I had stayed in the hotel room writing. She asked to see it. I was hesitant, because I hadn't even read it myself, but I fired up the computer for her anyway.

Her expression went from vague perusing to purposeful reading nearly immediately. Within moments, tears started forming in her eyes and rolling down her cheeks. When she finished, she wiped the tears from her eyes, and, while still staring at the screen, asked, "You wrote this?"

A little worried, I responded affirmatively.

"It's…it's beautiful, Matt. What is it about?"

I took the computer from her and read the opening paragraph for myself for the first time:

I had never heard a ghost before. I've heard them numerous times since.

And so began a ten-year project to face a truth long since buried.

§§§

A few weeks later, I was on a solo assignment in Louisville, Kentucky. By now, I had made it a point to try to write a little something about Rob each night in the hotel room. Nothing profound was appearing, and I didn't want to start buying beer just to free my mind enough to get to a state where the words would come. The little that I did commit to hard drive was pathetic, just random memories really.

But it kept me from diving back to old, bad habits.

I was particularly down this week because I was by myself. The words on the screen reflected my mood. Frustrated, I shut off the computer, grabbed my iPod, and went outside for a walk. It was a nice evening, and I was along a pretty busy section of the city with a lot of stores and restaurants. I could get lost in a crowd and be by myself.

Ten or fifteen minutes into the walk, with some good Blue Öyster Cult and Montrose jams lifting my spirits, I walked past an Applebee's parking lot. Getting out of a car to my left was a family of five, mom and dad laughing with their son and two daughters. The father gave his youngest daughter a kiss as she emerged, the son asked his mother if he could order a steak. The sadness that I always felt in going to restaurants while I was traveling kicked in hard at that point. I saw a different reality of myself in that family, one where I was with my children and sharing in their lives. Not one where I was an occasional visitor. As my surrogate family entered the restaurant, I suddenly felt very alone and not especially loved.

I was reminded of a sick joke that I would occasionally tell my friends when they asked about my frequent traveling and how we dealt with it. I would say that I was always surprised that one of my kids, when I was keeping them from doing something that they wanted to do, didn't respond by saying "our other daddy lets us do that!" I never once truly felt that Megan would do anything behind my back, but I certainly could understand why she might want to. After all, I thought, I killed one marriage that way already.

My iPod decided at that moment to change tracks from the Eric Clapton guitar solo that I was enjoying to a much slower song. The song fit my mood, but was not familiar to me. Trying to figure out what song the iPod chose for me, I listened carefully to the lyrics:

With music all around, His spirit enters my soul

Neal Morse was telling me about the peace that a relationship with God brought him. The song I was listening to, "Oh To Feel Him," suddenly sounded realistic. In my solitude, I remembered, if not peace, at least the feeling that I used to have in church. The feeling that there was something special going on. I always walked away feeling dissatisfied, though, because nothing ever reached me. (Of course, that could have been because my thoughts were frequently interrupted by a reminder from someone that we needed a twelve-pack that night.)

But Neal Morse made it sound so promising. I loved music, but he must have been listening to something besides the organ music and centuries-old hymns that I had heard. I had never felt anything in the music other than a desire to skip nine of the ten verses that were inevitably sung.

I was left thinking that I would love to find the feelings that Neal was expressing in a suddenly favorite song. As the iPod selected a Rush song for me next, I started heading back to the hotel thinking about what it would be like for His spirit to make itself present in my life.

The next day presented its own issues, and the longing that Neal Morse had stirred in me the previous evening was replaced with deadlines, travel delays, and the reality of a family of five that did not include laughter and kisses all of the time.

§§§

The kids were growing up fast. Things like scouts and sports and school kept everyone running. My feelings of being a spectator to my own life caught up to me, so I took a job at a local accounting firm to get off the road to be a part of it all.

Megan felt that the kids needed to be exposed to religion, to at least hear about God. Truth be told, I was beginning to feel the same way. Not for the kids, but for me. I would never admit that, though.

So we started going to a United Methodist church down the road from us. For the kids.

Turns out, the kids hated it. It was a struggle to get them to get out the door on Sunday mornings. After a half hour of bribes escalating to threats, we generally resorted to physically grabbing them to get them in the car with us. Which is why we had the worst parenting moment of our lives.

This particular Sunday was the worst yet. Church was to start at 11 o'clock and here it was 10:50 and we were only in the bribe stage of getting them out the door. I made an executive decision, and grabbed Derek's hand and screamed for everyone to follow me to the car.

Finally on our way to church, I sped to try to get there on time. Megan was trying to organize all the stuff that we would need to keep the kids entertained, making sure that we had coloring books, crayons, and whatever else she kept in her magic "mom bag."

Five minutes later, at 10:59, we pulled into the parking lot. I breathed a sigh of relief: we would only be a few minutes late for the service. Good job. Megan turned around to give the three kids a last-minute warning about their behavior and our (limited) expectations.

"Oh my God! Where's Maddie?" she exclaimed.

Matter of factly, Derek said, "She's still at home."

Evidently in our rush to get out the door, we forgot our youngest daughter, now aged five.

"Why didn't you say something?"

"We knew you'd figure it out eventually."

Back to the car. Speeding back to the house.

About a block before our street, there was a commotion. Lots of cars pulled aside. A cop car with its lights blinking. A policeman talking to a little kid on the side of the road.

Maddie.

Once we left her alone at the house, she had decided that she would just walk to church. She knew where it was. She didn't care that it was a four mile walk down busy streets. She just started walking.

Neighbors called the police when they saw a "toddler" walking along a major thoroughfare unaccompanied. "I am not a toddler," Maddie told the policeman indignantly. "I'm in kindergarten!"

Long story short, we had a lot of explaining to do to the policeman that day. Almost as much explaining as I almost had to do a few years earlier at the grocery store.

At that point, Maddie had yet to be born. Derek was about three years old and Lyn still an infant in a carrier when I took them to the grocery store. Earlier in the day, Derek had been pushed into a chair by a boy at daycare, and had a massive bruise around his eye. Thankfully, the daycare had provided us with an incident report explaining what had happened.

As I was going up and down the aisles of the grocery store, a nice elderly lady saw Lyn in the infant carrier and asked if she could say hello. "Isn't she a little cutie?" the stranger asked in her best sing-song voice. "What a beautiful little girl!'

Looking up and seeing Derek standing next to me, she saw his shiner for the first time. "Oh my! What happened to you, young man?" she asked.

Without a pause, without a smile, and apropos of nothing, Derek blurted out, "Daddy hit me."

"Derek!" I exclaim. "Why would you say that?" Looking at the lady pleadingly, I stammered, "I never hit him. It happened at school, I swear."

But to no avail. Quickly backing away, the lady made her exit down the aisle toward the front of the store.

That was it for shopping. I abandoned the cart in the aisle, still full of our much-needed groceries, and took the kids and exited the store as fast as possible. The last thing I wanted was to be confronted by the manager or the police to explain away an incident that never occurred.

Regardless, after clearing up the mess with Maddie's escape from the United Methodist church, Megan and I decided that church wasn't worth the bother. So we never went back there.

But Easter Sunday arrived shortly after, and we felt that we had to go somewhere, regardless of the struggle with the kids. After discussing the possibilities, we decided to go to Orchard Hill. It was big enough that even if the kids acted up, we could sneak out without anybody really noticing.

Surprisingly, the kids did not argue at all about church that week. They happily got in the car for the short ride, and walked peacefully to the doors into the large crowd gathering in the lobby.

At this point, let me break from the story.

I do not expect anyone reading this to be converted to the message of the Gospel. I do not even care if you think I'm delusional for believing it myself. I was one of you. I had nothing good to say about people like me for a good chunk of my life.

I write the next part of this as a continuation of a story. But I sincerely hope that, perhaps, you might be interested enough, or feel a calling, to see if there is something to it. Or that it might be the first in a series of steps that gets you to the threshold of a church and in the presence of God.

Sort of like *Testimony* did for me.

A band took the stage, just like many bands took many stages over the course of my life. At bars, arenas, outdoor festivals, and beaches. Some bands that I've loved, some that I'd never heard of, and, occasionally, some that I even disliked. I remember going to an Aerosmith concert because I was given free tickets. I had never liked Aerosmith, but the amazing show they put on made me forget that I disliked their music.

I had no feelings about this particular band. I knew nothing about them. They were just a church band. Granted, three guitarists, a bassist, two keyboard players, a drummer, a percussionist, and a violin player made up a church band like I had never seen before. But they were a church band nonetheless.

I was quickly blown away by how good they were. An upbeat instrumental featuring violin started the proceedings. I found myself actually tapping my feet along with the music. And this was church?

The music continued. A choir took the stage after the instrumental and my heart was opened. The message, both the music and the sermon, landed on now fertile soil. And I heard it! For the first time ever, I heard it! God loved me! Who knew?

A small voice reminded me of something I had heard somewhere: *With music all around, His spirit enters my soul.*

By the time the pastor began his message, I was willing to listen. His sermon was on the Ten Commandments, but he tried to make them relevant to real life in our times. In our world. He would read a commandment and ask "seriously?" While the answer of course was always "yes," the fact that he questioned the Bible was so unique to me. He made it clear that we needed to question the Bible as well, and that we would be surprised by how well the Bible could defend itself. He made it clear that he did not have all of the answers and to question anyone who told you that they did have all of the answers.

The last song after the message was called "How He Loves." The feeling was overwhelming to me. My life changed at that point. Never since have I doubted. Never since have I felt alone or unloved. I see my blessings.

Megan and I became very involved in the church, attending bible studies, serving in various capacities, and getting our kids involved in things. The funny thing is that they never complained about going to church anymore, and now they volunteer as much as we do.

And so god once again became God in my life. And so it continues to this day.

Chapter 18:
Back At the Bridge

Suggested Listening:
"Jesus Friend of Sinners" – Casting Crowns
"The Heart of the Matter" – Don Henley

There is therefore now no condemnation to those who are in Christ Jesus, who don't walk according to the flesh, but according to the Spirit. For the law of the Spirit of life in Christ Jesus made me free from the law of sin and of death.
Romans 8: 1-2 (WEB)

Stacy's dress lay crumpled in the corner, near my suit pants. She was naked and passed out next to me in bed. As hard as I tried to sleep, the bed was spinning too much. Closing my eyes brought with it the need to get sick. I had puked twice already.

We had barely made it home from the wedding. I should have taken the ride from my boss, but Stacy told him to mind his own fucking business. Had I been pulled over, which I should have been, I would have lost my license. Which would have meant losing my job. I had no idea what my blood alcohol level was at that moment, but it felt like it was critical. At that point, I knew that something was wrong. Really wrong.

I ran to the bathroom to puke again.

As I walked back to bed with the taste of vomit still in my mouth and my head pounding, I looked at my tiny, filthy apartment. In my bed was a girl who was there only because she was willing to get naked, next to a bedside-table drawer that held a ring that belonged to the woman that I had truly loved. A woman that I had let walk away. The rest of the apartment was littered with empty beer cans. The bathroom and kitchen hadn't been cleaned in months, thanks to the fact that I was rarely ever there. My real home was generic hotel rooms in cities where I didn't want to be. I ate (and drank) most of my dinners with strangers. Or by myself. Or with friends. Same thing.

I tried to wake Stacy up for another round. Of course, in my condition, I couldn't get it up anyway. But she was there, so I might as well try. I didn't know how many more opportunities I would have. With her or with anyone else. Stacy was passed out cold, though.

I didn't want to lay down again because I was afraid of the bed spinning.

Instead, I sat on the edge of the bed. I was ashamed. I knew I had hit a wall. Rock bottom. There was no going any lower than this. Even for me. I was debating picking up the phone and calling Mike Wolf, but I knew Cristal Myst was still on stage somewhere. I decided that tomorrow…I don't know. What? I'd get clean? I'd ask for help?

I'd kill myself?

I was doing everything I could to kill myself anyway, but I was taking the coward's way out. I was killing myself anyway with my drinking. Why not do it for real? Like a man. Get it over with. Tomorrow.

No, tonight. Stacy was not going to stop me, after all.

But I had no guns. My only knives were butter knives. Even the medicine cabinet only had Advil and Pepto-Bismol.

I started to cry. I was even a failure at suicide.

Come to me, Matt.

I felt something. A warmth, a peace. "But I'm a loser. A failure. No one could ever love me."

I do. I love you, Matt.

"But I'm too far gone. Look at me."

I'm only a prayer away.

"You abandoned me before. You abandoned me tonight."

If I'm not next to you, Matt, it's because you went away. But I'm here now.

"I'm just drunk. I'm hearing voices. Leave me alone."

As you request, Matt. Lay down now.

I crawled back into bed, where the spinning had mercifully subsided.

Go to sleep now, Matt. I'll be back.

§§§

Many years later, a while after our first visit to Orchard Hill Church, the kids began willingly and happily going to church, and Megan and I became actively involved in church activities. For the first time in months, Rob came to visit me.

> "I'm guessing that you don't want one of these anymore," he smiled, holding a Michelob Dark as he gazed down the creek from the bridge. "All the more for me, then! And the great part is that I don't get hungover!"
>
> No one played basketball or croquet tonight. The path to the fire pit was empty. The ghosts were long gone. Except for Rob.
>
> The creek trickled slowly under the bridge, past the weeds and the scrub brush, on its slow journey past the fire pit and beyond. My mind was clear, as it had been for

years, but I didn't know why I was here.

"Because you still doubt," Rob completed my thought as he took a drink. "Because, for some reason, you look at where you are as an ending. Did you ever think that your journey is just beginning?"

He threw a twig into the creek. It started on its slow journey to nowhere.

"That twig just had everything it knows taken away from it. It grew up as a part of a tree, but it fell off. Maybe it was pulled off, it doesn't matter. From the twig's point of view, it has been removed from the only life that it ever knew.

"Now it's floating away. I don't know where it will end up. Maybe there is a dam somewhere downstream, maybe it will wash up on shore. But it is going somewhere. Are you?

"You are starting a journey, Matt. I don't know how it will end. But I do know that it is just starting, so it can go anywhere. Where is it going, Matt?"

"What journey? Things have been going pretty good lately. My life finally feels like it is where it needs to be." My dream had now become focused. I was alone in some generic hotel room. Hardly surprising. "Why would I start a journey now?"

"You are always starting a journey, Matt. As long as you are blessed to be on this earth, you are starting a journey," he explained calmly. "That life that you are so content with right now? That is your OLD life. I say again, your journey is just starting, Matt. Where is it going?"

"How should I know? This is the first time I'm hearing

about a 'journey.' Am I getting a new job? SHOULD I be getting a new job? What are you talking about? You must know, otherwise you wouldn't be here telling me this. So why don't you tell me about this 'journey' rather than being all mysterious about it?"

"That's just it, Matt. I don't know where you're going either." He slowly placed his newly finished Mick in the bottle holder, and did something I had never seen him do in these dreams before. He looked directly at me.

It was funny that I had never picked up that little detail before now.

His face was not as I remembered it. He had not aged, and his features hadn't really changed. But his face radiated peace. Calm. There were no signs of worry, of stress, of care. His eyes were dark, but in them was a well of compassion mixed with sorrow.

"Matt, I will not be coming to visit you anymore. My mission has been accomplished. You have faced yourself, and figured some things out."

"What have I figured out?" I asked, if nothing else to keep him talking. He couldn't be leaving! He left me once before, and, while I saw him less and less over the years, I had come to expect the occasional visit from him.

He placed his weightless hand on my shoulder. "You are writing a whole book about it, Matt. Keep working on your book.

"More importantly, you have once again accepted your Father back into your life. My mission was to guide you back to Him. He'll take it from here.

"I was called, and I went gladly. You, too, will be called

someday. Then you will see the whole story, the whole journey, and you will see that this is but one point on a long line."

He turned and bent down to pick up the empty six pack. Not wanting him to go, I exclaimed, "Why do you need to leave? You bailed on me once before. Don't do it again!"

Rob remained calm. "I ask again, where are you going, Matt? Where is your journey going to take you?"

Now I was angry. Hurt. So, of course, I had to lash out. "Great, I'm talking to an apparition who is telling me how to live my life. I'm dreaming you, you know! Because I choose to! You left me, just like Jenny left me. You bailed. Now I'm forced to deal with some new reality in my God-damned life. Something that even you can't figure out."

"Let me correct you on something," Rob said. "Your life is not God-damned. It is God-blessed. You and I would not be here otherwise.

"There are two sides to every story, Matt, to every bridge," he said, now turning back to the creek. "We're watching the water flow on this side. From here, the water flows past the fire pit to join a river and eventually the ocean. Where has it come from, I wonder? What is on the other side of the bridge? Where the water comes from?

"You are spending your time on the wrong side of the bridge, Matt. You're always looking at, thinking about, the source of the water. Look over here, like I do. Haven't you ever wondered why we always meet on this side of the bridge? This is where we can see where the water flows

to. I watch the water make its way forward. I look at the journey ahead. That is where the hope lies. No one can live without hope, Matt. I tried. It didn't go well.

"*Move forward, Matt. Start your journey, whatever it is. We'll meet again soon enough.*"

With that, Rob grabbed his empties and started walking back toward the Becker house, into an impenetrable fog.

"Don't go!" I pleaded. "I can't do it alone!"

A different voice filled the suddenly cloudy vision. "*You're not alone, Matt. You never have been, and you never will be.*"

Suddenly, I awoke. And somehow, I now understood.

I was back on track. While I thought I had finally reached the destination, I had just reached the starting line. All the rest was a course correction. Now the real journey could begin.

It may have taken another 20 years or so, but He kept His word. He saved a wretch like me.

Megan and I have been married for more than 25 years now. Ours is a happily-ever-after story. A blind date made good. We've had our issues, but I am married to the most loyal and faithful woman on the planet. To my best friend.

I still travel too much, but now I cherish every moment I have with her. Many are the nights that I wake up alone in a strange hotel room somewhere. I long for those nights when she feels me next to her, puts her arm across my chest and sleepily whispers, "I love you, husband."

My story continues, and I look forward to every page He chooses to write for me.

God is good! I take that back. God is great!

EPILOGUE:
FREE WILL

Suggested listening:
"What Faith Can Do" – Kutless
"Free Bird" – Lynyrd Skynyrd

For God so loved the world, that he gave his one and only Son, that whoever believes in him should not perish, but have eternal life.
John 3: 16 (WEB)

<u>MEMORIES OF A MARRIAGE (PART ONE?)</u>

…de mortuis nil nisi bonum…

Bitter memories to be exorcized
Over the course of a life
A brief love which flourished and had its day
And which then laid down and died
Tender memories to be set aside
And remembered secretly
A public masque to protect yourself
And allow good memories

The courtship, the thrill of the chase
The sensation of brand new love
The friendship: secrets, private jokes
Phone calls to hear the other's voice
The dreams which two alone can dream
The world which two alone can share

The first time, my folks were away
On their bed, middle of the day
The closeness, the sacrifice of
Virginity to growing love
The wonder of two joined as one
The passion two alone can give

The chapel, white gold rings exchanged
Kisses from friends and family
The wedding, all our friends are there
And toasting our health and good cheer
A party of two among all
Private party in public hall

The mountains, our honeymoon and
Our first attempt at family life
Waking to find I am not alone
Feeling safe in your loving arms
Our pillowed fort of lifelong dreams
A lover's linen sea of two

The snowstorm, five days together
With nothing to do but explore
The card games with the stakes so high
Payment and reciprocation
An igloo of newlywed lust
An act of God for two in love

One last hope, to wake up with you
After four months by myself
Florida, one last love affair
Finale to eternal love
One made two by breach of trust
One made two by misguided lust

Bitter memories are the public masque
The shield which must not be dropped
For friends take sides in a battle not theirs
But in which you need support
Tender memories are a sign of weakness
A signal that you've forgot
The pain of the wound to be cauterized
As if it's their's

...say nothing but good of the dead...

I wrote that poem while I was still going to counseling with Lois. She thought it was a significant step in letting go of the past. Of saying goodbye.

But of course, I never did. I never do. It's too easy to look back and see where you messed up, even if you didn't mess up. Sometimes it's easier to take responsibility for messing up than thinking that something happened for a reason. Because then you need to figure out the reason.

I now know that I was not ready for the personal devastation that I felt when Rob passed and Jenny left. I would like to think that I have gotten better about handling tough events in my life. I probably haven't.

§§§

One day, years ago and years before I met Megan, a letter came to my apartment. I have never told anyone about this. I had been divorced about six months and was drinking heavily. The return address showed me that the letter was from Jenny Whitehall. I recognized the writing on the envelope.

Luckily, I was just coming home from work, so I had a fresh twelve pack with me. Evidently, I was going to need it.

> *My Dearest Matt,*
>
> *I guess by now you would have heard that I got remarried. I'm not sure how you would have found out, but I am sorry that I was not the one to tell you about it.*
>
> *I am Jenny Whitehall now! A new name for a new future! My husband, Mark, is the guy I told you about when we were standing in front of the courthouse after our divorce. Weird, huh? He's great, Matt, you'd love him.*
>
> *But I know you, and you would not love him. Because I'm his instead of yours. And that is why I am writing this. To let you know that you are still in my heart, and that you always will be.*
>
> *But you also need to know that he treats me great. He loves me, he honors me, he cherishes me. All of the stuff in*

the vows. I wanted to let you know right away that I am in good hands with Mark. I am happy. You always told me that you wanted me to be happy. I am.

And that's what I want for you, Matt. To be happy. That's why divorcing you was so hard. I knew what I was doing to you. You may not want to believe this, but that whole situation hurt me too! You'll never know how much.

And it still hurts, Matt. I see things every day that remind me of you. I hear songs that we used to listen to together, see places that we used to go. I can't go into Perkins anymore because of the memories there.

At this point, if you're still reading, you're probably wondering why I am telling you any of this. I'm questioning myself too, but I think that you need to hear it. Hopefully, it will help you move on.

Matt, our marriage was a fantasy. I still don't think it was real.

What I mean is that you came along and saved me from a bad situation at home, from some pretty crappy boyfriends that came before you, from a neighborhood and a school that were often depressing and difficult.

You were everything I wanted: good looking, polite, intelligent. You were going to college. You were a GREAT kisser!! You were respectful and caring. I don't know. You were just everything that I had dreamed of as a teenage girl.

You were my knight in shining armor. And you swept me away to our castle on Ashton Street, where we lived in our bed and where you fought all the monsters and *dragons that tried to take me away. You fought them off, every one of them. The low paying jobs, the horny drunks, the overbearing parents, the unknown future. You took on each one in my defense.*

And for a year or so, you won every battle. Like I said, fantasy land.

Then you started changing. You took the job on the road and you weren't there when the bad guys came. You started drinking too much and were passed out before the bars closed and the real battles started.

Somewhere around that time, I woke up from the dream. You kept living in it, thinking that somehow we would magically end up in the happily-ever-after-land where you hid.

I wanted to go there too, but my heart had turned cold. Dark. Coal black. I saw you as a fraud. The monsters were approaching on all fronts, and you no longer saw them. I saw them all too clearly.

Many were the nights while you were gone that I fought some demon of my own making. And my hero, my rescuer, my knight in shining armor was battling the corporate world in a faraway land.

And I learned to hate you, Matt. I HATED YOU!

Of course, now I see that it was love. Longing. Loneliness. Not hate.

But by then, I had done the unthinkable. I had let the monsters win, Matt. The bad guys had captured me and stolen my heart. Darkened it. Hardened it. And still you had your multi-million-dollar battles that you were waging to help others get filthy rich.

I'm hating you again now that I think of what you cared about more than me in those days.

And you were oblivious. You still are. You think yourself the victim in what happened. That you are squeaky clean, somehow spotless.

Things don't just happen, Matt. You reap what you sow. And you sowed the seeds of my loneliness. You abandoned me to the monsters, Matt, while you swam with the sharks!

What I am trying to tell you is that somewhere along the line, I stopped believing. In them. In us.

I stopped believing that my knight in shining armor was anything more than an imposter. And through your actions, I went from being your princess, the princess that you were always there to rescue, to being just another peasant girl working in the fields. Just like that. Without you noticing. Without you caring.

My heart broke and I became an empty shell. I felt hollow. The fantasy died.

And you never saw it. Not once. You just hopped on the next plane that some faceless corporate bigwig told you to get on. And you didn't look back.

That, my love, is what I was trying to tell you on the courthouse steps. I knew that you needed and deserved an explanation. To know where my heart was and, more importantly, why. Why it was empty. Why it could not continue into the darkness that I saw, and that you were oblivious to.

My heart is filled again, though. Mark has poured into me the way that I needed you to back then. And I can love again.

I also can love you again, Matt. I regret the hurt that we went through. That I caused both of us. That we caused both of us.

There was a time during that period that I thought that I was just mistaken that I loved you. And I saw the pain in your eyes, and I damned myself for causing it. I wished that we never had committed ourselves to each other, made vows, that we then let break.

And we both broke them, Matt. You promised to love me, honor me and cherish me til death do us part. But there I was, and you didn't see me needing loving and honoring and cherishing. You went on and on that day at the courthouse about honoring your vows. All proud of yourself, you were. I hate to break it to you, but you broke your vows too.

I forgive you, Matt. You may not think that you need forgiveness, but you do. We all do.

And by writing this letter, I am hopeful that you will learn to forgive me at some point.

I wish you well, Matt. More than that, I wish you love.

I still love you and I always will. I will cherish every memory of ours for as long as I live, even as I make new memories with my new life. I will try to go back to Perkins and not be sad that you are not sitting across from me. I will look at my new husband (and who knows, maybe someday, my kids) and be in the moment. But in those quiet times, with a glass of wine and maybe feeling a little blue, I will remember your goofy smile, your stupid jokes, and your awful taste in music!

I pray for you every day, Matt. I truly do. I know that someday, God will bless you with the fantasy world that we almost had. But this time, it will be real for you and for the lucky woman who God has blessed to be your partner!

Heaven is real, Matt. But while we are still on this earth, we have to find what little slices of it are there for us. And love is as close to Heaven as we will ever get. Go find love, Matt.

May God bless both of us!
Love always and forever,
Jenny Whitehall (Christopher)

What I have learned with the help of Rob, of time, of Megan, and of God (now a capital "G" once again), is that there is always a path forward. A future. And, unlike a previous version of myself who was always trying to figure out the destination before taking the first step, I am now content to take the next step in faith. The next steps.

I don't know what tomorrow will bring, but then again, I never did. I only *thought* that I did. Hell, I'm lucky I know what today is bringing. Don't get me wrong: I would love to know. But I will find out as it is revealed to me, and that is kind of exciting!

What I have learned over the years is the Truth of what the Bible was teaching. Jesus loves me. God loves me. In fact, God loves me so much that He sent Jesus, His only son, to die on the cross on my behalf. And through His resurrection, He conquered death for all time. Only by believing in this, was I (or anyone else) saved.

I was given free will. God gave me a choice: Him or me. Once Rob and Jenny left, I chose me, thinking that I could do this whole life thing better than Him. After years of choosing me (complete with failed relationships, drinking issues and fractured family matters), I finally chose Him.

THAT is the lesson that Father Paul was trying to teach so many years ago.

That is what He was telling Neal Morse. And that is what Neal Morse was telling me. That is what the music at Orchard Hill was telling me. That was the message that I finally heard, after 16 years of formal religious education and hundreds of unproductive trips to church.

That is the whole Christmas thing, not the presents and the tinsel and the carols. That is the whole Easter thing, not the bunnies somehow making chocolate eggs.

And then there is the forgiveness. Again, I had been praying "forgive us our trespasses, as we forgive those who have trespassed against us" for most of my life without realizing its implications.

I still sin. Not something that I am proud of, but I am still a sinner. Always will be. I will, despite my best intentions, hurt someone through acts of omission or through acts of commission. Through words or through silence. Through pride, greed, lust, envy, gluttony, wrath, and sloth.

But I have been forgiven by God because of my belief in His Son. Even after everything you have read in this book, I am forgiven. Maybe not by the people in this story, but by my Heavenly Father.

And so I, too, must forgive. As much as I resent, or was hurt, or was betrayed, I must forgive. Knowing this makes all that I see in the rearview mirror different. Jenny hurt me, Mom hurt me. If I'm honest, Megan has hurt me many times. They all need to be forgiven. And forgiven unconditionally. Just as I was.

I'm not saying that it's easy to do. Jesus Christ, it's hard. But how hard do you think it was for Jesus Christ to go to that cross for me? "Father," He prayed in Gethsemane, "everything is possible for you. Take this cup from me." Then comes the command, "yet not what I will, but what you will."

And He has told me what I need to do. "Love your enemies and pray for those who persecute you."

I still get stuck in the past (look at the previous few hundred pages). But I do things in the present. And I enjoy them. And I cherish them. As they are happening, I make a mental note so that when the inevitable challenges come, I have defenses.

When the kids get in trouble, or when Megan and I fight, or when work sends me to some backwater town 30 miles from the nearest decent hotel, I have a storehouse of good memories to bring up to remind myself that "this too shall pass."

After all, those challenges are the result of being blessed. The kids wouldn't be giving me headaches if I wasn't blessed with them to begin with. My fight with Megan is because I was blessed with a strong, loyal, intelligent, loving wife who wants the best for me and our family. And that job that sometimes can be so annoying is only possible because I was blessed with the abilities and intelligence and health that allow me to do it as well as I do.

Rob has not returned. I miss him dearly. But I know where he is. He is waiting for me. Rob, Marino, my parents, and any of the rest of the crew that goes before me. The reunion will be spectacular. Legendary. And we will have Canadian Grizzly, and Mick Dark, and whatever else we want (a good bourbon would be appreciated as well). Maybe even some Phoenix Cream Ale for Dad (although, hopefully, he has discovered something better in Heaven).

I know that, one day, I too am going home. Have you ever felt (say, on a perfect summer day with your friends or family nearby) the peace and beauty of nature? Has a song ever touched you with its beauty and taken you away, even momentarily, from the reality of your day? Have you ever seen a baby, or a sunset, or a beautiful woman, or a tree in its autumn finest and thought about how it got there?

Those, friends, are just some examples of a glimpse of Heaven. Our true home, the one we all long for, whether we are believers or not. We have all felt it, regardless of our religious beliefs. And that is the best argument that I can make for the reality of God.

That, my friends, is my ultimate destination. Still decades away, I pray, because I am looking forward to many more adventures before I check out.

I write about yesterday, because yesterday taught me not to live for today. Yesterday taught me to live for eternity. Which then brings Hope. And we all need Hope.

Won't you fly-y, free bird?

About the Author

Michael Lauer grew up in the Buffalo, NY suburb of Cheektowaga in the 70s and 80s, when life was simpler and the music better. A graduate of St. Mary's High School and Canisius College, he is an accountant who recently became creative. But rather than go to jail for tax fraud or something exciting like that, he published his first novel, The Complete History of Cheektowaga (As I Remember It), in 2017.

Michael now lives in Southwestern Pennsylvania with this wife, 3 children and 2 dogs. This is his second novel.

Made in the USA
Middletown, DE
23 May 2019